The Essence
of an Hour

SUSAN FURBER

Valley Press

First published in 2021 by Valley Press
Woodend, The Crescent, Scarborough, YO11 2PW
www.valleypressuk.com

ISBN 978-1-912436-49-1
Cat. no. VP0169

Cover design by Jamie McGarry.
Cover image from the Everett Collection.
Text design by Peter Barnfather.
Edited by Sam Keenaghan.

Printed and bound in Great Britain by
Imprint Digital, Upton Pyne, Exeter.

THE ESSENCE OF AN HOUR

Susan Furber was born in Buffalo, New York, in 1992. She holds a B.A. in English and Philosophy from Saint Mary's College, Notre Dame, and spent a year at the University of Oxford. Susan is an editor and lives in London with her husband. This is her first novel.

for my mother, Kathleen

'Both have sin'd, but thou
Against God only, I against God and thee.'

– John Milton, *Paradise Lost*, Book X, 930-931

'As imperceptibly as Grief
The Summer lapsed away.'

– Emily Dickinson

'Press from the petals of the lotus-flower
Something of this to keep, the essence of an hour!'

– F. Scott Fitzgerald, *The Last Day*

Chapter One

I took out a cigarette and lit it. The knack of breathing in while clicking the spark wheel was not a natural one for me, and my thumb grew sore from failed attempts. At last I managed.

It started to rain, but I didn't care. My makeup had worn off back in the coat closet and my hair looked a wreck. And anyway, it didn't matter because the evening was over. At least for me.

The party had been a failure. There was no way of salvaging it, no bright side to look on. All I could do was reconcile myself to it and smoke my cigarette. Tomorrow I'd wake and think I was happy and alive, but the headache would creep in and remind me. That's how it always starts, though I didn't know that then. I was new to drinking.

My first college party, and the Yale Club at that too. Not some sordid dormitory boozer like Ellen bragged about going to on the weekends up in Albany, trying to drag me along. That was for getting tight and going off with some boy. This required an evening gown.

I'd bought a new dress, had it tailored until it fit like a glove and gave off the illusion I might have a bustline of sorts, but I had a nervous stomach for a week, as I do, and lost five pounds just like that. It hung a little in the shoulders, gaping under the arms, but I didn't mind. I loved it too much. Champagne pink and a faux diamond-encrusted collar. I slipped into it every night before I went to sleep along with my first real pair of high heels. Dads probably thought I was up there saying my prayers. If I was praying for anything it was that the divine will of the Lord be done, that I grow breasts in a fortnight, and for Mark Hamilton to kiss me. But the Lord can only do so much; we're not in the age of miracles. Besides, I was taught He helps those most who help themselves, so I stuffed a few tissues in before leaving for the evening.

I'd been kissed before – I wasn't a complete virgin – but I was waiting to be kissed well enough for it to be worth remembering. I mean, I'd think about what dress was in the laundry so I couldn't wear it tomorrow or something really mundane like that, while some boy was making at a pretty sad excuse for kissing. I knew that couldn't be all there was to it. People were crazy about sex stuff. It started wars and caused suicides and practically every joke an adult told was some sort of double entendre not so coyly referencing it, so I figured once I met the right guy, I'd be crazy about it too and stop thinking about dirty clothes and the washing basket. Or maybe I was dysfunctional or under-sexed or suffering from some sort of textbook psychosis. I'd heard Freud was out before I had a chance to read him, and behaviorism or something like that was the rage. Not that it mattered much. Dads was not one to pay for psychotherapy.

So, I went on keeping those thoughts to myself and waiting to pick up crumbs of conversation. Mark Hamilton promised me I'd meet a whole bunch of people who'd read Freud and Jung at the party, but of course I didn't talk to anybody but Tom Westerby. And he wasn't interested in anything other than his pecker.

I'd taken the train by myself to New York and kept the money Dads gave me for the porters. He hadn't mentioned how much to tip, and I was too shy to guess. Besides, Aunt Jo and Uncle Bill picked me up from the station and took me for lunch at the Plaza, so I didn't need to pay a penny.

Aunt Claire bought me a traveling suit for the occasion from Myers in Albany. Not the sort of thing a schoolgirl would wear, but a real grown-up woman – I was Anna Karenina on the platform, waiting to meet Vronsky in Moscow. Aunt Jo said it was a coming-out party of sorts, my debut if you will, like my mother had before the war, and like many of the girls I'd later meet at Vassar had still. Prized cupcakes to be sold off to the highest bidder and fast.

Four hours I'd spent getting ready for this. After lunch, it was straight back to Aunt Jo's and Uncle Bill's on Sixty-fourth and Park to bathe and primp. And for what? Frizzy hair, smeared lipstick, and an odd feeling of oozing blood in my panties. And it wasn't close to being that time of the month.

Mark Hamilton was a dud. That's all there was to it. You go ahead and think you're falling in love with a nice boy, the sort of boy Dads might approve of, which at eighteen really is a rarity, and that's the very boy who abandons you five minutes into a party, leaving you an open playing field for any stranger who wants to step up to bat. Excuse my poor baseball metaphors; I've never understood the sport. But what I did understand was feeling a pathetic hag; deserted, alone, and with only a drink to keep my hand occupied, making it look like my date was in the john and he'd be back any minute.

I also had plenty of time to consider why I loved Mark Hamilton, but I couldn't come up with much of an answer. It was very likely owed to the mole situated under his left eye, which crinkled into the fold of the skin when he smiled. Jesus, I know, but I've loved worse men for far more asinine reasons than that since. Or perhaps it was due to the time we spent together on the debate team those two years at St. Anne's and St. Luke's before he left me for

Yale. And by time spent together I mean him saying things to me like, 'You really are living proof that women's minds are illogical.' God, it was terrible, but he said it with that mole winking, and I thought it was a joke. Standing next to the punch bowl alone, I began to think it might not have been.

When Mark wrote to me in February, inviting me to this literary society night at the Yale Club in the city, I thought hell, he's starting to make advances towards me. And that's when Aunt Claire and I went out and bought the dress and the heels and the traveling suit, and she lent me the valise she used when she and Uncle Rory had gone to Europe back in '34, the year before his illness started.

I never considered the boy might only be being friendly or kind-hearted, a gesture made to an old school friend and childhood companion. Hell, he'd probably have invited Constance Mitchell who sang in the choir with her stumpy excuse for legs and close-knit eyebrows just the same. But this didn't occur to me when he asked; I didn't think of it until I was sitting in the rain, cursing my fingers for not getting the knack of flicking a lighter.

I was eighteen years old and wearing a pretty new dress and my first real pair of high heels. I was tipsy, and I wanted to have fun. I wanted to be noticed and complimented and petted. I wanted to laugh and be gay. I wanted to dance and flirt. I wanted to enjoy being an eighteen-year-old girl wearing a pretty new dress and her first real pair of high heels. I certainly did not want to waste my time and efforts making myself up only to stand next to some bar, afraid that some slob might spill his drink on my dress.

Though really, what had been the point in any of it? Mark was practically a saint and no amount of faux cleavage could entice him out of his celibacy. The whole affair had been a farce from the start. He'd promised me a party when I saw him at Midnight Mass over Christmas, talking up the superiority of minds at Yale and how I'd get a kick out of meeting some of the guys. Well, maybe I would have if he bothered to introduce me to any instead of ditching me like a bad outfit you wear to get out of the house while your parents are watching, shedding it as soon as possible for the real set of clothes underneath.

I mean I did take comfort in observing that he wasn't speaking to any other girl. It wasn't like he preferred some Joan Crawford type to me or anything as cliché as that. I don't think he liked girls or something, our minds not being logical enough for his notice.

Anyway, there I was by myself, too shy to bombard Mark's conversation and, as I hate other members of my own sex, I couldn't exactly go up to the group of co-eds timidly gathered on the fringes of the dance floor, turning their heeled ankles in circles as a sign of impatience. Three more hours of this. Standing, waiting, drinking what I could only assume was gin, getting fairly tight and wondering when the spread might be served. After weeks of eating very little, I was starving.

'My, my, where's your date, pretty lady? We can't be having girls like you as wallflowers, can we? We're gentlemen here.' That's exactly what he said to me, straight out of some Western or sleazy paperback novel, the kind with red covers and yellow lettering and blazoned with breasts and steely-eyed men. Certainly not the stuff of great poetry, but I fell for it.

Because I thought he was beautiful for talking to me. And he looked rather suave standing there, his jacket gone and his tie undone. He was tall, what some might have called gangly – but beggars can't be choosers – with black hair, thick, and very long eyebrows, and deep-set brown eyes. Tom Westerby, that was his name. Tom Westerby.

He led me to the dance floor. I don't remember if I said anything before that or not. I was swept up in his lean arms, the chiffon of my dress pressed to my skin by the palm of his hand. I felt his sweat through the thin material, but wasn't this supposed to be the very essence of romance? So, I went on trying to imagine it that way.

We chatted about something or other because that's one of my big faults. I can never shut up, especially when I'm nervous. You can tell when I'm scared by the things that come out of my mouth. My green eyes go wide and my lips fold into one another, and I'm off. And I'll talk about anything. Literature mostly, but sometimes politics too which is really bad because I've never been that knowledge-able, only opinionated. And I'll wake in the morning with a head pounding at the regret of things said.

He was leading me away from the dance floor, and I didn't feel alarmed. He was confident, and I was confident too, or at least I thought I ought to be, so I pretended on. Well, that and I was tight. My heel nearly snapped, and I swayed in his arms. I gave him a dreamy look, or what I could manage of one anyway, a sort of drunk, dewy-eyed heroine. I'm sure it was repulsive, but he didn't care.

He kissed me hard against the mouth, and his tongue slipped in and it was very, very wet. It must've been drenched in alcohol. It tasted of sugar and tobacco and a hint of sick, sweaty somehow, but I kissed back. We ended up in a coat closet of sorts, but hell if I know or care for that matter. His hand slipped up past my garters and into my panties, and he started to put a finger into, well, the part that distinguishes me as female. And all that while his other hand was smoth-ering one of my breasts. I couldn't even imagine I liked it.

But was that right? Was I meant like it? Were girls supposed to turn to mush at this and be in love? It wasn't as if I were such an innocent as not to know about these sorts of things. Madeline Evans whispered about this stuff during lunch every day, and she hadn't been so much as kissed – she thought she was a sex expert because she read about it in her filthy women's magazines. Maybe I knew less than her in theory, but I certainly had more experience.

I pushed him away, but he pulled me in closer, his tongue delving further. It felt like he was performing surgery to remove my tonsils the way that tongue kept probing. And that horrible finger. I was to later learn from Teddy it hurt because the guy hadn't waited until I was ready. Everything I was to learn about sex I learned from Teddy. Though that in itself was limited.

'Please,' I whimpered.

'You want more, baby. How about me? Dontcha think I'd like some too?'

I could see his hand reaching to undo the fly of his trousers. Dear God, not tonight – I was not about to see my first one of *those*.

I took my fist, the one that wasn't pinned back against the wall, and punched him neat in the gut. Praise the Lord, Teddy had taught me to fight. It came in handy to know stuff like that.

His face flew up, and his hands instinctively grabbed at his stomach. I hoped it made him go soft too, though I didn't know too much about that at the time.

'Hey, where do you get off? Bitch.'

'I don't like *that*, and I don't like you,' I said with narrowed eyes and a mean mouth. 'Get off of me!'

I thought he might hit me back, but he didn't.

'You cut my lip, you bitch.' I hadn't punched him there,

so I didn't know what he was on about. I was not a particularly ferocious kisser.

I wasn't frightened, or I don't think I was. He was a drunken fool, and I had the right of way, or so it seemed. If I could only manage to get past him and out of the closet, I'd be all right. I felt sore, you know, down there, but that was nothing that couldn't be forgotten with time.

'Get out of my way.'

He pushed me back against the wall, holding at my arms.

'You think you can cut my lip and leave?' He studied my face. He knew. 'You're a virgin, aren't you?'

'I ... yes.' I admitted to it. What could he do? He wouldn't. Surely boys didn't really do such things. This was the territory of bad novels and nuns' warnings. But I was getting a terrible suspicion some boys did. And that it wasn't so clear cut as it was in novels. That it left you feeling not quite certain of what had happened, if you'd wanted it. And if you had, where did that leave you when you didn't want it anymore?

'If you don't stop squirming...' His breath was on my neck. He stank of cheap beer mixed with vodka and Coca-Cola.

'Please,' I whispered. 'Please let me go.'

He slid his hand, his fingers smelling of me, to my throat.

'You're not worth it.'

The fingers loosened from my neck, and I felt the weight of his body suddenly slump against me, as though he had passed out. I felt something wet at my shoulder and realized he was a goner, his penis still pressed hard against my thigh.

I waited. His swollen face was inches from my own. So close we were to one another. He wouldn't remember, and yet ... I had seen those eyes for what? An hour at most, but I knew them. They've stayed with me. I've not forgotten.

They were almost pretty when they were shut, framed with long eyelashes.

I ducked my head beneath his arm, picked up the hem of my dress, and left. It was not the time for trembling.

He hadn't done it. There was that. For whatever else he'd done, he hadn't done that.

I tiptoed my way through the revelers. I couldn't meet their eyes. They would know. They mightn't care, but they would know. Something to be made light of perhaps, or scarcely observed. An inevitable casualty when hosting a party. That was me.

I should have gone to find Mark, I knew that. But I could not endure his hollow face and his certain lecture. He didn't approve of drinking, at least not in excess. And if he knew … God. It was easy for him to sit locked away, debating the problem of good and evil with his fellow eunuchs. He didn't have to recognize the world as it was; he wasn't a girl.

But I didn't hate Mark, and I didn't pity him. I couldn't even pity myself. I wanted to go home, that was all. I'd think about the state of my dress and my underwear later. That could be seen to in the taxi.

What I needed was air.

I fumbled for a cigarette and a lighter left on a side table, fishing one loose from a packet half soaked through with spilt punch. I was going to smoke my cigarette and sober up and wait for Mark to go home.

I sat outside, my back against the clubhouse, my dress on the pavement. I wasn't scared. I was too tired for that. The night air was thick and painted on my skin. The humidity had turned to rain. I didn't care. I smoked my cigarette. When I finished it, I wished I'd grabbed two. It gave me something to do while I waited for Mark to come searching for me. In the end, the doorman asked what the matter was and found my date for me. 'That's why girls shouldn't be allowed,' he mumbled or something like it, 'they get too tight and stumble off on their own.' Mark slipped him a dollar and took me home.

That's when it started to fall apart, I think, on that warm night of early spring 1941. It was only March and already it felt as though it were seventy degrees. That's unusual up in New York, you have to understand. I mean some years it's still snowing. But in that year and on that night, I remember it being insufferably hot. Our memory often lies to us, but, then again, our memory is the only form of truth we can and always will trust.

I was drunk and tired, and damn, I wanted another cigarette. That part is clear to me even if the rest isn't.

Chapter Two

I was sent to the bathroom to scrub the lipstick from my mouth. Sister Margaret sent me to the bathroom every time she caught me wearing lipstick. It was against the rules, but some of the nuns didn't mind it. As long I steered clear of Sister Margaret, I was usually safe, but this morning she'd come up to me as I was reading the morning prayer over the P.A.

I'd been chosen the previous fall to read the announcements as I have such an even voice and fine diction. Sister Mary Catherine set me up for it, saying I could have a career in radio. I knew she meant it as a compliment, but I resented it.

'Lillie Carrigan.'

I cringed. I used to do that when people said my maiden name, no matter the tone, reminding me I am in fact Irish on my father's side and not French, as I am on my mother's. Common Catholic rather than elite.

I'd inherited that from Dads too. No one hated being Irish more than he. I mean he had an English mother, buried in the Episcopalian cemetery instead of with her husband, a fact he was very proud of, and my father was proud of few things. It was that and the city of Albany where he was born and raised before moving out to the sticks of the Island. He thought Albany was a cultural haven, which it wasn't, or not to me anyway. I knew that from the first time Aunt Claire took me up there to see a touring production of *The Importance of Being Earnest.* But I guess you find funny things to take a heartened interest in when you're from nowhere. I know I did.

'Lillie Carrigan,' she repeated. 'Please go to the bathroom and wash that vile substance from your mouth. School is not a dance hall and think of the sort of women who paint themselves. Do you aspire to be such a woman, Lillie Carrigan?'

I knew my answer, and I knew the right one. I answered as I was expected. 'No, Sister.'

'Good, now please cleanse yourself of that painted sin and report to your homeroom straight after, no dawdling, Lillie Carrigan. Confession at four o'clock.'

Confession was Sister Margaret's usual punishment. It was as painful as a rap of the knuckles, leaving bruises on the soul instead of the hands.

'Yes, Sister.'

I'd go to confession, all right. I'd make up some venial sins, the way I usually did. I mean, really, what did they expect me to say? 'Bless me Father for I have sinned. It has been three days since my last confession and in that time, I got tight and fornicated. Right, yes, how far did I go? Well, I don't really know how to describe it. I guess it was halfway, but I didn't like it much. Does that redeem me? I guess not. Anything else? Oh, yes. I wore lipstick this morning like the whore I am. That's it, Father. Three Hail Marys and three Our Fathers again? Great. Now for the Act of Contrition. O my God, I am heartily sorry for having offended Thee ... Father, I'll see you on Saturday afternoon if Sister Margaret doesn't send me before.'

I didn't mind having to wash off the lipstick; I knew there wasn't much of a chance of getting away with it in the first place. Besides, it bought me five extra minutes away from homeroom and having to sit next to Mary Elizabeth Donahue, saint in the flesh that she was. I absolutely hate people who can't be mean or selfish. I think it's a sign of a lack of passion or too much self-control. Either way, I don't imagine such a lifestyle can be healthy. It clearly signals a bad case of repression. And if anyone was repressed, it was Mary Elizabeth with her dull brown hair worn in braids and her face as plain and unremarkable as the Nebraska landscape. Jeremy Collins said that once about her. Cruel but true. She was the Irish immigrant Pollyanna. God, I hated her.

'Good morning, Lillie,' she greeted me, filled with genuine joy. Her smile was too full of teeth for my taste.

'Morning,' I echoed, miserable.

The bell would ring to dismiss us from homeroom in exactly eight minutes, but I had chemistry next and Mary Elizabeth sat next to me in that class too. Damn alphabetical order. There was no escape until second period French. She took Italian.

I felt a pencil jab into my back, and I turned knowing it would be Ellen. She passed me a note, and I smiled. I was tempted to read it immediately, but I knew from experience Mary Elizabeth would ask, 'What's that about?' with her idiot's grin and clear eyes. She was a curious girl, and while I think most other girls could have guessed the note contained something dirty (Ellen's notes were naturally scandalous), I don't think Mary Elizabeth's mind went to that sort of thing. I mean, hell, maybe she knew more about sex stuff than I gave her credit for. She did once ask me if it was unnatural and unholy to have a woman on top. I think I shrugged, too frightened to reveal my own ignorance on the subject. I wasn't daft enough to think it unholy or anything like that, but I wasn't too aware of the possibilities in sex positions. I was hardly Madeleine Evans with her magazines. I'd only learned at the age of thirteen, from Lara Marcelli rather than Teddy, that sex required a man's pecker to be shoved into a woman, connecting the two together. I'd imagined lovers rolled around for hours kissing and cuddling as the sperm sort of swam into the womb like Gertrude Ederle crossing the Channel. The thought that something would have to stab into me like that, like that nasty finger wriggling around until I bled, well, it sounded like hell.

I thought of Madeline with her smug kindergarten face curled into a grin, claiming the feeling was like being full, the pleasure coming from the pain, but I didn't trust her. That was from one of her magazines too and not experience. Not that I would have trusted her experience. She once told me I was lucky being tall and everything, unlike her. She said if she married a tall man, being petite, they could only have sex with her on top because otherwise their bits would never line up. I didn't know if this was true, but I decided never to dwell on it for too long. Besides, as Madeline said, it would never be a problem for me.

I waited until Mary Elizabeth was absorbed with copying down the 'saint of the day' before I read the note. Sister Mary Catherine insisted on instructing us daily on a different saint during homeroom. I suppose she didn't know how else to fill the fifteen minutes. Idle hands make the devil's work or something like that.

The note was short.

How was weekend? Any action? Stories later please. E.

I sat there rubbing my plain lips together, pushing back my cuticles, trying to forget, but it proved impossible. A memory once recalled must play itself out.

That finger. What was I supposed to make of it? I'd never felt anything like it before, and I was sure I had hated it. There wasn't anything in the least bit enjoyable about it … the way he had snapped at me and pinned me back … I shivered; I mean on the inside because it didn't show. No, I couldn't possibly have been expected to have liked it, to have been flattered by it. I mean, were we girls meant to feel honored every time we made a guy's pecker hard? I didn't know.

Would a normal girl, who wasn't suffering the thousand neuroses I'd self-diagnosed myself with, have enjoyed it? I thought not, but I couldn't be sure. Ellen might have known, but I suspected she was well in the camp of it should have felt good. I knew Ellen ran a little faster than some of the other girls at St. Anne's. She knew boys outside of St. Luke's, so I didn't blame her. The only boys I knew who didn't go to St. Luke's, *had* gone to St. Luke's.

Life was dull on Mohawk Island, and the population low. There were about fifteen hundred of us in 1941. One thousand five hundred people on an island – that was it. I was no better than some pokey-town Victorian who didn't know a man had to stick it in you for a baby to be made. Practically. But I'd read novels – I had that much – and I should have known somehow.

I mean, Jesus, here I was supposed to be some sort of modern young woman, no longer buying the myth of lie back and think of England. I should have enjoyed being petted. This was the time of liberation, or so I'd been told, doubtless by Madeline Evans. Why then had it felt so damn uncomfortable? And scary too.

Maybe it was Tom Westerby's fault. Maybe he wasn't any good at making love to a girl. Yes! I could tell Ellen during passing that Tom Westerby, a Yale man, had gotten fresh with me, but hell, he wasn't any good! That was it.

But the thing was I didn't exactly know what good meant or felt like, and I was afraid Ellen might know that I didn't know too. I could've told her nothing, but I liked telling

Ellen things. She was my friend, not my closest because that was Lara, but I liked hearing her tell me about when boys petted her, and I didn't want to disappoint her by being such a hopeless virgin with no stories to dispense in return. And besides, I had to tell someone about it. Call it misapplied Catholic teaching, but I never feel quite right about anything until I've laid it before someone else.

Ellen grabbed my arm as we left homeroom. We stood at about the same height, so I guess Ellen also didn't need to worry about being on top if she married a tall man.

'Tell me everything about Saturday. Did you get any action?' asked Ellen as soon as we were out of earshot.

I shook my head.

'Come on, Lil, I need details!'

'I drank a lot,' I confessed. 'Or I think I drank a lot. It was gin or something.'

'Mmmmm, gin is nice, but you know I'm crazy for wine.'

Ellen loved to drink and she wasn't picky, a good quality to have when you can't buy alcohol for yourself. She liked to say she was crazy for wine because she thought it made her sound sophisticated, but she would have drunk anything as long as you told her it would give her a buzz. I bet she couldn't have named one specific type of wine, other than red or white. She claimed to prefer red.

'I think it was gin. It tasted all right.'

'Nothing else is quite like whiskey for our Lillie.'

'Beer's all right.'

Ellen stuck out her tongue. 'Beer is for poor folk.'

'And wine is for dirty old men who touch up kids,' I said. I didn't mean it. I liked wine too.

'To each her own,' she said with a raised eyebrow, plucked and drawn on. She'd come back from Christmas made up that way, and Sister Margaret must have been too busy handing out confessions for lipstick and rouge to notice it. 'Come on, really, I want details. How were the boys? I've never been Ivy before.'

'It was what you'd imagine. Tuxedos and combed back hair. It was the literary society party of the year or something like that. It was nice. There was lots of dancing. I liked the dancing.'

'Lil, that tells me absolutely nothing! You may as well have stayed home in your room if that's what you're going to tell me. Come on, what happened? Who'd you dance with?'

'Only one boy, really.'

'Right, Mark. Of course. Well…'

'It wasn't Mark. Mark isn't one for dancing. He prefers talking.' I attempted to hold the encroaching bitterness in my voice at bay. 'No, there was another boy.'

'What did he look like? Did he ask for your number?' Ellen was predictable in her questions. The next would be, 'What does his father do?' We weren't old enough to be with men who held their own jobs.

'No, but…' Here was where the story needed to be told, and I was reluctant to proceed.

Ellen looked at me, expectant for me to continue, but I still couldn't figure out how. I was going to have to approach this story from a different angle if I was to get through it.

We'd arrived at our chemistry classroom, but the bell hadn't yet rung. I had two minutes to get it out. Mary Elizabeth, God bless, was already seated and chatting to Dottie Duggan on her right about some summer camp for orphans she was planning to work at that summer or something. Mary Elizabeth was crazy about orphans and stray dogs too.

'Hey, Ellen, I've got a question for you.' My tongue felt large and my mouth dry, my spit thick. I pushed back a cuticle.

'Stop that,' said Ellen. She hated when I did it. Said it gave her the heebie jeebies to watch me inflict pain on myself with such nonchalance. I stopped.

I took up the question again. 'Have you, umm, has a boy, umm, ever put his finger in you?'

She laughed. 'Are you asking me if I've been fingered, Lil?'

'Yeah.'

'Of course, silly. A girl's got to have her needs met every once in a while.'

For as much as Ellen knew and talked about sexy stuff, she never spoke of it with much love or passion. It was a natural thing for her. Desires met, cravings satisfied. All carnal, no love.

'Oh.' I didn't know what else to say. It was clear enough – I should have enjoyed it. I sat there, in my first-row chemistry seat with thirty seconds to the bell, half listening to Mary Elizabeth prattle on about the disadvantaged youth in this country, and I knew I wasn't normal. I couldn't be a nice girl like Mary Elizabeth, and I couldn't be like Ellen either. I was lost some place in the middle, damned to limbo.

'Wait, Lil, were you?' Ellen's eyes went wide, and she had to cover her mouth with her hand. For Ellen, the next best thing to receiving pleasure herself was to hear about her friends being pleasured. You sure couldn't call her selfish in that regard.

'No, Lillie! I can't believe this!' She had to cover her mouth again as the bell rang, and I knew if she didn't bite down on her hand hard at that very moment, she was bound to cry out something which would humiliate me to the abyss of hell.

I couldn't talk about that sort of thing without others covering my voice with their own. I waited until later in the period, when Sister Agnes was drawing out an orbital diagram on the blackboard, to turn long enough to read Ellen's lips as she mouthed the name: Mark Hamilton. Ha! What a laugh! Mark would never be that intimate. Maybe I would have liked it if he had. I thought I might've, but I couldn't be sure. I shook my head and mouthed no. That was it.

Ellen rushed to me at the end of the period. She had English next. We had but a minute left to speak. By lunch she wouldn't care.

'It wasn't Mark Hamilton? Wow, Lil, I didn't know you had it in you! Who was it?'

'Just some boy,' I said. I thought it was a great line, establishing I could be casual about this sort of thing.

'Well,' she shrugged, her shoulders already starting to turn left, 'as I said, a girl's got to get what she can get sometimes. You know?'

'Oh, I agree.'

The conversation was over. We parted, and she winked at me, evidently more joyful at the prospect of my conquest than I had felt myself. Lillie Carrigan had been casually fingered by a Yale man at a New York City party, who could have imagined it?

Practically every girl at St. Anne's – and there were only sixty-three of us in the high school – was determined to let every other girl know she was not some ignorant sexless nobody, that she'd done *something* beyond letting a boy hold her hand. But a girl would have died if her peers thought she'd gone all the way. There was a difference between messing around with a guy and actually having sex, but where the difference lay exactly, I wasn't sure, and I don't think the other girls knew either. But we knew we would have to confess to having sex. That was a mortal sin. The other stuff we thought probably qualified somewhere along the lines of venial, but since we figured the priests and nuns didn't know what any of that stuff was, we needn't confess it. The appetizers were free and supposedly tasted every bit as good, if not better for women so said Ellen and Madeline, with half the sinfulness and almost none of the guilt. Or so we thought at eighteen.

I told Lara the whole story as we walked home together along the river that afternoon, the day fresh, one of the first of spring. I told her the truth. No flippant words to disguise my shame. There was no need for it. Lara understood. She was my best friend, better than Teddy.

'I've never had that … was it terrible? It sounds terrible,' she said.

'Yeah, I don't know. Maybe something's wrong with me, Lar. I'm starting to be afraid. I've never been kissed and actually felt a thing. What if there is some sort of sexual malfunction in me or something?'

Lara pursed her lips together, forming an 'O' with her mouth. She'd never been kissed full stop.

'Maybe you haven't been kissed by the right boy.'

There was Ellen thinking a woman's got to have her needs met wherever she can get it while Lara still believed in Prince Charming kisses waking you from your slumber.

I did a mental tally of all the kisses I'd received in my brief eighteen years. They had either been childish pecks or confusing messes with poking, slimy tongues. There had to be more to it than those limited options. Love, or at least genuine affection, had to make it better. I had been treating kissing as a game, daring boys to see what moves they might make, and surrendering easily. I had never been much interested in the act itself, and less interested in the boys.

I may have gone up to New York City and fornicated, or whatever way you want to look at it, but I was hardly some

Persephone returning from the underworld, rich in know-ledge and experience. I knew very little more than I had on Saturday morning, and for everything that had happened, I remained the same naïve convent girl, looking for comfort from a child who had never been kissed.

Chapter Three

My first kiss had been from Teddy when I was twelve and didn't know about the jabbing truth of sex. So, it hadn't counted. Or that's what Ellen said two years later when I told her I had too been kissed by a boy. 'No tongue? Doesn't count,' had been her harsh verdict. The fact that there could be tongue involved was something I wasn't to discover for another two years. Ellen already had, or so she claimed. You never knew with Ellen. I'd later ask her if she was a virgin and she asked me where I technically drew the line, to which I didn't know how to answer, my technical knowledge on the whole thing being poor.

But it didn't matter. I thought Teddy's kiss counted. I didn't see why it shouldn't. What if it had only been a peck that hit the corner of my lip more than anything else? It was worthy of great romantic literature what had happened between Teddy and me. I was sure of it.

I mean how many girls can claim they received their first kiss and drag on a cigarette on the same day? All right, probably a lot. But while in the midst of family grief? Okay, fine it wasn't my grief, not at the time. That would almost have been *too* literary.

Teddy's brother Adam had died three days earlier of a congenital heart condition. He'd been the one to find him in the morning, the same way Dads would find my own mother when I was fifteen. But that hadn't happened yet. My mother was inside the McCalmans' house that day with the rest of the adults, pretty in her good black crêpe and shy and not having a drink (she'd only drank champagne once, on her wedding day, and she'd hated it, or so she said) while the rest of them drank like fish. Not that Dads drank much, especially not like the McCalmans. Though very few couples I've met, my own husband and I probably being the exception, can drink like the McCalmans.

Teddy managed to get a tumbler full of whiskey which we shared between us. I hated it and only had a few sips, but it certainly didn't put me off for life. Lord, if only it had. He lit a cigarette and passed one to me. 'You said you wanted to try, remember? I'll teach you.' I coughed and spluttered, and he finished it for me, after his own.

'That one's nicer than the first.'

I knew he meant because it was mine, and I thought my God, he's going to kiss me, and he did. And that was that. We never said a word about it.

But when my mother died three years later, I held a brief hope he might kiss me again. It was a really sick thing to think. And he didn't anyway.

Teddy hadn't kissed me since that first time, nor had he made the slightest romantic overture other than to offer to deflower me if I was a virgin at thirty. That's how he said it too.

I'd be lying if I said I never had a thought about Teddy in that way. I had. Especially after that kiss and again when my mother died. I remember wanting to go to him that night, the first night I had to sleep in the house with my mother downstairs in the living room displayed in a coffin ready for the next day's mourners, and ask for him to hold me. I was lonely, and I could not ask for Dads. But I didn't go.

I never could go to Teddy like that, or really anyone for that matter. I still can't. I've always been too afraid.

But it was all a long time ago, both of our childhood tragedies.

I rarely saw the three McCalmans together after Adam died, though I spent most days after school in their living room raiding their bookshelves. Mr. McCalman appreciated European literature. Dads read detective novels, and my mother, God rest her soul, had gone in for Georgette Heyer, never Austen.

Mr. McCalman had a whole library in the living room, and a secret stash of a whole other type of literature kept in his study. I knew Teddy looked at it sometimes, but I was too scared to ask if I might have a peek. I wasn't sure I wanted to.

I knew little of Teddy and his family, he knew little of mine. We spoke rarely of the hours we spent away from one another except to mention what we'd been reading.

And it wasn't as if there was much to say about my family anyway, if I had wanted to tell Teddy about it. Lara understood it better, having spent more time with them. But I said nothing. It was Dads and me, and occasionally Aunt Claire and Uncle Rory for Sunday dinner, but they too were quiet by nature. We are a silent, unassuming, and polite people.

The McCalmans, though, they were different. It wasn't that they were passionate or violent, they didn't go in for the hysterical dramatics, no, but you knew from their frosty looks they hated each other. But they weren't always like that. Every few months, I'd be over on a Saturday afternoon reading, listening to them getting tight together in the kitchen, planning where they could go for the evening with a place like Albany being such a dump. And they'd get dressed up to the nines and go out, and Teddy would sit home silently drinking and smoking and saying nothing of it to me.

Dads and Mr. McCalman should have been natural friends, I guess. Neighbors, both lawyers who commuted to Albany, though Dads came home every night, something Mr. McCalman reportedly only did twice a week, if that, and they were graduates of Fordham Law. Different years, of course.

Dads didn't care much what I did, or other people either. I mean he let me go along as Teddy's date to his cousin Martha's engagement party the following Saturday without troubling me over the particulars. It had been the same when Mark asked me up to New York.

That's not to say he didn't notice things, because he did. He just didn't say much about it.

What he did notice was the way I looked when I appeared at the foot of the stairs that evening, ready for the McCalmans to pick me up for the dinner.

'Very nice, honey.' It was the best he could manage. 'Here, come over to the living room while we wait.'

I knew what to expect when he said a thing like that. It would be his version of a talk. Because every once in a while, he did give voice to his observations, mostly about other people's drinking habits. Thankfully, and to this day, he's never mentioned my own.

'Sit, sit,' he insisted, fussing over the pillows on the chaise longue, moving them out of the way. 'Don't wrinkle your dress.'

I gave him a weak smile.

'Honey,' he began, taking a seat himself, 'does Teddy drink?'

Dads was hardly a teetotaler, not like my mother had been, but he didn't approve of boys who drank before going to college.

'There might be champagne tonight,' I confessed. 'It is an engagement party.'

'Well, that's okay. But be sensible.'

'Okay.'

I thought that would be the end of it, but he continued speaking – a rare moment for him.

'I had lunch with Jim McCalman last week, we were both on a case down at the Court of Appeals. And you know, I like Jim, he's a nice enough guy, but well, he ordered a whole bottle of white wine with his lunch, and I had a glass, but you see… He's one of those types, though she is too. Hmm, grief strikes people in different ways,' he concluded, his eyes fixated on the carpet. It was the closest he'd come to revealing how he might be dealing with his own or perhaps questioning me. I was glad he had stopped.

'That's true,' I said. It was best to give him short replies and duck out of the conversation as quickly as possible. I'd learnt this in our three years together, alone. How my parents endured twenty-three years of marriage is beyond me. But then my mother had had the Church.

'Well,' he said, slapping his hands together, 'I'm going to go do some work in my study, but you let me know before you head out, won't you?'

'Mmhmm.'

I wasn't sure why I'd agreed to go, other than it was an excuse to put on makeup and a dress. I usually went for that sort of thing, but not tonight. It'd only been a week since New York and the thought of slipping back into the same dress made me feel ill. There hadn't been time to dry clean it, so it smelled faintly of cheap alcohol. I reached into my clutch purse for the perfume and put on more scent while I waited.

I'd met Martha McCalman, Marty for short, twice. She was a perky and sporty girl who'd finished up at Saint Mary's the spring before and was announcing her engagement that night to some big slab of a Notre Dame man who apparently worked in Chicago as a lawyer. Every Irish man I knew was a lawyer, or so it seemed. I didn't understand why that was.

Marty was only four years older than Teddy and me, but twenty-two felt a vast and grown-up age at eighteen, the great divide being twenty. I couldn't imagine it – being engaged to a man in four years' time, all thoughts of girlhood behind me.

It wasn't going to happen like that for me. But I wasn't planning to be a virgin at thirty either. I was hoping not to be one by nineteen, if I'm being honest, but I wasn't quite sure how that was to be accomplished. I figured once I was at Vassar there might be looser morals, being around Protestants and all.

Mrs. McCalman had been the one to ask me to the party. The assumption was that I was close enough to family or I would be one day, that was clear. Everyone thought we'd marry, Teddy and I, and maybe I was counting on it somewhere deep inside of me. It's hard to tell now. I think I must have been. Or at the very least that he'd live up to taking my virginity, if it came down to it.

Some people said we looked like brother and sister, both with green eyes and dark hair, but it was always the same people who insinuated we'd end up husband and wife.

'It's evident you have some sort of connection,' said Mrs. Grieger after three glasses too many of champagne one New Year's Eve party. Teddy later told me that was the night he lost his virginity. Not to Mrs. Grieger, of course. It was to a married woman, though. I knew that much.

Teddy and his parents picked me up to drive over at quarter past seven. His mother told me I looked lovely while Teddy smiled, his eyes flickering like the first orange embers of a lit cigarette. Whenever I think of Teddy that's how I see him with those sleepy hazel green eyes, the hint of a grin pulling to the left, his large white teeth, the edges stained with nicotine, peaking through.

He held my arm as we walked into the dinner, touching the crook of my elbow where my sleeve ended and my glove hadn't begun. Bare skin. With another boy it would have felt intimate, but hell, this was Teddy.

We were the only kids our age at the affair, as I'd suspected it would be, and it was a bore all right. We weren't halfway through the first course, a grand total of five were to come, before Teddy began to figure out a plan of escape. No one would notice or care if we left, he whispered. Hell, it might have been expected.

I left first, excusing myself to the bathroom, rather obviously bringing my clutch purse with me. Teddy followed a few minutes later, meeting me in the library with a bottle of champagne in hand.

'I think you can have some of this, little girl,' he said, uncorking the bottle. The bubbles stung; I drank it down fast. He smiled and poured us each a second glass. I knew we'd finish the bottle.

I slipped off my heels. Teddy was tall and even with the three extra inches on my natural height, I didn't come close to looking him square in the eye. Without heels, I came to his shoulder. I liked that about him, his height and his lithe body. He was a runner, though Lord knows how he managed it with a pack a day. He'd probably have smoked more if it hadn't been banned during the school hours. I could scarcely finish one and the taste would linger in my mouth for hours after. But glamorous women in magazines and movies smoked and drank from long-stemmed glasses with olives resting on the sides. I was determined to get there one day, and I was counting on Teddy to show me the way. Someone like Mark Hamilton sure as hell wasn't going to, with his stuffy Yale Club and pretentious chatter.

The room was overcrowded with chairs, two coffee tables, and a chaise longue in each of the three windows, but nothing looked so inviting as the plush carpet. I laid down on my side, sinking into its softness, enveloped and happy. I was tipsy and giggly, the very sort of girl I despised.

Teddy eased down next to me.

'Hell, I better keep an eye on you, or you'll be drinking my family out of house and home. Run away with the gardener too. Don't think I don't know you Lillie Jane Carrigan. You're the type.'

'Hmmm.'

He loosened his tie and threw off his jacket, sinking further into the carpet.

'You're quite a gal, you know that?'

'Using a line like that Edward McCalman, I expected better of you.'

'Oh, yeah? And what did you expect?'

I didn't answer.

'What would you do if I were to kiss you right now?'

I wasn't listening to him. Not really. I was much too absorbed in my study of the white plaster moldings on the ceiling, very nouveau riche, and laughing at the thought of some Irish immigrant house in the suburbs of Albany aspiring towards sophistication with their library and champagne and plush carpets. I must have heard him and registered it someplace in my brain, though because I replied, 'I suppose I wouldn't mind.'

He pulled my thin-framed shoulders to him and looked me in the eye. Sometimes I think back to this moment knowing what I know and knowing what we've lived, and it's impossible not to see sadness in the smile he gave me.

That may sound silly and hell if it isn't sentimental, but it's one of those thoughts I have for so long attached to the memory of the story that I can't go unthinking it.

His lips were soft, and I didn't think about laundry that time. Hell, I didn't think. I didn't have to go imagining it was magical, forcing my body to react. It had never happened to me like that before, and it has never quite happened to me like that since, not with any other boy or man.

It's funny. I can never quite remember what it felt like to kiss Teddy that night until another man kisses me, but then it all rushes back, and I know that it isn't right. It isn't Teddy.

'Well, how was that? Or did you expect more?' he asked, the words coming out slowly and pronounced.

'Edward McCalman, I have a question for you,' I said, raising my body weight onto my elbows. 'Was that planned this whole evening?'

'No. Completely spur of the moment. But I bet you've been wondering all night if I would kiss you.'

I breathed heavily, and I knew exactly how my face looked – blotchy. My stomach dropped, and I felt the rash spread across my chest and neck.

'No. It was completely spontaneous.'

He drew me close and whispered, 'We're both pretty bad liars,' and kissed me again.

'I better not kiss you anymore. Not tonight anyway. You're not ready for me to kiss you the way I want to,' he said, his breath heavy on my neck.

It was a terrible line, the sort he himself had read in a book and adopted for his own. I wondered if he used it on all his girlfriends. But what does it matter? I thought dreamily. He's using it on me now. He's a romantic like me. He can't help speaking the language of books and films. Is he living this moment the same as I am, wondering how he'll write it up later?

I knew he was. I could be confident of that.

I sunk into the carpet, drunk with love. I remember thinking the air was full of contentment, whatever that meant to me at eighteen, my child's heart pounding. Never again was I to live a moment that was in such accordance with my girlish delusions of what love and romance should be. I lay there recalling his kisses already, romanticizing what had not yet passed. Formalizing every detail. Or really, deciding on the exact words I'd use to describe it to Lara. Not to Ellen. This was too beautiful to ruin with her sordid mind. And I certainly couldn't mention this to any of the other girls. They'd only think of us as another of the St. Luke's and St. Anne's romances. And I hated that sort of thing. I never went in for it.

'I need a cigarette,' he said, rising from the ground to look around for one.

'Light one for me too.'

'You're a funny kid,' he said, but he lit one for me.

We sat side by side, smoking and smiling. And he leaned over and kissed my neck, a quick peck. The sort of thing that at eighteen I took to be the sign of an assured and sophisticated lover.

'If you can't finish that, I'll take it back,' he said.

'I can handle it. I like a cigarette. It's almost post-coital.'

He smirked.

'And how much do you know about that, Lillie Jane Carrigan?'

I steadied my voice, trying to sound sexy. 'Pour me some more champagne, won't you?'

He leaped up to grab the bottle and poured us each another glass.

I wanted to make some sort of dumb toast but held back. I waited for him to speak.

'This is nice.'

I agreed. It was true.

We looked at each other, green eyes meeting green. I knew what I wanted to say and what I longed for him to, but neither of us spoke. But I knew he knew, and he knew I knew too. And that was enough.

'Had we better go back? Won't they miss us by now?'

He drained his glass. 'Let's finish the bottle. Then we'll go back for more booze.'

Another silence.

'Come here, Lil, you look cold.' And he enveloped me in his arms, and he pushed me back into the carpet, placing his body on top of mine. He kissed me, but it wasn't soft or kind as it had been earlier. I clung to him, knowing I liked it. I had never liked it before. I had always been scared. Scared I had already conceded too much, and the inevitable fumbling would continue until I screamed. But I didn't feel as though each movement were a sin. I hadn't known kissing could be like that. And maybe that was the trouble, or the beginning of it anyway.

He tore himself from me, suddenly, and lit another cigarette.

'You better go back, Lil,' he said. 'I don't want to take your entire innocence in one night.'

I wanted to stay with him. I wanted to be kissed. I wanted another cigarette, though I knew it would leave my mouth dry for the morning.

But I went.

I couldn't stay. I don't remember feeling frightened of what the moment could have led to nor anxious it would never be repeated. I was too happy for that. It was the first time.

Chapter Four

I told Lara the next day as we waited for our parents after Mass. Mr. Marcelli could hold an hour-long conversation with a plaster wall, or so claimed Lara. Dads spoke to few people, instead loitering by the flowers in the Lady Chapel where my mother had spent a great deal of her short life. He never liked Mass, I knew that, but he never missed a week. Not even for golf. It was part of his way, at least until I left for college.

Lara couldn't believe it when I told her. It was a warm spring day, and we took a lap around the churchyard, suspicious of others overhearing. Teddy's parents rarely went to church, the occasional Christmas or Easter, certainly not both in the same year, and Teddy never did after his Confirmation. Typical lapsed Catholics.

'And then, Lar, he leaned over and said, "What would you do if I kissed you right now?" I don't know why, but I was so invested in studying the ceiling and absorbing every detail I could. I must have known it was coming and that's why I wanted to soak in the details, to impress the memory of it to me forever, like a flower in a book...'

'Lillie, get onto to it!'

'Lar, it was the most beautiful thing that has ever happened to me. All I could say was "I suppose I wouldn't mind" and then there he was kissing me. Loving me! Holding me like I weighed no more than a leaf. It was as though it were his mission from the gods to kiss me like that.'

It was overkill. I can see that clearly now, but, at eighteen, that was how I felt. Cross my heart. I wish I was exaggerating. Lara too was a romantic, or really a senti-mentalist (I always do think of that line by Fitzgerald in his first novel – Jesus, I've repeated it drunkenly to enough men when I see the inevitable kiss in their eyes), which made it worse. You need one cynic in a friendship to level things out. We were damned by our optimism.

'That's beautiful. Too beautiful! I bet he's been thinking about this for years. Planning it. Waiting until he could.'

I too had harbored this thought but knew it couldn't be true. It was the sort of thing boys laughed about girls thinking of them.

'I'm inclined to think it suddenly came upon him. I did look very nice last night and…'

'Psshaw! He loves you. That's why he hates me. He thinks I'll steal you from him.'

Lara was right about that. Teddy did not like Lara and begrudged her company whenever I insisted on doing some-thing with the both of them. A picnic when we younger, a trip to the zoo, my rather failed sixteenth birthday party when Dads let me invite boys for the first time and only Teddy came. Their civility towards one another was cold at best. I used to think it was because Lara couldn't give him anything. And by that, I mean neither interesting conversa-tion (Lara didn't read as we did) or sex. But who knows. Maybe he did see her as a threat. 'A threat to getting in your panties,' as Lara remarked later that summer.

I'd known Teddy longer, but I loved Lara more. We'd been best friends since the third grade, ten years, and I used to think her the prettier of the two of us and I the smarter. She was plump with strawberry curls and large brown eyes, the color of black coffee. Lara had beautiful clothes sewed by Mrs. Marcelli, each garment embroidered with roses and butterflies. My own mother did not sew, and I was jealous. All my clothes were store-bought from Myers.

Lara's house was wonderfully loud and smelled forever of asparagus and lemon. The Marcellis mightn't have always said what they meant, but they spoke to one another, which was more than I could say for my own home, even when my mother was alive.

Lara had three older brothers. The eldest two had wives who we'd once thought to be the most gorgeous women we'd ever seen, with black hair set at the hairdressers every Friday afternoon and a different pair of high heels for each new dress. They must have been all of twenty-eight when we were eighteen, but, with their heavy breasts now sagging with babies, they seemed practically middle-aged. They proved to us that time would not be kind, and we must start young if we wanted to catch a man, as they had.

I loved the Marcellis. They were not neglectful as the McCalmans, nor cold and pious as my own family. And yet, they were more fiercely religious. They had an Evangelical thread to their faith, an obsession with the fire and brimstone side of Catholicism. Lara was never allowed to go to parties or to see boys. Maybe that's why she lived vicariously through me, but I don't think that was it. Or not all of it. She'd been that way before we thought of boys.

Lara, who had never been kissed, knew more about the facts of life than I did. Her brother Jimmy, who was the closest in age to her but still five years her senior, knocked a girl up from Rensselaer when he was eighteen. She had peroxide-bottle blonde hair, and her scalp was perpetually peeling because of it. Her name was Antoinette, and Lara hated her.

Antoinette wasn't so bad. I mean I never liked her, but I hate all women, especially blondes. My opinion here should be discounted. But Lara hated her and for good reason too. Because Lara knew after Jimmy and Antoinette, she would never be let out of the house. This is what happened to girls who were allowed to go around with boys while they were in high school. Boys were expected to make a few mistakes and have lots of dates, but not good girls like us. We had to stay home and wait until those same boys were ready to settle down.

Maybe Jimmy told her about where a pecker had to go or maybe Antoinette did. But either way, Lara cried when she learned of it and rang me up on the telephone to confess the facts of life. I cried too. I felt a sick cramp in my stomach, similar to the dull ache of my monthly pains, which had started the summer before.

While I grew thinner in the years of puberty, Lara grew thicker, until I rather vainly thought I took the crown for both looks and brains. I mean I didn't think of myself as the class beauty or anything like that. Just between Lara and me, I knew I was the more attractive. I was tall, and, on good days, I convinced myself that the pale skin and dark hair made me look French. On bad days, it was undoubtedly Irish.

We spent most of our time dissecting what the matter was with us and why we couldn't find boyfriends even if we had been allowed to have them. For me, it was the lack of a chest and too big of a nose that turned up slightly at the end. For Lara, it was her eyebrows. They were very thick but then also sparse in sections – an absolute anomaly for her to pluck, and pencil couldn't help much.

We didn't make the nicest looking of schoolgirl companions. It was clear each of us had a lot of maturing to do in our faces and our bodies too, but we didn't know that then. We thought at eighteen we were at the height of attractiveness and that left us fairly frightened. If this was as good as it was going to get, then we needed to resign ourselves to the fact that we hadn't turned out as well as we dreamed in our pre-pubescent years.

But I knew Lara did think I was pretty. Not pretty like Alison Montgomery or Lena Brennan in our year at St. Anne's, they really were gorgeous creatures, but pretty enough to have Teddy McCalman secretly in love with me for years. I was the heroine of the story, she the best friend, and I had at last been kissed by my hero. There couldn't be a better story than that.

'Does this mean you two are going together?' asked Lara.

'I don't know. I don't think so. I mean I don't want it to have to. It would be ordinary, typical St. Luke's and St. Anne's.'

Her eyes narrowed. She understood. 'I think that's much more romantic.'

'But I don't know. I haven't … I haven't spoken to Teddy about anything yet.'

'Well, don't look at me to speak to him for you. He hates me.'

'I won't. I'll go and see him after school tomorrow, like usual. I'll act as if nothing happened and wait for him. But, Lar, what do I do if he doesn't remember or bring it up?'

'Not remember! I bet it's all he can think about. He's probably planning on how he can get you alone to kiss you again. Boys can't think about anything other than sex. Well, if you ask my dad anyway.'

It is very difficult being an eighteen-year-old girl. We cannot imagine that the opposite sex does not dwell on us in quite the same way as we do on them. It is not lack of imagination, I assure you. It is lack of exposure.

Sometimes I wonder if Lara and I had known more about the opposite sex, if we could have understood them better, then we could have avoided our tragedy. Was it really our innocence that ruined us, or was it something deeper? It's what after all these years, I still can't decide.

But I didn't think that then. My thoughts were filled with dreams of Teddy kissing me and making love to me. I felt my face, tender from the night before. I was in love. And Lara knew and approved.

*

I went over to Teddy's the next day after school and waited for him to finish with track and field practice. I was reading *Lady Chatterley's Lover*, skimming for the sexiest parts or what I could get of them in the expurgated version, the only version available to me at eighteen. I twitched uncomfortably and felt my panties pressing against my skin, my eyes flying over words I had never encountered before, wondering if they meant what I thought they did.

'Another dirty sex book?' was how he greeted me.

I looked up at him from where I was draped over a chair, my legs one way, my arms another, my skirt hiked up past my knees.

He disappeared before I could reply. Already messing around in the kitchen, grabbing something from the pantry and a beer for himself from the fridge. I felt my neck flare up with heat. I buttoned my top.

He came back, and I smiled. He handed me a slice of coffee cake and a glass of milk. And that's when I lost it.

'Hey, Teddy,' I said, willing my body to sit up. 'I don't understand it. Why do you get to drink beer every day, and you come in and give me this damn glass of milk? It's not like one beer is going to get me high.'

I don't know why I had to go and pick a fight with him.

I know I wish I hadn't. I knew that the moment I started to speak, but I had to. It was insulting to be treated like a child when I'd spent the last two nights imagining myself a woman in love.

He sat down, propping his legs up on the coffee table, casual and undisturbed. His mother would never notice the scuff marks.

'With you I don't know.' He said it with a smile. His voice had this underlying jocular tone no matter how serious the words coming out of his mouth were. I remembered that from when Adam died. I hated it about him.

'You think I'm a drunk because I had a glass of champagne and let you kiss me, don't you? You think I'll hand my virtue to you if you so much as let me have a sip of beer. That's why you threw me out of the library and sent me back to face your family alone, and you didn't come back for another forty-five minutes. We were on dessert. What were you doing? Did you find the liquor cabinet and drink it yourself?'

'Come on, Lil,' he said, his mouth lifting to the left. He wanted to laugh. I could tell.

But I couldn't stop. It's a thing about me. A thing I don't like very much about myself, I'll admit. And it probably is what got us is into the whole mess in the first place. Oh, not the fight which was happening then – it didn't matter later on, not really – but what was to follow in the months to come, the summer and the autumn. If only I could control myself. Not get so het up in imagining the way life was going to go and throwing a tantrum, because that is the word for it, every time reality varies from the dream.

'Why do you think I'm a child? You do. I can see it in your eyes. You think I'm a little girl who you have the power to decide when to ruin and when to not. Well, I'll tell you something, Teddy McCalman. I don't need you to ruin me. I can do that plenty well enough by myself.'

'I know.'

It was stupid. I was nervous. But hell, I doubted he would light me a cigarette to calm me down.

He was looking at me, but, then again, he wasn't. It was as though he were looking straight past me, or through me or something. Looking at a me who didn't exist anymore or maybe one who didn't exist yet. Perhaps both. I don't know. He didn't say anything more. Why wouldn't he fight back? How could he sit there, smiling in his smug way, knowing full well I might go off to cry but I'd come back to him, like a child seeking reconciliation with its parent after a fit?

'And now you're sitting there, peaceful and calm. Nothing can shake you, Edward Joseph McCalman. Always goddamn calm and peaceful and judging me for all my wildness and…'

He rose, the floorboard creaking, neither of us thinking of his mother upstairs. He walked over, bent his lanky body, and kissed me. It was light and did not linger, and I knew he meant it. If I'd been a good girl, I would have allowed him to continue. But I wasn't a good girl, and I didn't want to be quieted. I threw him away from me with foolish violence.

'Go to hell, Teddy.'

I stormed out of the McCalman house, and I didn't go back until Easter Sunday. It was a long and sad two weeks, and I know I suffered more for it than Teddy did. Because he knew I'd come back. All he had to do was sit and wait.

He knew me, you see. But I don't know, maybe he didn't. I never really could understand Teddy, so it's difficult to know the extent to which he could have understood me. I often made the mistake of thinking he was a man. I forgot to remember he was only eighteen too.

Chapter Five

The next morning found me in the bathroom scrubbing lipstick from my mouth. I had been caught on purpose. I couldn't bear Mary Elizabeth for the full fifteen minutes of homeroom. Chemistry would be bad enough.

I had a rotten headache too. I had spent the night crying, followed by a sleep of bad dreams. I thought about feigning sickness – Dads never cared much about that sort of thing even if he saw straight through the lie – but I knew that the next day would be no better. And so, I faced the day.

'Lillie,' whispered Mary Elizabeth as I slid down next to her at our desk, 'I thought you'd never come. Are you feeling all right? You look very frail.'

Mary Elizabeth was never pale or wan or really that skinny either. It wasn't that she was fat exactly. She had a thinnish build leaning on the side of stocky, boyish but not in a sexy flapper vamp sort of way. I mean she always looked very healthy; maybe that's where she got her obsession for asking me if I was feeling ill. 'You know, you look like if the wind blew, it would knock you right over.'

'Well, good thing there isn't any wind,' I muttered, trying not to sound too cagey.

She grinned with that stupid smile of hers filled with teeth. I have an overbite too, you see, but I leave it at only showing my top-set. Mary Elizabeth had this thing of jutting out both layers, forcing her lower jaw out, showing off how white and healthy they were.

'Wait until you hear my news – it might well bowl you over.'

I narrowed my eyes. 'What is it?'

'Guess!'

'I don't feel well. Come on, tell me.'

'Guess who is going to Vassar too?' She teetered around on her chair like an overly excited child, the exact replica of a third grader waiting for her class picture to be taken.

'Oh.'

I was probably meant to congratulate her, but the words did not come. I'd been the first girl from St. Anne's to try for Vassar and only because of my mother. All right, I had heard rumors that Mary Elizabeth might try to go Seven Sisters too. Her college boards were nearly as good as mine (fine, she did better in chemistry and calculus, I'll admit to that), but still – Vassar? There were six other colleges she could have tried for, but she had to pick the one which I'd been destined for since I was born a girl.

This life outside of Mohawk Island was to be mine alone. Two more months of purgatory, wearing doll clothes and waiting to grow up and have some semblance of my own character, and then it would be my reality rather than some adolescent daydream of living. Soon there would be no more punishments of confession, no more Holy Roman Catholic Church, except for when I came home on the vacations. I could have been raised Protestant like the rest of the girls, that's what I planned to tell them anyway. But now, Jesus, there Mary Elizabeth would be with her toothy grin and cow eyes, handing out Rosary beads. Any hope I had for a new beginning was shattered. I wanted a drink. Nice and stiff.

'Congratulations,' I managed.

'It came as a surprise to me too, you know. I mean I knew I was accepted ages ago but didn't say a peep because, you know, the money and all.' Mary Elizabeth's family were poor, or much closer to it than mine. Her mother was a seamstress and her father was injured at the Ford plant before she was born or not long after. But being good Catholics, that didn't stop the Donahues from pumping out the kiddies.

'I was all prepared to go to Saint Rose's, but Sister Agnes told me I should try. I told her we don't exactly have the money, you know, but she just said the Good Lord will take of that if it comes to it, and how right she was.'

'When did you find out?' I said, trying not to look upset. It's a real problem with me – any emotion I have is apparent on my face and in my voice.

'Only yesterday, after school, there was a letter for me when I got home. I've won a scholarship, you see. That's what I've been waiting on, praying for for months. Isn't it wonderful news, Lillie? It means that you won't have to be lonely up there by yourself. My mother said she would pack me with plenty of cocoa and an extra coffee cup for any time you want to come to my room to visit. I told her you were going too, you see, and that made her feel a lot better about sending me with all those girls that, well you know. They won't be like us, will they, Lillie?'

At least I didn't have to go on a scholarship. At least I didn't have to show up with some stupid tin of cocoa to make friends because it was the only luxury my parents could afford. And Mary Elizabeth was such a simpleton. She'd tell people she was on a scholarship and a Catholic and poor and couldn't afford to have nice clothes or manners. But she wouldn't be ashamed of it because Mary Elizabeth couldn't understand meanness in others.

Yes, at least there was that to think on and comfort me. Not that it helped much.

*

'You'll be glad to hear you've lost Mary Elizabeth as a future classmate at Saint Rose's,' I reported to Lara during fourth period drawing. It was the only class we had together besides the lunch hour.

'How do you know that?'

'She's been offered a scholarship to Vassar in Chemistry.'

'What? You hate her.'

Lara knew me well.

'It's awful. I'll have to have Mary Elizabeth trailing after me like a puppy dog. It's practically unbearable to imagine.'

'Maybe she'll find a new group of girls to go with,' suggested Lara.

'She'd better. I can't imagine who would like her, though.'

Lara shook her head back and forth, her eyes widening as her chin folded into her neck. 'That type of girl always finds friends. They're better at it than you and me.' She was right. Neither of us were popular nor exactly had a talent for making friends. Oh sure, we had a group which included Ellen, Madeline and, most regrettably of all, Mary Elizabeth, but we didn't really like them, and they probably didn't really like us either.

'Saint Rose's won't be so bad for you now. You've decided on there, haven't you?'

'It's either that or secretarial college, and my mother was a teacher before I was born. I mean before any of us were born.'

It was true. Mrs. Marcelli had taught kindergarten and adult education courses at night up in Albany. It's how she and Mr. Marcelli met. He was studying to take his citizenship test and trying to learn English. She was the pretty, young teacher. It was very romantic, or so I thought as far as parents meeting stories went. Mine had been set-up for some Christmas dinner dance held by the Rensselaer chapter of the Knights of Columbus.

'Here's to us becoming our mothers,' I sighed. I mean no girl wants to be her mother at eighteen, least of all me. I didn't want to be dead at the age of forty-four, though I did like having her graceful collarbone. And her eyes. But that was about it. I certainly didn't want the loveless marriage and succession of miscarriages.

'Vassar isn't practically a nunnery like Saint Rose's,' said Lara, choosing to ignore my comment. 'Did I tell you what my dad did a few weeks ago after Mass? It was the Sunday you were up in New York.'

I shook my head. I would've remembered.

'All I did was say hello to Michael Reilly. Hello, nothing else. And I only said hello because I help his mother teach catechism on Tuesday evenings, you know that. But my mother saw it and on the drive home told my dad she had seen me talking with a boy.'

'Why did she do that?'

'She meant it as a joke. She said, "Oh, Joe, Lara was talking to a boy." I said I wasn't, it was only a hello. It would have been rude if I hadn't. My dad wouldn't have any of it and said if I was going to talk to a boy and be ashamed of the young man enough to deny it, then I should not have been speaking to him in the first place. And I started crying and we didn't talk over lunch. It was horrible. I almost threatened to eat it in my room, but I knew it would make it worse. And my nonna was over, so I couldn't.

'But what do they expect of me? To stay in my room and die? Wither up into a shriveled old maid like my Aunt Joan?' Her brown eyes grew larger and looked on the verge of tears. Up until we were fifteen or so, I had never seen Lara cry except for when her grandfather died. She used to seem much more stable than I. Then something switched in her. And now she could barely get through a story about her parents without welling up, and it didn't help that Lara was an ugly crier.

She calmed herself.

'At least they care. I mean I'm sure Dads hates it too, me talking to boys, but you know how he is. He never says a thing until suddenly you're finishing your dessert without a word throughout dinner and then it's, "Honey, are you seeing a young man? Well, you know you have to be careful. They don't think like girls." And that's it. Nothing again.'

'He lets you go on dates. I'll be forty before my dad will let me out of the house with a member of the opposite,' she couldn't bring herself to say the word, 'well, you know what.'

I didn't want to tell Lara about what had happened with Teddy. I couldn't bear the humiliation of having only two days before confessed my love for a boy who the next day threw me over. Well, maybe I'd thrown him over but that didn't change the fact that I'd gone around kissing yet another boy who I wouldn't be seeing again.

Lara continued, 'They want us to get married, but how do they expect us to if we aren't allowed to say hello to boys? I don't even want to talk to boys. I think they're scary. But it doesn't help for my dad to assume I'm boy-crazy.'

'I guess we'll be free soon enough,' I said without conviction.

'That's not what you were saying earlier.'

'Anything has to be better than this hell and curfews with parents.'

Lara froze, very suddenly, and shook her head violently. She did things like that sometimes.

'Let's talk about something else. This is making me sad.'

I knew I couldn't mention Teddy then because that was sad too.

I felt us growing separate, Lara and I, but I said nothing of that either.

*

It is difficult to decide where to start a memory. To recall what the important parts of it are and to filter out the bits which do not contribute much. When remembering, I am inclined to see a through line in the narrative, and I am desperate to forget anything which happened that does not add up, that seems a contradiction of sorts. I know we are supposed to contain multitudes and all of that transcendental nonsense I was once hooked on, but there are simply things I do not want to admit to.

And you would think these would be the sins I committed, or anything that would make me less than the ideal heroine of the story. The thing is though, I don't mind admitting to that sort of thing. I don't mind confessing my sins. The whole point of this thing is that I do like that – I get some sort of gratification out of recalling the most painful wounds, rubbing salt in them.

No, what I hate is the banal. I hate the wasted pieces of conversation we have to have with each other every day. I hate the motions which get us from doing one thing to the next. And I hate that I have to confess to having insipid moments, times not impinged with beauty or poignance or pain. In novels, we do not have to worry about how our heroine brushes her teeth or sits through chemistry lessons or has to go around with ladders in her stockings. And yet, this is what makes up life. But I refuse to allow it to enter memory.

In my memory, everything is leading towards what happened, and I desperately seek symbols and signs of foreshadowing everywhere. I have concocted the structure of the narrative for so long and believe it in so deeply and convincingly, I cannot detach myself from it now. Whether any of it really happened as I remember, I do not know. And certainly events did not happen in such a domino-effect fashion as I think. Or maybe they did.

The funny thing is usually I impose the narrative structure onto a string of memories after I see the story as finished. But it wasn't like that with this story, these memories. I saw myself writing it as I was living it, somehow grasping the significance of a moment before I understood its consequences. I felt each layer building on top of itself, another sign that I was losing it.

Ellen convinced me to go out with her the next Friday. I who had never so much as stayed out past nine o'clock on a Friday, except to go to the movies, was becoming quite the socialite, or so it seemed. Dads thought I was spending the night at Ellen's, and I was in a way. That's why I didn't dare to get ready at home but waited 'til I could breathe freely before Ellen's own vanity, crowding in for space at the mirror.

The party was at Ned Halpert's. The heatwave of early spring was holding, and I wore a summer dress from the year before which Ellen had deemed not too youthful. Ellen usually thought that while my clothes weren't exactly dowdy, they hinted of the nursery. If only we'd been the same size, she'd have lent me clothes of her own, but it always annoyed her to see pieces which were tight on her, swallow me and leave obvious gaps under the arms and at the neck. Luckily, we were the same shoe size, and she leant me a pair of pumps.

I'd left the house around six while Hetty was finishing up dinner. I hadn't said goodbye, but, all the same, she might have been suspicious if she'd seen me in a pair of high heels on a Friday evening and mentioned it to my father. I never trusted her to be on my side. She'd been with us for years, but I did not like this woman from the old country. Her eyes were pale blue and seemed to be made of glass. Another cold permanent fixture in the Carrigan household.

Ellen painted on her eyebrows and offered to have a go at mine, but I didn't let her. I liked mine as they were. 'Suit yourself,' she said, though she must have thought it a mistake.

I worked for over half an hour to get my curls to produce the effect I wanted, studying a print of Rita Hayworth clipped out from *Life*. Ellen's hair was curlier, but she shook out her ringlets and let them hang loose. She said it was very bohemian of a style and let boys know you weren't like all the other girls. I wondered if that meant easy, but I didn't dare ask. Ellen put on red lipstick. I only had pink.

We weren't late or anything, but the party had started by the time we arrived. I could tell as soon as Ned answered the door, a stupid grin on his face and glazed-over look in his eyes. A few drinks deep already, and it wasn't yet nine. It was sure to be a real baller of a party, I could tell that much.

'I could kill for a good glass of wine,' said Ellen. I had been waiting for her to say that. She always did.

'Drinks are this way, ladies,' said Ned as he led us through the foyer into the living room where there must have been thirty-odd people or so, most of them the same lot as usual – mostly St. Anne's and St. Luke's but some public-school kids and graduates too who'd stuck around to work at the Ford plant or were a year late in leaving for college. Teddy wasn't there, I saw that right away. Fixing my hair had been a waste.

A Benny Goodman record was playing, but no one was dancing. The room was full of excited voices – talking, laughing, signing, the sounds of aggressive kissing. It was the first time drinking for some, while others were old veterans, as I felt myself becoming.

Ned was a friendly fellow, and he told me to take anything I liked. It must have been his father's liquor cabinet, and I knew he might have hell to pay for it, but I took out the scotch and poured myself a tumbler. I didn't know then that one was supposed to have water with it or ice. I drank it down neat. I don't know if I actually liked the taste of it, but I had bragged to Ellen about how I adored whiskey, and I thought I might as well prove my point.

'Ellen, what are you supposed to do at a party like this?'

'Have fun! Come on, don't be such a Debbie Downer. And don't get drunk and start reciting poetry or whatever it is you did last time.'

The memory of James Moore's Christmas party stung. It had been a particularly humiliating night ending in vomit and tears.

'I can't help it, you know that. My mind gets jumbled when I drink sometimes and it's the only thing I can do to keep it thinking straight.'

Ellen laughed. 'There's James over there. Why don't you go and recite *The Battle of the Ancient Mariner* to him again? He seemed to enjoy it the first time.'

Ellen was thick, and she was tight, but I didn't feel like correcting her mistake.

'James! Get over here. Lillie's here, but she's left her poetry book at home this time.' Then, to me, 'Go get him. He loves you.'

I felt myself pushed towards James, though not physically by Ellen. James and I had happened twice before. The last time I let him touch my left breast but not my right. Maybe tonight's the night, I thought. Hell, he's all right.

I liked James. I always had. He wasn't tall and thin like the sort I usually felt myself attracted to, but he was kind of sexy. He wasn't much taller than I, shorter in fact with me in heels, and he was verging on the side of pudgy. He'd have a double chin by twenty-five; that was a certainty. But he was funny and clever and would tell me how lovely I looked. He also had very pretty and sympathetic blue eyes and was reported to have socialist sympathies. He wasn't my absolute ideal, but I was attracted to him.

James came over, kissing both Ellen and I on each cheek, the way he must have read Europeans did it. 'I like Lillie's poetry recitations,' he said. 'Her expressions are so … vivid.'

'Ha! You only like it when I forget a line and you can supply it.'

He smiled. 'Yes, I like that too. It reminds me that, every once in a while, a man's mind on liquor does prove superior to a woman's, but only very rarely, of course.'

'Of course.'

'You two are too much for the likes of me. I can't understand a thing you say, and I don't much want to either.' Ellen laughed and left. It had been her plan all along.

James didn't mind. He took me by the shoulders, pulling me to a corner where we could hear one another better.

'Drinking whiskey? You really are a girl straight out of a Hemingway novel.'

'I like it. It's better than weak beer, and that seems to be the only other option.'

'In that case, I'll pour myself a glass.'

Confidence oozed from James in a way not suited to a boy of eighteen. Speaking with him was like trying to impress one of my father's partners in his firm. He was destined for law school. It was the only thing he could have done. Well, either that or politics.

I don't remember how it started exactly. We were talking, but I knew he wanted to kiss me, and I knew I would let him. I didn't want to at first. I liked having the memory of Teddy's kiss resting on my lips and didn't want to corrupt it. I was high on strange romantic ideas like that. A lot of bullshit, maybe, except somewhere inside of me I still do believe in that sort of thing.

But James Moore had kissed me twice before, and I knew it wasn't an unpleasant experience. Franky, up until Teddy had kissed me the week before, it was the best kiss I'd had. James was a good kisser. He ought to have been considering he claimed to have kissed twenty-seven different girls, which I do believe was true. For all of that, though he was a virgin. Like me.

And there he was kissing me, his tongue in my mouth. With James there was a certain joy in kissing back sloppily too. Kissing James made me forget a whole lot of things including how lovely kissing Teddy had been, how markedly different. Then bang right in the middle of it, everything came crashing back and hurt twice as much. But for the first minute of the kiss, intoxication hit hard and I fell into that delightful state of inebriation, giggly and content.

'Shall we go someplace a bit more comfortable?'

I nodded my consent.

He took my hand, winding our arms together and led me back to the foyer and up the stairs to one of the bedrooms. It didn't look like the master, thank God, or Ned's either. It was probably some sort of guest room, I don't know. I didn't take the moment to study the decor too seriously.

I felt James rubbing against my thigh, his penis hard beneath his trousers. I knew that much about sex, though I had yet to see one. I was sighing and breathing hard, more for dramatics than from actual feeling. I thought that was what a girl was supposed to do.

'You're so goddamn pretty,' he was mumbling into my hair, and I knew he meant it.

Everything was happening too fast, and I didn't know how to stop it, but I knew in my little girl heart I wanted to stop it very badly. But then again, I didn't. I liked James and liked feeling pretty and sexy and wanted. I liked how he slyly unzipped my dress half-way and deftly unclasped my bra. He cupped my left breast and started to rub his thumb across the areola. I let out a sigh of genuine pleasure. I had not felt that before.

He then drew us closer together, until we fell onto the bed, his bulge against my thigh.

'Lillie,' he whispered, 'I know we can't, but there are other things we can do.'

I nodded.

'Do you mind if I, umm, free myself up a bit?'

I did it for him. I took my shaking hands and undid his belt buckle and unbuttoned the fly of his trousers. He took my hand and cupped it over his crotch. I didn't know what one was supposed to feel like; I'd forgotten there were balls and all of that. I guess I'd never really thought about it.

He pulled down my dress, revealing my garter belt and underwear. He undid my stockings.

'Shh, don't worry. I'm not going to. I just don't want to get you messy.'

I don't remember if I really understood; I suspect I didn't. I didn't have much knowledge of ejaculation back then, only that it could make you pregnant if it went inside.

I felt his whole weight collapse on top of me. It was a very different feeling from when Teddy had done the same and not only because James was heavier. But I didn't mind it, not really. I felt charged and sexy, and I continued to like his kisses for what they were. I was tight, and I didn't care.

He started to move on top of me. I felt the bulge rubbing against the bone of my mound, like how my hand did when I touched myself. I only knew how to do that, not the other way like what Tom Westerby had tried with his fingers.

This felt good, though; I remember that. And I remember not having known that this feeling could happen with a boy until then. I thought it was shameful and sinful and meant to be kept secret, but here was James showing me he too knew the possibility of it. He smothered me with his weight, and we kept on kissing. It was very wet.

He rocked back and forth, faster and faster. I felt him growing sweaty, and I admit I did not fully understand what the inevitable conclusion of this was leading to on his end or my own. Then it happened. I came. I cried out, timidly at first, afraid to make much noise now that it was genuine.

And he came too. I felt my panties growing wetter and when he pulled away, I saw the damp on the front of his own boxer-shorts. He kissed me again, saying what a girl I was and all that sort of shit which I knew somehow would be said to me by many boys and men again and again.

But what did I feel? That I remember perfectly. It was the same mixture of pleasure and guilt I had often felt when I had done that to myself, except I had never allowed for it go over the top. I always stopped. And so, for the first time I felt full of wonder at the power of my own body, fascinated by what it had achieved and suspecting that was the whole point of this sex business. Ellen had long understood.

But I knew it was a sin. I did not love James and that made it worse. Better or worse than doing it with my own hand, I did not know, but somewhere in between perhaps.

At least I wasn't stupid enough to think I could get pregnant from a thing like that. But it was no good, even that was not a comfort.

I dressed despite James' protests that I should stay. We could have a lover's cuddle and speak of poetry, he suggested. He liked me and did not want me to go, but I had to flee.

I zipped up my dress and pulled up my stockings, not bothering to re-fasten them to my garter belt.

'I'll, ahh, I'll see you around, James,' I mumbled and left. He was in his shorts and could not follow.

I needed to get some air. It was cooler, the heatwave of earlier had broken, and I wished I had thought to grab my coat before stepping out. Not like I knew where Ned had put it. I wanted a cigarette too, but I never had any on me, and I'd forgotten to ask James for one. He smoked, if only reluctantly as part of his pose of masculinity. But then he would have followed me out, and it wasn't worth it. I didn't want him kissing me again. I never wanted to kiss him again or see him.

What was I doing? It was like I was running madly towards some distant cliff, daring myself to jump, and crying with fear every time I reached the point of it. I was afraid, is the simple truth of the matter. Recklessness with a conscience never works out well. I didn't know what to do or where to go, and I sure didn't know how to get home. I didn't have my driver's license.

I collapsed on the front lawn of the Halpert's house, crying for I don't know how long. Only two weeks later and here I was again. I couldn't take much more of it. The drinking and the sex and the guilty conscience. At least this time I knew I had enjoyed it; I didn't have to contend with the fear of abnormality on top of it all, but I didn't know. I didn't know how I was going to stop myself from ending up the next week on a stoop, crying and wishing for a cigarette. And the sad truth is I still haven't learned.

Chapter Six

Aunt Claire insisted on accompanying me to pay my annual Easter duty. I think she suspected if she sent me on my own, I might spend the hour loitering around Delaney's looking at lipsticks and never stepping into church. I had been very quiet about my religious crisis and subsequent waning faith. I was afraid of being forced to have a long conversation with Father Kavanaugh. And I knew that wouldn't help.

Aunt Claire had been wary of my behavior since she'd observed my negligence in crossing myself after receiving the Blessed Sacrament, and she told Dads about it. Not that he cared much, the Protestant in him always seemed to win, but not in his sister.

I dread confession more than most Catholics. I mean some actually look forward to it, take my mother or Mary Elizabeth for example. They liked having their soul cleansed and momentarily living in the grace of God. There is a whole other sort of Catholic who enjoys it because it's the equivalent of spiritual bail. That's why we go on Saturday afternoons, cleanse the soul before a big night out. Though how some manage to take communion the next morning, I've never understood.

I am a good Catholic, am still. Even if I have given up on God. That's not the important part of it, as I see it. I learned my doctrine too seriously as a child and took it to heart, and I am not willing to play fast and loose with the rules.

Except for lying by omission, I've always done that.

I knew I couldn't tell the truth. Confession couldn't erase

the terrible feeling I had when I laid awake at night and wondered if I was supposed to like that thing Tom Westerby did to me. It could not wash away memory.

I recalled his face with fear, a sick feeling growing in my stomach, a paralysis in my legs. I wished to forget it and him and the whole damn evening and return to a state of innocent girlhood where I needn't worry about a boy whispering in my ear, 'If you don't stop squirming, I'll rape you.'

I never have told anyone what Tom Westerby said to me that night in the closet in New York until now. I never could. I tell a version of it perhaps. There he is, a slick, slimy boy, drunk and confident. And there I am. A shy, sad girl, also drunk. But I am not weak. Oh no. I punched him. But you know all of this. I've told you before. But what I didn't tell you is everything he said. He had power when he spoke those words, taunting me. Reminding me that I was nothing but a whim to him, helpless. I couldn't let it all in. I couldn't accept what had happened. I could not bear the thought of my own innocence, because to admit to it rendered me powerless. I can't, still. I was a scared child whose will was taken from her, while he, the guilty one, held the power.

It'd gotten worse in the remembering of it. I thought maybe with Teddy and romance or with James and pleasure … But I couldn't stop it. And I knew Father Kavanaugh would fare no better in banishing the demon. I could not confess, and he could not absolve.

Because had I sinned? I don't know why that mattered so much to me. But it did. I felt fragile and thin and I thought of my mother in purgatory and if she knew … If she knew I'd gone to the dogs on my own accord, then so be it. It's my own will. But what if it wasn't…

It must be a venial sin, I thought. A mortal sin must be

committed with intention. This was very elementary catechism, but much harder to apply than to recite before First Communion. What I did with James, all right, fine that was mortal, but then again had I really wanted that to happen? No, I complied because I was drunk and I was lonely but … Had there been intention to commit sin? Had I put myself in the position to allow sin to happen, I could imagine Father Kavanaugh saying. Well, yes. But I had done that with Tom Westerby too. Did that make it mortal?

I stood in line, waiting my turn, deciding on a few venial sins I would confess to. Sometimes I thought Father Kavanaugh was disappointed when he heard a young girl's voice listing off the usual transgressions of lying and not being the nicest to her friends and parents. 'Is that all?' he was known to prompt. I never went further, though I knew some girls, Francis Tooley, for one, who had. Francis went ahead and confessed to having sex with her boyfriend at summer camp, but then it turned out she hadn't. It was only a case of impure thoughts, but for her that was the same as having done it. Which I mean it was, in a way. A sin of the mind. Dear Lord, though if I had to start admitting to sins of the mind…

On that spring day of '41, the Saturday before Easter, I exited the confessional and knelt before the tabernacle, mumbling the words of the Hail Mary, pretending that in saying this ancient incantation I was transforming my whole being to a pure and innocent state. I wanted it to work, but it didn't. I never thought it could. And so I pushed back at my cuticles and waited for Aunt Claire to finish.

I kept my eyes on the confessional. Aunt Claire, for all her adherence to religion and its doctrine of humility, really was a stylish woman. She had a thin frame, much like my own. No breasts, no hips but prominent shoulders, arched back in perfect posture. The other grown women I knew, including Mrs. Marcelli and her daughters-in-law, were short with pudgy legs and figures that had been weighed down at the center, forcing their large bottoms ever closer to the ground. They could wear nice dresses, and they certainly would be on Easter Sunday, but they'd look like a dollar fifty compared to Aunt Claire.

She knelt next to me in the pew, her back rod straight. I adjusted the position of my rear meeting the seat to match her own one of piety. I knew she wouldn't be long at her prayers. She never was. And I was grateful for that.

Jesus on the cross and all of that suffering, and the moaning and the thunder of Tenebrae two nights before. And the candles later that night, the welcoming back of Christ, the stripping of the purple cloths, pulled away by hook. The joy which would soon refill this church. And I would be there for it in a matter of hours and again the next morning. The Passion completed. The spring come.

If I could have believed in it, surely it would have helped. But I couldn't. I couldn't turn to God when I did not understand his forgiveness. And I'd given up on the Virgin Mary a long time before that too. She was to be a mother to the motherless, but she wasn't. She did not have a breast at which to cradle your head.

My mother would have brushed my hair and told me … No, she wouldn't have listened. She would have stuffed her ears with cotton balls, refusing to recognize there could be such evil in the world and that it could touch her daughter. She wouldn't have blamed me, no. But she would have told me it hadn't happened or begged for me to tell her that instead. That it was another one of my stories I was working on, and I really ought to use my talent to glorify God and not write such smut. Yes, that was it. Another of my stories.

And it is. Though it is one of my true stories. A memory.

No, I've never told anyone. Not Lara, not Teddy, certainly not Father Kavanaugh, not my husband, nor my God. What would be the point? They could offer no absolution for a sin I could not – cannot – understand if I committed.

And so I did what I have always done. I took the memory of it, and I stuffed it away in the recesses of my mind and of my heart. Do not touch this, it said.

But sometimes I do flip through these files of pain – that's how I see them laid out, organized and labeled according to particular episode, stored in a cabinet without a lock. I grab at one, skim through the contents of the memory, wonder if that girl and her story enclosed within are true. And if that girl could have been me.

Chapter Seven

Easter came in the middle of April that year, and Mark Hamilton rang me up the week before to ask me to his parents' Yacht Club dinner on the Island. Not that they had a yacht. No one did. It should really have been called a boat club because all they had were dingy little dinghies you could take out for a few hours, but someone got it in their head that that wouldn't do and went ahead and decided on a name which denoted prestige rather than accuracy. It was a funny club at that too because few Islanders belonged to it. Mostly it was Albany families who came down to enjoy the pathetic excuse for a beach (man-made the decade before on the southwest side of the Island – one of Roosevelt's projects) and take in a dinner and a drink at the club. My father, like most male Islanders, belonged to the Knights of Columbus which held its meetings in St. Luke's rumpus room and stank of thin beer and Pall Malls.

I'd never been to the Yacht Club before. There had never been a reason. But here I was to be the date of Mark Hamilton for their special Easter Sunday lamb roast and to meet his parents too. Ellen was of the opinion that a guy didn't ask a girl to meet his parents unless she was something special, and I got it in my head that for once she might be right.

I mean I really thought he liked me. Sure, he might only be a stop gap between the boys I'd meet at Vassar but ... I had no other boys to dream of other than Teddy and ... I knew *he* could not end well. Still, I didn't know about

Mark. I couldn't understand why he never gave me his full attention when we were together. To me it seemed, if you liked a girl, you'd talk to her. Or, if not talk to her, at least try to get her into bed like most of the other boys I knew did. Not with his parents there, of course, but on the drive back home. But Mark was more interested in the Catholic Church than in me.

Oh well. Having a date gives you something to talk about with your girlfriends, if nothing else. So I'd gone up to Albany to buy gloves with Lara after paying my Easter duty. Lara had to buy a new girdle which she hated because she said it made her feel matronly. She'd been stuck in one since she was fourteen despite not having any appearance of a chest whatsoever. But Mrs. Marcelli insisted. I've never worn more than a brassiere and do not understand the horrors of the contraption which Lara called her chastity belt.

We spoke of Mark and the Hamiltons as we passed by the pretty pastel dresses displayed in Myers that season – just arrived the week before. We did not speak of Teddy. Lara preferred Mark anyway, though as she said, 'He can't hate me because he doesn't know who I am.' I wondered how Lara managed to get lost in a town of so few people, but it was true. When you don't have a personality other than being the companion to another girl, you're fairly forgettable.

'I like this one,' I said of a pale blue dress with a tight taffeta bodice and blue tulle skirt.

Lara laughed. 'You'd look like a five-year-old in the ballet.'

I didn't care. I bought it with the excuse of the Spring Formal. Sure it was premature but buying clothes without having an occasion to wear them to first is a particular vice of mine. It's the only experience I have of love at first sight.

How Lara and I were to get dates to the thing, we didn't know. It seemed an insurmountable problem and the threat of wallflowerdom was quite likely. That was unless Mark Hamilton asked me after the dinner, or if I could get up the nerve to ask him. Ordinarily a girl couldn't ask a boy for a date, but in the instance of the dance being her own she could well go ahead and do so. Which I thought I might do depending on how well the dinner went.

I bought a fresh tube of lipstick too. Red. Like Ellen's. I felt myself to be a woman.

I wore it on Easter Sunday, thinking I looked rather glamorous in my pale-yellow Easter dress, white hat, and white lace kid gloves. I looked fairly awful with remnants of baby fat and teeth too eagerly spread in a grin. But hell, I was eighteen, and I thought this was the height of my allure. And it is for some girls, but my God, if it had been for me...

When Mark Hamilton knocked at the door, I spied right away that he hadn't brought flowers. I was disappointed. I had daydreamed for the last week about him doing so, but it was all right. He'd borrowed his mother's car for the evening which was open-topped. I knew it would ruin my hair, and I didn't have a scarf for it, but I didn't care. I was determined to enjoy our drive to the club because it might be the only time we had to ourselves all night, until the drive back that was. But drives home are different from drives to a place. Drives to, if they're good that is, start with small talk and open into a proper discussion. Drives home can really only be filled with polite conversation of how lovely the evening was, that's until they descend right back into small talk, or so I find.

I'd never met Mark's parents before that night. They were Episcopalian, and lukewarm at that, but Mark was a Cardinal John Henry Newman sort of Catholic, converted by the Oxford movement, as I would later learn to call it, at the age of thirteen. How they all got on and lived in the same sphere, Lord, I don't know, but I've never been that good at discerning how other people's home lives are possible. It's enough to bear through my own.

They were a very funny couple, the Hamiltons, not much different from my own parents – not in terms of money or education anyhow – but Protestant and therefore more acceptable, and invited to join clubs the way Dads never had been.

His mother was thin and had a Hollywood sort of face. She was blonde and that instantly put me off her, as with all blonde women. She looked better at forty than I did eighteen. But she told me how lovely I looked. Perhaps she was being kind. A mother has to say that sort of thing to her son's date, but I took it as a real compliment and beamed, color rising to my pale cheeks.

Mr. Hamilton was a man with a hearty laugh and a middle-age gut held in with a waistcoat. His light brown hair was thinning on top and he had a mole, much like his son, but not so well placed between his eyes. His hands shook as he grabbed his tall son to him, squeezed his shoulders, and complimented his choice of date for being exceptionally pretty. I blushed again.

I've known his type too often since. One look at me and they think they have a pretty girl who will fall straight into their lap and lick them up with praise. Not me. It was the first time I encountered someone of Mr. Hamilton's ilk, and so I didn't know how to behave, which I guess explains what happened, in a way. I did learn, I'll tell you that. Probably about the only mistake I've gone through often enough and finally stopped repeating.

'What do you want to drink, Miss Carrigan? Or is it Lillie? Have anything you like.'

This meant that I could order alcohol. No adult had

asked me that before. I really must've looked to be a grown-up woman.

I didn't think about it for a second. 'I'll have a whiskey, neat, please.'

Mark gave me a look. I wasn't sure what he meant by it, only that I must've done something wrong. Mr. Hamilton laughed with genuine good humor. I thought it was an endearing laugh, very welcoming, but now I know it was it was mocking me, labeling me in a certain way. I don't think he was proud of his son's choice of date after that.

'Wouldn't you rather a nice sherry, or perhaps a bit of fine brandy if you are inclined towards the darker spirits?' I looked at his hands. They were gross, stumpy things. And still they shook.

'No,' I said, 'I'm afraid I've never had very much to drink, but I know I like whiskey without anything. It is very nice, don't you think? I'll drink it very slowly.'

Mrs. Hamilton smiled. 'Why look at that. A girl who knows her own mind.' I smiled too, though I didn't want to.

'That's Lillie for you. Do you know she's read practically the entire English canon?' added Mark in an attempt to pacify his parents.

I cast my eyes down. I never know what to do with myself when people are heaping praise on me. It doesn't seem polite to agree wholeheartedly with everything they are saying right away. And, besides, what Mark was saying was, and still is, a lie. I've never read *Tom Jones* or *Clarissa*, and I don't intend to.

'I don't know about that,' I said, slowly, shyly.

'Mark tells us that you are expected to be valedictorian of your class,' said Mrs. Hamilton in her sweet but distinctly Manhattan voice. I wanted to like her, but something about her lacked warmth, much like her son in that way.

75

'Yes,' I murmured.

'And Vassar too. Did Mark mention I'm a Vassar alumna myself?'

'Yes, my mother was as well. What year were you?'

'Class of 1920. I was there during the war. A very different place it was then. Let's hope it won't be like that for you.'

'Well,' said Mr. Hamilton, choking on his saliva. It was the first sound out of him in over five minutes, but he looked the sort of man who only felt comfortable when speaking. 'Who knows, Helen, with Roosevelt in office we could be in the war before Lillie here goes up this September.'

'What are you reading, Lillie?' asked Mark, derailing the conversation from politics. 'She's always reading something.'

It was odd. Mark was not trying to show me off; he was attempting to justify me as a choice of date. Justify my very existence by making me out to be some sort of whizz kid, the added novelty being that I was a girl from a Catholic family, I guess.

'I'm reading *Tender is the Night*. I've only started.'

'Explains the whiskey,' said Mr. Hamilton.

'I like Fitzgerald,' I said, a hint of aggression in my voice. Though with me the hint couldn't have been that strong. 'I think he's a genius. Or was.'

'Didn't he die of alcoholism?'

I saw that Mark's aggravating obsession with morality came from his father. Denouncing art because he'd read something of the artist in the papers.

'Heart attack, I believe, but yes, he certainly was young. It's a shame. After this, I'll have read everything he has written, and I wish there was more.'

'You see, Lillie reads everything,' said Mark.

'I don't read everything. I only read things I like.'

'And you like that sort of thing?' asked Mr. Hamilton.

'Don't you think all this sort of stuff is a fad? Surely they won't let you read modern trash at Vassar?'

'Yes, they will structure my reading at Vassar; it'll mostly be the classics, I suspect. But I do hope to have time to read what I please, when I can.'

'And your parents don't mind?'

'I'm afraid it's only my father at home. My mother died when I was younger.'

I relish revealing this detail to people I dislike. I wait for the sympathy to enter their eyes but refuse to accept it. I also never say passed away. No, always dead or died. It packs more of a punch.

I continued without hesitation, 'He doesn't like it either, but he appreciates that I am eighteen, and it can hardly be helped.'

'If it's only youth, then it will pass. That must be a comfort.'

'No, I disagree. I hope never to lose my ability to discern what is good and what is not. And I know Fitzgerald is good, as is Hemingway, as is Joyce, or what I can get my hands on of his. It is very difficult to get everything he's written.'

Mr. Hamilton did not reply and neither did Mark attempt another desperate and asinine comment, hoping to turn it into conversation.

It was Mrs. Hamilton who spoke next, soothing us all with anecdotes of her Vassar days, claiming I would adore it and how jealous she was of me to be but eighteen and have the happiest of days ahead of me. It was kind of her, but I could not warm to the woman. She did not invite it.

'Another whiskey then?' said Mr. Hamilton.

I met his gaze. I could see he had already evaluated my breasts and decided they weren't much. I knew the night was over and I knew I hated this man and he had no use for me. I thought I might as well agree. Give them their dancing monkey, if that's what they all wanted anyway.

'Well, if you insist, yes, please. Thank you.'

The air in the room was close, and I felt ill. I drank the second whiskey faster than the first, and I knew I would be positively drunk by the end of the dinner. I wanted nothing more than to crawl beneath the table and pray to a god I scarcely believed in that I might cease to exist.

I knew I seemed a danger to these people, a poor excuse for a rebel. But they labeled me one because I drank my whiskey neat and read modern literature. Funny things to hate a person over, though to their credit, I've hated a lot of people for far less sensible reasons.

I had to be humiliated and taught that I was setting out on the wrong course of life and best to change directions fast. How could a girl of eighteen be allowed to expose herself to uncensored ideas? I bet they would have loved a girl like Mary Elizabeth, Catholic and all. She would have fitted their expectations.

'You are a free spirit, I believe,' said Mrs. Hamilton with a little smile. She had the same soft eyes as her son.

Yes, that was the consensus. I was a free-spirited intellectual who if she hoped to marry and rejoin society would have to abandon such foolish notions. Mr. and Mrs. Hamilton thought, as I suppose Dads hoped, that college would sort me out and send me away a young lady rather than a modern woman tempted by the rhetoric of socialism and, God forbid, the lure of the diaphragm. Any sort of girl who hoped to have a chance with a Mark Hamilton ought to use her education to lessen her mind rather than to broaden it. I knew I could not ask him to the dance after all.

The ride home was miserable. I knew Mark was ashamed of me, but I didn't mind. After all, he had been the one to abandon me, the very person to expose me to how the adult world functioned. I expected him to scold me, to lecture me on my sins, but he said nothing. Not until the end, when he opened my car door and said, 'Thanks for being such a good sport about it all, Lillie. I hope it wasn't too horrible for you. See you around some time?'

It had been a failure of a night and didn't I know it.

I waited until he had backed out of the driveway, a whole hour before he had been expected to drop me off, and crept the three doors down to Teddy's. Teddy was at the piano, in the living room, his fingers causally landing on notes. He was alone. I knocked at the window. He turned his dark head, and I could see from the way he squinted and screwed up his mouth that he was confused by the rapping. His eyes scanned the room, looking for the source of the noise until at last he fixed his gaze on the window and saw me standing there in a nice dress.

'What's the story, Lil?'

He was on his knees, speaking through the crack in the window he had made. I bent my head, unwilling to tear yet another pair of stockings by kneeling in the dirt.

'Can I come in? I've had a night of it.'

'Damn, you think you're Cathy or something. Have you been drinking?'

I scowled. 'How did you know?'

The left corner of his mouth raised in a grin. I knew we were all right again.

'You reek of it. Come in.'

He let me in at the door, but I paused before stepping across the threshold. I was unsure of how to greet him.

'Come on, stop playing all shy and regretful. There's some wine left over from dinner, we'll have that. Mother fell asleep early.'

I found my voice and tried not to squeak. 'You're giving me booze?'

'It's Easter, why not? And, if I remember correctly, the last time I denied you your precious *booze*, you told me to go to hell. Can't be having that sort of behavior on the day the Lord has risen, can we? Especially not when you've already had a good head start. No reckoning what you may say or do.'

'All right then, I get it.'

'Come on then.'

I caught up to his pace as he led me through the house to the kitchen.

'Teddy, I have to say…'

'Yeah, I know, you're sorry and all that bullshit.'

'Well…'

He pulled me close in what resembled a brief hug. 'Is that enough? I don't want to keep on with this sentimental crap. Let's drink. You left your book here too.'

'Oh.'

I was rendered dumb. Teddy had touched me, and his scent lingered.

'What's the matter, anyway? Raiding Daddy's liquor cabinet again?'

'I had dinner with the Hamiltons.'

'That useless prick Mark Hamilton? No wonder you're drunk.'

I sighed. 'They don't think I'm a lady, whatever that's supposed to mean. Not suitable for Mark as far as they're concerned.'

'And Mark's a bastard. Come on.'

'That's not entirely fair. He's an intellectual.'

'He's a nobody who read some books the wrong way.'

I laughed. He smiled.

'What's funny about that?'

'I think that's exactly what Mark would say about you and me.'

He smiled again and lit a cigarette. 'That's another thing he's wrong about then. Hey, you want one of these?'

'No, I'm okay. Dads will smell it when I get in.'

'Suit yourself.' He poured me some wine. 'Here you go.'

He didn't kiss me then as I hoped he might. But it didn't matter, not really. Because I knew we were friends again, and I had missed that most.

I went home, and I read my Fitzgerald, and I went to sleep a happy girl.

Chapter Eight

But now we must turn to Lara's story, as I have neglected her. Lara in the background all this time, studying her Italian and French conjugations, plucking her eyebrows and silently feuding with her parents. Celebrating my romantic successes with little hope of her own.

Lara, what is there to say of her when she knew so little of herself? Her character was malleable, determined by those around her. She liked the usual sort of things other girls did. Movies and puppies and kittens. And she liked to laugh a lot. Most people knew her as the laughing girl who had peed her panties in the fourth grade and needed to be issued a new skirt in the nurse's office. I couldn't tease her about that, though.

I sometimes think it was this very quality in Lara, her inability to decide on a fixed personality, which drew us together and made us friends. I was then the dominant one of us, the one with the stories and the ideas. Every once in a while, Lara had an idea, like when we were eleven and she decided we should have tea parties and pretend to be grand ladies with children and marital problems. I took the idea and ran with it, inventing a whole other world for us to inhabit. In that too I became the main character who she called on once a week to hear how my affair with Lord Salisbury was progressing. She'd add some asinine details about how her children were teething or asking my opinion on how one politely refused the advances of a husband's friend, but I was the star of it, and we both accepted it.

We weren't eleven any longer and we weren't playing tea

party, but little else had changed. Lara remained the one who had never been kissed, and I the one who, until recently, had simply not been kissed by the right boy. But really, we were in the same position, mine slightly better perhaps, but not by much.

She was losing her baby fat, but her figure, much like her personality in those days, had yet to develop and emerge. Lara always wore wool stockings and never shaved her legs. 'The hair grows back in an hour, what's the point?' Her school uniform blouse suffered from yellow stains at the armpits, but despite great effort, she was never able to scrub them away.

A person without a definition. A problem I could never grasp. I have, for better or for worse, always known who I am. Nothing much has changed since I was eight or eighteen. My virtues, though few, and my vices, which are many, have remained. The same cannot be said of Lara, a person who, beneath her face, though thinner, and her laughter, now scarcer, I can barely recognize.

Lara was not weak so much as a person without firm structure. She fought to have her own will, but, as she lacked her own character, she was in constant debate between whether to concede to her parents' wishes for her or to follow my lead to the way of all flesh, though she innately sensed she wanted neither.

That spring I asserted my dominance, and she followed. I've always seemed stronger, in Lara's eyes too. But it wasn't true. We were both scared little girls. I only had the upper-hand in my determination to ruin myself. That was all.

In the end, Teddy asked me to be his date to the Spring Formal, which solved a lot of problems, though like everything, invited more.

'Don't get any ideas,' I remember him saying, 'this isn't

romantic. But hell, if we both have to go, we may as well go together. I'll bring a flask. We'll need it.'

'And you'll let me have some of it?' I asked.

'Why not?'

Months of agonizing on how to get a date and there it was. Teddy would take me. It had all been so easy. So easy in fact that I hadn't dared to dream it.

That evening, when I told Lara over the telephone I'd achieved a date to the Spring Formal, and Teddy no less, she launched into her complaints of how she would never receive an offer. Her joy at my success was shattered by fear of her own inevitable failure. That was the way with Lara.

'I don't know who would be enough of a fool to ask me. Really, Lil, the guy would have to be crazy. And I don't want to go with a crazy person. Not like I'll even have the option of that, though.'

'There's still plenty of time. Tickets don't even go on sale until the end of next week. Some guy is bound to ask you.'

I mean I wasn't that certain of it, but I thought with myself knocked out of the way I could turn my attention to Lara. It would give me something to think about which was good because there were many things at the time I didn't want to think of.

'Who? Come on, Lillie, be honest. I don't know any boys. How could I? We go to a convent and when I try to say to hello to someone my dad has a heart attack.'

She laughed about it a little, but I knew the worry was eating her up inside.

'I don't even want to go. It's all pretty silly, isn't it, Lil?'

'Yeah, I guess so.'

What was I supposed to say at this point? She was growing near to hysterics, which I didn't exactly blame her for because I would have been much the same, really, I had been. But that was Lara. She took a topic and harked on about it at every angle for an hour until you threw up your hands in surrender.

'It isn't silly.' And here we went again. 'You're going with Teddy. You'll waltz off like Cinderella at the end of the night, he'll propose, and you'll never have to worry about a thing again.'

'Hey!'

'Okay. Fine. Maybe that won't happen, but you know you have a guy interested in you. You're not going to die an old maid with cats, the mockery of your nieces and nephews who have to take you in when you're senile.'

'Lara, it's a dance!'

'Lil, it isn't just a dance, it's the whole facts of life.'

I rolled my eyes, thankful she couldn't see.

'I'll find you a date.'

'Who? You don't know any boys either except for the ones you've already kissed. I don't want your leftovers like that, thanks anyway.'

'I'll ask.'

'Like I'm some desperate crone? Don't you dare!'

It was impossible.

'You're lucky. You've always had Teddy to fall back on.'

'Lar, I can ask Teddy if he has any…'

'Don't. Teddy already thinks I'm a pathetic creature. Don't go giving him more reason, please.'

I didn't have to. It was Teddy who brought it up. It turned out that Jack Allen, a friend of his from the track team, needed a date having recently split from his girlfriend, Catherine Spence – she broke up with him – and feeling pretty hung up over the whole thing.

I knew Jack well enough from the few parties I'd been to with Ellen. Ruddy faced, tall with the build of a chubby man but somehow slender. The type of boy who said 'jeez' to be polite but who was thinking stronger language in his head.

I thought I remembered liking him well enough, but, in truth, he was a fairly forgettable sort of person. And in that very way, he was perfect for Lara.

When Teddy said to me one afternoon as I was reading in his living room, sans kiss or lovemaking of any sort, 'Hey, Lil, do you know of any girls who would go with my friend Jack Allen to the formal? He knows a lot of girls and everything, but he doesn't want to take any of them. He had Catherine Spence last winter, you know her? Yeah, I know, she's a bitch. But he hasn't felt like getting romantic with another girl after that or something. Do you know anyone he could take? You know, as a friend?'

I smiled because I knew. Here it was.

'Lara hasn't got a date either. I think they could get along very well,' I said.

'Sure. I'll suggest it.'

And then he went back to his book and we spoke no more about it. I couldn't read, though. I had to ring Lara, and Teddy knew it all too well when I begged off five minutes later.

'You and Lara better not have any of your secret plots at the dance,' was the last thing Teddy said to me as I dashed out the door, nearly forgetting my book.

That's how we really come onto Lara's story because it is difficult to untie her from Jack. Their lives were to be inflexibly bound together after that. Two people set up out of mutual desperation. And from that was born what I have long thought of as the happiest days of our lives. And what I know now to be our ruin.

*

It started with ice cream.

It was to be the first time Lara and Jack were to meet, having both agreed to go the Formal blind. Teddy hadn't thought of introducing them to each other beforehand, but he didn't oppose when I suggested it.

'You think they can meet for the first time at the Formal? That would be humiliating. What if they have nothing to talk about or…'

'I don't see why. Come on, it's not like this is some arranged marriage, Lil. Some people do that too, you know.'

'That's fine for some people but not for Lara. Christ, Teddy. Do you ever think of others? Have some imagination! She'll drive herself mad with worry, and me too. Come on, can't you ask Jack if he might like to go for an ice cream or something, the four of us?'

'Jesus, an ice cream?'

'Teddy, please. After all, I found Jack his date. It's only fair that everything is done on my terms.'

'Some matchmaker you are. Jesus, Lil, fine, I'll ask him tomorrow. We'll go on your ice cream double date like something out of Andy Hardy.'

It was all coming together very nicely, I thought. Teddy had said double date.

But then it was almost as difficult to convince Lara to go along with the plan. Which was fairly ungrateful considering she'd been the one to ring me on the phone for weeks and complain about how no boy would ask her, wallflower status, inevitable spinsterhood, etc.

'I can't do that,' she blurted out when I told her during art class. 'What if someone sees us from church? They'll tell my parents.'

'How exactly are you expecting to go to the Formal then if no one is allowed to see you?'

'That's fine,' she said with a change of tone in her voice, now almost cheerful. 'It's supervised by the nuns. My mother probably would have thought it strange if I didn't. But a date beforehand? They'll think that means dates after and then I'll have a boyfriend and boys only want one thing and all of that, and they won't approve. And if they think we're serious about each other, they won't let me go to the Formal just in case he wants to go all the way that night. Don't look at me like that, Lil, like I'm ridiculous. I know that's exactly what they'll think. I've lived with them for seventeen years, and I know.'

I knew what she meant. Other girls, hell most girls, had parents who thought it was sweet to go with a boy, and if you had a proposal before a high school degree all the better. Not our parents, though. The Marcellis were too worried about babies and Dads about my education – a fact I should have been grateful for but wasn't. I was eighteen and a jerk.

'Listen, Jack's got a car. What if we met the boys outside of St. Luke's, that way none of the sisters will see us, and we can get off of Mohawk Island and go someplace else where we won't know anyone. Hell, we could go to Albany.'

'That's worse. What if someone saw us getting into the car with the boys or drove past us on the road?'

'Christ, Lara. What do you want? For us to hide you underneath a blanket in the car?'

She didn't so much as hint at a smile.

'Come on, I'll be there too. Won't that help?'

'Your father won't like it either if he finds out you've been driving with boys.' She shook out her hair, loose curls falling across her cheek. 'Maybe,' her eyes brightened, 'maybe they could meet us at Delaney's? But like as an accident, you know, don't you think?'

'I don't get it. How is that any better? Surely someone will see us there.'

'Well, if they do, we'll say we bumped into each other and were being friendly, and seeing as he is going to be my date for the Formal and all that, it would be rude not to stop and say hello. But I mean this, Lil, it can only be about fifteen minutes. I know once you get around Teddy you'll want to stay forever, but it's got to be quick. Okay?'

'If that's what you want.'

And that is how it went. Lara and Jack met accidentally at 3:35 pm on the last day of classes, a week before the Formal. I knew Teddy wished he'd been able to celebrate with a beer and a funny cigarette, but he could do that sure enough later. I didn't know then what Jack liked, but I guess he'd probably have preferred that too. Well, too bad, I thought, they'll have to meet us for a wholesome ice cream cone, by accident. If they want good girls like us, pretty and nice and from respectable families, then they'll have to make up their minds and put up with it. That's all.

My only regret at the time was that we hadn't had a chance to change out of our school uniforms and look more glamorous instead of the pathetic and eager virgins we were. But that would have raised suspicions, and besides, we didn't have the time.

I remember the boys were there first, leaning against the counter with ties undone, jackets thrown into the corner of some booth and shirt sleeves rolled up. It was the last week of May, and the weather had picked up again. They must have looked painfully young to everyone else, boys imitating the ways of the men they were not, but to Lara and me they reeked of masculinity. I sensed Lara freezing beside me. How were we to approach these gods and dare to speak to them in our Peter Pan collars and dowdy worn-through grey woolen skirts?

We saw them first through the shop window, and if they had not seen us too, I'm certain Lara would have grabbed my hand, and we would have fled. Even with a rose-tinted memory, it would be impossible to recall the beginning of that first meeting without a shudder.

'Hello, Teddy. Hi, Jack. Fancy bumping into you two here.'

'Come here often?' asked Teddy with raised eyebrows.

Someone needed to be brave here, and it was going to have to be me.

'Jack, this Lara. Lara, this is Jack,' I said. 'Funny you two have never met before.'

Lara gave a tight-lipped smile, the best she could muster.

'Jeez, where are my manners,' said Jack, running a hand through his sandy-colored hair before offering it to Lara to shake. 'It's really good to meet you. I, ahh, I hear you go to St. Anne's like Lillie.'

'She did, until today,' I answered for her. 'We're all done. That's something to celebrate.'

'Why, ahh, yes. Come on, Jack, pull yourself together man,' he said with a little laugh that came out as a phlegmy clearing of the throat. 'What would you two like? I can, ahh, I can get it for you.'

Teddy said nothing of paying for me. Not that I had expected him to, but after all, he had said it would be a date and that's what we were taught on the Island. It's a date if the man pays, and it is something else entirely if he does not.

Lara lifted her eyes to meet Jack's. She hadn't dared to before then.

'I never know what I want,' she said with a shy giggle.

'Do you know Lillie and I come here practically every day, and every time, I swear, I never know.'

'I'm exactly the same,' said Jack. 'With too much choice, I'm lost. Maybe we should sit down and talk over the options first? I think it could possibly take hours, with a decision like this to make. What do you say?'

I could see Lara faltering. If we sat, there was no hope of getting out in fifteen minutes and to be caught sat down would be too much.

'I'm afraid Lara and I have to be getting home soon so we better order. Lara, come on have the pistachio, like usual.'

She nodded. 'Yes, that's best. I'll have pistachio.'

I don't remember Teddy saying a word. He mightn't have either. He took out a cigarette and smoked it, wrinkling his eyebrows, making it clear to the rest of us his mind was elsewhere. I didn't care. I'd see to that later.

We stood around, hands awkward in pockets, eating our ice cream, Jack agreeing with everything Lara said. He never tested out an opinion first. I found this to be a deeply irritating quality, but one which I immediately recalled about Jack when I had met him without Lara previously. He was not a man to think for himself. But for all of that, he was exceptionally intelligent, or at least good at school. Maybe because he could repeat back to the teachers exactly what they wanted to hear.

'Wow, you must be really smart,' he said to Lara when she told him she was planning to study to be a teacher in the fall.

To this Lara laughed her genuine laugh.

'No, more like patient.'

'Yeah, I guess you have to be to deal with kids all day. That would be difficult. Think about how much of a pain we've been to our teachers, Teddy.'

Teddy said nothing.

Perhaps it was because Teddy refused to speak and Lara spoke in single sentences, that Jack's other dominant quality emerged that afternoon. He had the ability, as Lara would later say of him, much like her father, to speak to a brick wall.

'I'm sure glad I'm done with having teachers, I'll say that. I mean high school teachers. And the priests. Jesu – jeez. Professors will be different. More elbow patches and scotch. Don't you think?'

Teddy's ears perked up. 'You just want the scotch.'

'Hey, that's not fair, I never drink anything stronger than…'

Lara's eyes were wide with attention, awaiting Jack's next words. Teddy must have warned him about Lara's parents being stricter than most.

'Root beer,' he finished.

Teddy grinned. He was starting to enjoy himself.

'And that's why you're valedictorian, Jack. Like Lillie here. Though Christ knows she doesn't like sticking to root beer.'

Usually I would have struck Teddy for a comment like that, but I was so glad he'd finally decided to speak, I didn't mind.

'It doesn't count at a girl's school. Being able to read a whole sentence alone qualifies you for the top five per cent of the class. Coincidentally, that's mutually exclusive from the quarter of girls who already have marriage proposals, or who will after the end of next week.'

'Hey, perhaps they're lucky – they don't have to meet accidentally at soda fountains.'

Jack had said it as a joke. Overexcited and overeager to please, he'd stepped in it.

Lara turned her usual horrible shade of tomato soup red, the same as when she cried. I felt her humiliation too. They were right to laugh at us with their casually rolled up sleeves and their long legs and non-virgin statuses. I knew Teddy thought it was stupid, but he thought most things were stupid, and I hadn't minded until then.

I wondered if Jack were a virgin, but I thought not. He had been with Catherine Spence through to last winter. And she was the only one in our class who was actually a socialist and practiced what she preached. She'd been sending her birthday and Christmas money for years to the Republicans in Spain and the Jewish refugees of Europe. She'd made a big fuss on Class Day the week before when she announced her plan to abandon Mount Holyoke to go to England and train as a nurse.

No one at St. Anne's applauded her heroics, though as no one particularly liked Catherine. She had a reputation for being easy and popular with boys, both St. Luke's and the public-school ones in Troy. She was also filthy rich and had been known to invite groups of boys over to swim naked in her swimming pool when her parents were off in Albany or New York, or so was rumored.

Her leftist politics informed her general feelings on morality and, in particular, on free love. How was Lara to compete with this when she had not kissed a boy? And what did it say about Jack's character to have gone with a girl rumored to hold naked orgies? I did not know.

I could not look up until Jack, very pale, spoke. I noticed his teeth then too. Jack had good teeth, much better than Teddy's. He must not have smoked.

'Jeez, that sounded pretty bad. Let's pretend I didn't say that, can we? I've been looking forward to meeting you and all...'

Lara's blush deepened. 'I've, I've been looking forward to meeting you too.'

It was all right after that. Lara had never spoken to a boy

before, not like that, and I was very proud of her. All right, I was really proud of myself for having matchmade so well. And I had done well. Lara looked practically like the Madonna with her curls coiled up on top her head, her face bright and white, her thin lips parted, and that had to be attractive in some sort of way.

As for Catherine, well, it wasn't exactly as if she was much to be compared to looks-wise. She had close-cropped, straight black hair, quite sexy if no longer fashionable, but it didn't suit her square face to have such short of hair. And besides, her breasts were already giving into the inevitable decline. It wasn't so much that they were large and full and thus inclined towards sagging, as some girls. They weren't much bigger than my own, but she didn't wear a bra after school hours. The nuns hadn't approved of her going without during the day. They said it was a sin to be too enticing. Enticing to whom we never learned. I suppose Jack Allen for starters.

They'd broken things off for reasons I didn't know at the time, but which Jack told me many months later when we ate breakfast together in Midtown, lingering over coffee. A very odd morning, the only one like it. I was hungover, my mouth dry from too many cigarettes, and a feeling of sick in my throat. Jack was hungover too from the party the night before, and he was more vulnerable, more honest, more willing to express thoughts of his own rather than simply commenting upon others'. That's when he told me.

It had been he who finished things. She'd wanted to get married after they graduated and go to England together. But Jack being neither particularly political ('I mean I'd vote for Roosevelt if he runs again, but I'm not going to fight in some war if he gets us tied up in that. No, sir.'), nor inclined to a premature marriage, ran. Most everyone thought it had been Catherine to end it, though. She was the type.

But I didn't know that story then or that Catherine Spence would later die at Bethnal Green tube station in March of 1943, crushed to death while on leave. And I didn't know that by Jack meeting Lara at half past three in the afternoon on a day in late May, the sins for which I am still paying would be put into motion.

If I had known then what I know now, or think I know, would I have pushed them apart, if I could have? Have never played matchmaker? Would I even have had the power to stop it or were they destined for the other? To look at them as they are now, I would hardly call them soulmates, but perhaps that is what several years of marriage does to a couple.

But how had I seen them that summer? Before it happened. Before I knew too much. When we were the four us, gangly and loose-limbed, and terribly green, meeting for the first time and, for Lara and me, falling in love for the first time too. The boys supposedly had beat us to that.

Were they soulmates, Jack and Lara? My God, no. They were two kids who happened to meet and get on and not find anything better. I must have thought that then too. I know I must have. But I can't remember if I did.

It's true I never viewed their romance as great as Teddy's and mine. They were common cogs in the machine passing their time along until the eventuality of marriage and babies, forming suitable enough love stories to amuse their grandchildren with in later life. Teddy and I were nothing of that sort, or I believed as much – we were violent, passionate, unique. A story that could never result in grandchildren to tell it to. Superior in every way, except for in practicality that is.

Our love could only end in one way. All right, I was eighteen and very prone to melodramatics, yes, but I did sense it, somehow. Maybe it was because Teddy and I had both known death already. Our lives were tainted by it. And so, it was impossible to not allow the mind to wander there.

But how could I have known about Lara and Jack? I scarcely could have guessed he and she would make it through the Formal with enough to talk about, let alone that he would kiss her for the first time on July eighteenth, or any of the rest that followed.

Lara and I were crazy. We were always going around thinking any boys who said as much as hello to us or passed us on the street for Christ's sake might be our future husbands. Well, that's what Lara thought. I rather cast the man as one of my many future lovers, having the mind at eighteen never to take a husband.

But here we were, and neither of us knew that in our Peter Pan collars and grey skirts, we had met the man Lara was to marry. The very father of her children who were not yet to be.

Chapter Nine

There have only been three times in my life when I wanted to be kissed, when I yearned for it. The first kiss I mean. All the ones after that are imitations of the first one, seducing us back. And of those three times, never once did the man – or boy, really, in two of the instances – do it.

One of those times was the Spring Formal.

I don't remember much of the evening. There wasn't much worth remembering, except that as I stood swaying under the dimmed lights of the gymnasium, I desperately wanted Teddy to bend down and kiss me. He didn't.

Every girl had a gardenia pinned to her bosom or fixed to her wrist. I wore mine in my hair and Lara against her pancake chest. The smell of gardenias is synonymous with that of school dances, they being the cheapest of the respectable flowers. Lara's fell out, and she never recovered it. She later had the flower at her wedding, her only allusion to the past and the early days of her and Jack, and it made me ill. I've never worn a gardenia, or really any flowers for that matter, since.

I don't remember if at the time I thought it was a special evening to hold dear to my heart forever. I think I wanted to believe that nonsense, I could see most of the girls there did, but I mustn't have bought it. All I remember was touching up my lipstick in the bathroom and pressing a cloth under my armpits to cool off, wondering if the kiss would happen or not. It was quarter 'til ten at that point and the dance ended at half past. A whole group was headed over to Jacob Finney's after, but I didn't know if I wanted to go. Lara couldn't, and James would be there.

God, I did not want to see James. I'd seen him in passing, a hello and how are you. He was off to Georgetown in the fall. But to be drunk around him again ... Lord, no one likes to be in a room where she has been romantic, if that's the word for it, with more than one boy in it. It's too much to take in, especially when you're tight.

There was the nagging question of whether people knew about James and me anyway. They must have, Teddy included, but he never mentioned it. I never asked him if he knew, and I never told him. I never told Teddy about any of my past romances, nor did he mention his to me. I knew about his earlier adventures at fifteen with housewives and public-school girls, but that didn't seem to matter too much. Not at the time.

But there was to be no kissing that night, and no after party either because Paul Andrews, who I'd always thought a loud and smelly boy, spilled punch down my blue tulle dress, ruining it. The dry cleaner tried, but it never came out. Another failure.

So Jack drove us home, dropping Lara first for decorum's sake. Her father had been welcoming enough when Jack and Teddy picked Lara and me up from her house earlier that evening, but Mr. Marcelli would have pumped Hitler's hand and invited him over for dinner, if he met him. Not Mussolini, though. That's where he drew the line. He distrusted any Italian who had not had the good sense to come to America when he could.

'You don't drink and drive with my daughter,' he called out as we left. We'd gotten off light.

Dads was home when I got in. He wasn't waiting up for me, or so he would have said if I'd stopped to speak with him, as it was only eleven o'clock on a Friday night. He was in his study reading when I came in, deflated. I'd asked Teddy in for a cup of coffee and to listen to some records, but it wasn't any good. The boys would go ahead to the party, probably, or some other one perhaps. They didn't have to say anything. I knew they would. They were boys. Girls expected gardenias and kisses; boys wanted booze and sex.

I took the flower out and pressed it against the pages of my English Romantic poetry anthology. It seemed fitting. I brushed my hair and went to sleep. Another night of anticipation wasted. It would never happen now.

I could have cried, but I'm glad I didn't because forty-eight hours later, after the graduation ceremony, a very happy girl went to bed. The happiest of girls I must have ever been.

*

It sounds stupid to think of how happy I was, but I was. I floated home. I rang Lara and fell against my bed, my sweaty legs creasing the bedspread.

'A girl in love can't be anything other than a girl in love,' I blurted out when she answered. 'Lar, it's true. He loves me. He didn't say as much, but the way he kisses. You couldn't kiss a girl like that if you didn't love her. I should know. I've been kissed by plenty of boys who certainly did not love me.'

'It's like a story.'

'It's better than a story. Because it's real. It's like when Anna is sitting on the train when she leaves Vronsky for the first time after meeting him, and she can't concentrate on the book she's reading because she's too excited by the life she is living and – oh.'

'You've lost me there. Who's Anna?'

'It doesn't matter. All that matters is I am in love and he must love me too.'

I knew I was getting ahead of myself, but I couldn't help it. My heart soared and my stomach ached.

I had been kissed. I had been kissed, and I hadn't needed to be drunk for it to happen. And neither had the guy. There had always been alcohol before, every single kiss, which was pathetic, but it was true.

No other girl I knew had this problem. Ellen went on nice, sober dates every once in a while, but not me. I'd never been on a date, but I wasn't like the other girls who hadn't. They were kissing virgins like Lara or Mary Elizabeth or Madeline – girls who lived in delusional daydreams about frogs and Prince Charmings. That was not me. I lived in some nightmare purgatory, halfway between innocence and knowing.

But no longer.

Teddy came to see me after our separate graduation ceremonies. He'd changed out of his blue suit to casual linen trousers, but I remained in my fluffy, gaudy white dress. The sort of thing more suitable to a deb ball than a graduation. But it's what the sisters made us wear because we were young ladies and young ladies graduate to every new phase of their lives in white. With red roses. Something practically out of Hardy. I had a blue ribbon pinned to my breast to denote my valedictorian status, and I hadn't taken that off either.

I hadn't seen Teddy since the night of the Formal. I hadn't wanted to. It had been nothing but disappointment. Not an outright humiliation, of course, as those dates with Mark Hamilton had been. I'd managed not to get drunk and end up kissing some slob I didn't care about and didn't want on me in the first place. And seeing as how a great many of my nights ended in such a way at that time (or maybe for me, for all time, who knows), I frankly should have viewed the evening as a success. Except I didn't.

He'd walked the three houses down to see me. It was four in the afternoon, the height of the heat for the day. The sun had saturated the black asphalt of the road, and my hair was thick with humidity.

We went for a walk down the street, me having slipped into my sandals beforehand, my height greatly reduced to Teddy's shoulder. I could feel the heat of the asphalt on my feet, the soles inevitably blackening.

'You know I've never noticed how much I like these houses,' said Teddy.

Was this a coded message about me? How could I know? I'd never thought about the styles of the prairie boxes and the bungalows – that's what a house looked like to me.

'They're no different than the ones in Albany,' I said.

'No, they are. They're wider. In Albany and New York, they're narrower. You have to fit more on a street. And they're split too. You don't see many families living in a whole one of these in the city.'

'I guess.'

'I don't know what I'm going to make of New York. I think I'll like it all right, but I've never been away from here for more than a week. And I don't know how long I'll last at college. I might drop the classes as soon as I get there and live on the money my parents'll give me until it runs out. Cigarette?'

'Someone might see.'

'Suit yourself.'

'Drop the classes, really?'

'Why not? Can you see me as a lawyer? I mean, I know I could do it, but do I want to?'

'I can't see myself as a lawyer either, though it's what my dad wants. No, but you want to write.'

'Yeah, there's that. But really, I want to live as a writer. I don't know if I've got it in me to do the work.'

'I think you do.'

He knitted his brows together and raised the cigarette to his lips to light. 'You think too well of everyone, Lillie Jane Carrigan.'

I choked on a laugh.

'I do not.'

'Well, of me anyway.'

'I feel sorry for you is all.'

'Is that right?'

He stopped walking and squinted his eyes. The frown returned. He took another drag of his cigarette.

'I don't need this stupid thing,' he said and put it out. And then he kissed me.

And that was it.

I was normal.

And I could be wanted too.

I could be wanted not because I was there, or because I seemed easy with my modern ideas, or because I was naïve and corruptible. Or gullible. Or a girl so drenched in the sorrows of life that she didn't care what happened to her. I suspected boys could smell that on me.

No, there was none of that. I was happy. I was eighteen, and I was happy, and I knew how a normal girl could feel. It was the pure joy only first youth can know.

'Was that okay?' he asked as he pulled away, kissing the corner of my eye. I could feel his heart beating rapidly against mine. He was frightened too.

'Yes,' I breathed.

'It's nicer to kiss out here, I think. There's something,' he paused as he studied the cracks in the asphalt brought on by years of winter erosion, 'not romantic about the whole thing. I think that's what I like.'

My heart swelled. This boy who had understood me since I was a child, educating me in literature and four-letter words, who knew what it meant to lose a family member close to you and remain in a small town where everyone knew your tragedy and shook their heads with gossipy sympathy each time they saw you. I was going to have this boy for my own, and he wanted me.

The summer stretched out with the possibility of happiness, a path I had never allowed myself to traverse before. A whole three months of happiness to be had. No longer a drudgery to be endured before the freedom of leaving Mohawk Island for what I could only hope would be forever, as it turned out to be.

I saw before me not a tragic ending but a time to be spent together, growing closer and more tender in our feelings. I was going to fall in love.

I was determined. And I was happy in my determination.

Teddy asked me if I wanted to go to a party with him that night, but I could not. The Marcellis were throwing a barbeque at theirs at which Dads and I would be the only non-Italians, as usual. While I regretted we could not be together longer, I knew the next day we would be again and not as friends sitting in separate chairs in his living room. No, from then on it would be different, and I was right about that.

Never again would Teddy and I pretend to be platonic. Our romance had begun.

I grabbed Lara's arm close to me that night and whispered to her that I was falling in love, and she swooned along with me but told me to be quiet otherwise her parents might hear. I did not think of September. It was June, and I was a girl of eighteen. And that was all.

Would I bargain for less misery in the months that followed, which I confess I still feel the aftershock of now, by returning those brief moments of bliss? I don't know. I never know what to think. What could have been possible otherwise?

Chapter Ten

I don't think Dads particularly liked the idea of Teddy. I mean all he said about the whole affair was 'Okay, honey. You be careful.' Once during dinner, without prompting, he put down his knife and fork which had been cutting through his steak, and looked straight at me. 'Now, Lillie, let me give you some advice. I don't know much, but I was a boy once. And there's two things you need to know about boys. Talking about him to your girlfriends behind his back never helps. So don't do that. And if you want to be loved, you need to be lovable.'

He never expounded upon the second point except to say, 'You are smart and very pretty, and you have a bright future ahead of you. You don't have to marry at twenty-one like your mother and I did. You can study or you can have a job, or maybe once the war ends in Europe you can travel like your Aunt Claire did, but I don't want to see you stuck on one boy.'

'I know. And I don't want to marry at twenty-one. I don't want to marry.'

'Hmph,' he gave a satisfied smile, 'we'll see about that.'

I think I was supposed to translate this into his attempt at a sex talk. No one had mentioned the mechanics of sex to me, aside from Lara and the girls, but certainly no adult. Nor had I been told by anyone specifically that I need wait until marriage. Celibacy was rather taken for granted.

As Dads said, I had a bright future. If the thought of hell wasn't enough to keep me away from the evil deed, the threat of winding up pregnant and having to drop out from Vassar should have done it. What could be done to rectify the situation of a bright young girl getting knocked up had never been mentioned to me, but I knew about it all the same. I had Jean Rhys to thank for that.

But for the most part I was left alone to enjoy my first bloom of young love with Teddy without the interference of concerned parents. Dads assumed we'd break it off at the end of the summer, sensibly, and I could go to Vassar and try to find a nice Protestant boy instead. The McCalmans didn't take notice of me being around as I always had been. Besides, Mrs. McCalman would have been thrilled to call me daughter-in-law.

And so I was lucky in that way.

Lara was not.

'They keep asking about Jack,' whispered Lara one after-noon in the last week of June as we ate our lunches across from each other at my desk at the *Mohawk Island Dispatch*. We both had peanut butter sandwiches and apples, and I drank it down with my third cup of black coffee for the day. Lara had tea.

I had been at the *Dispatch* for about two weeks and had braved inviting Lara in to have lunch with me while she was on her break from the A&P. I noticed the two secretaries on staff did it with their friends, and I couldn't see why I, as a temp copyeditor for the classifieds and personals, shouldn't be allowed to do the same. I sat out front with them. The four men of the paper – Mr. Jacobs who ran it, Mr. French who did most of the editing and opinion pieces, Bryce Edwards who wrote the features and covered the baseball matches over on Starbuck Island, and Jerry Ryan who set the press each Thursday morning for the paper to be ready for Friday – sat behind the door in a cesspool of tobacco and gaseous smells. There were only two rooms to the whole office, aside from the bathrooms, and the sexes had no desire to mix.

I was glad there were no men around to hear our conversation. I was suspicious of Julia and Fran overhearing, both being seriously middle-aged (over thirty, or at least appearing to be), but they were absorbed in their own gossip. Fran was married and her husband worked over at the Ford plant, which she blamed for him never being home and thus why, after four years of marriage, they were still childless. Julia wasn't married so she and her girlfriend were constantly on the hunt for men. Every Friday her friend would stop by to pick her up at five, and Julia would remove her small table mirror from within her desk and fix up her face and freshen her lipstick. They served as warning signs to Lara and me, as most women did at the time, representing some undesirable fate.

'They're convinced we're sneaking out to see each other,' she continued once she had assessed that neither Julia, Fran, nor their respective friends cared to listen to the woes of a seventeen-year-old girl. 'But how can we when the whole town has eyes?'

Julia was a Methodist, and Fran didn't go to church. They were safe enough to talk in front of in that case, even if they did hear.

'I told you, Jack has a car. Can't you go over to Troy to see a film some night?'

The Troy-Mohawk Bridge had been completed in 1935, courtesy of President Roosevelt and the WPA. The only direct effect the Democrats seemed to have had on my life.

'Forget it. If my parents found out...'

'They won't.'

'But they will. They suspect everything. This morning when I told my mother I'd be eating lunch with you, it was

"Are you sure Lillie won't be a boy?" One of them is bound to walk by here in the next hour to spy. My mother tells my dad everything.'

'Walk to the next town and have Jack pick you up there.'

'Lil, we live on an island!'

'Fine. Take the ferry.'

'The ferryman will ask where I'm going.'

'Lar, I give up. I can't help you unless you are willing to help yourself. That's it. I cannot be responsible for the future of you and Jack.'

'How am I going to marry if I can't have a boyfriend? I may as well be a nun.'

Here we went again.

'You don't have to be a nun.'

'It's better that than an old maid.'

I looked around swiftly to ensure Julia hadn't heard.

'You can't be a nun unless you have a vocation, you know that. And I don't think you have a vocation, do you?'

'It's what they want. All right, maybe not to be a nun, though I am sure that my dad would be delighted. He wanted one of my brothers to be a priest, prayed for it every week, and look how that turned out. But no. They want for me to die a virgin, whatever I do.'

Julia was entrenched in her own, likely similar conversation, thank God. I didn't think she was a virgin, though. But I didn't know. I assumed that after twenty-five no woman was.

'You're not going to die a virgin.'

'That's easy enough for you to say. You're not even going to have to go to college as one.'

'Lara!' I hissed, horrified but mostly flattered.

'Well, isn't it true? Aren't you and Teddy,' and here she paused to drop her voice, 'well, you know?'

'I … I don't know. I haven't thought about it.'

Hadn't I, though? Hadn't I been thinking of how romantic it would be to lose it to my first love at the end of summer? A perfect memory to dream on cold winter nights when huddled next to the dormitory radiator?

It's true that up until then we'd done little other than kiss, and it had been nearly three weeks. Three weeks of snuggling up on his back porch by candle rather than electric light so as to ward off mosquitoes and prying eyes. He'd started to touch my breasts over my blouse. I mean not that there was much to touch, but it was driving me crazy. I wanted him to rip the thing off but feared his disappointment after the bra disappeared. It didn't help much, but it did help some. I hadn't a clue what he was thinking other than that I assumed he wanted sex, eventually anyway.

I'd told him that the next time his parents went out, and we could be alone together inside, he could see them. But Lord knew when that would be or why I had promised it in the first place. Sure, James Moore had seen them and seemed approving, but that had been in a drunken frenzy, and it had seemed easier to show him my breasts than to allow him to show me his pecker. I wondered if one could have sex without having to see one. I hoped so.

But I could not mention these things to Lara.

And I certainly couldn't confess to her that often, late in the evening, I'd lie naked on the floor of my room, the carpet scratching my cheek and my body flushed from the heat of the night and my young passion, burying my mound in my hands, moving in circles until I felt the first twinge of pleasure. That's when I stopped.

'Shh, Lara. You know I wouldn't do that. Not until I'm engaged and there is no threat of that happening.'

'Really? I thought maybe...'

'Hell, I'm eighteen. That might be fine for some girls but

not for me. I don't want to go from daughter to wife and never be me.'

Lara turned down her gaze. 'But all it is is killing time until one can be a wife. It's only when one is a wife that she can start living. No one can care what she does then.'

'Plenty of people can, including her husband.'

Lara picked at the leftover crusts of her sandwich, dissecting them as though the crumbs were petals of a flower symbolizing the tradition of 'he-loves-me-not.'

'If you married Teddy, you wouldn't have to go to college.'

It was true. If I married him, I could follow him to New York and keep house up in the Bronx. Nothing could be duller than that, I thought, love or no love.

'I don't want another four years of being around girls whose dreams extend only as far as a ring on their finger, that's all. But...' I paused because I knew I desperately did want to go away in September and be able to read and to learn and to shed everything that was in me of the Island girl. 'There'll be a library, and I can keep myself entertained. And besides, if I marry, how am I going to go to Paris and write as soon as the war is over?'

Lara pursed her lips together as she did when she was thinking. 'I'm sure Teddy would love to go with you.'

'But if I'm married there'll be babies, and I can't go to Paris with a baby.'

I was eighteen and naïve and somehow believed that babies came within the first year of marriage, despite knowing of girls on the Island, mostly the ones who went to public school in Troy, who had had babies out of wedlock, or my own parents who hadn't had me until after they had been married eight years. Hell, I mean I could have looked over at Fran just then and known better, but I couldn't connect anyone else's lives to my own perception of the future.

I could hear Lara talking again, bringing the conversation around to her predicament with Jack.

'Think about it, Lil. Jack had Catherine Spence. I'm sure her parents aren't crazy, keeping her locked in the house with a chastity belt around her waist. How is he supposed to go from her to me?'

'But you did say he came into the A&P yesterday and asked if you might like to go for an ice cream or something again. See? He is interested.'

'A boy like Jack after Catherine Spence is not going to settle for an ice cream with a nun.'

'I don't know, Lar. Maybe he does want you. Look at Teddy and me. I'm hardly like some of the other girls I know he's gone around with.'

'But you could be a bad girl if you wanted. That's the difference.'

I inhaled, bracing myself for what I knew was coming next. And there it was.

'You're lucky you don't have to worry about what your mother would say.'

That's how these chats with Lara always ended. She'd wind herself up until she spun out with the usual hurtful comments, though I knew she didn't mean them to be. She genuinely did believe I was luckier to be without a mother. Perhaps I was. I don't know. I think I would rather have had a mother, but then maybe she wouldn't have allowed me to go around with Teddy. It's difficult to think like that. One or the other. That's it. But, as so often happens, the two alternatives in the fantasy do not align on the cause and effect chain, so you can never really be sure if they were mutually exclusive worlds to begin with. But that doesn't stop you from playing it out over and over again in your head. I tried not to let it get to me, but it did.

'I know, Lar. Anything else?'

I saw the stray smudge of peanut butter sitting on her lip. We were little girls, pretending to speak of love and act the parts of grown-ups, but that didn't feel quite right either. I wasn't a little girl, not exactly. I was a girl, yes, but wishing I could be a child with my friend who was still one, refusing to recognize that in some ways I was grown up, even if I hadn't asked to be made so.

'I'm sorry, Lil, but you have to admit it makes things easier for you when it comes to boys.'

I folded my bottom lip against my teeth and slowly let them scrape across the edge. I wanted to cry, but I couldn't. Not in here.

I glanced up at the clock above Fran's desk. Quarter 'til two. Nearly there.

'Lar, look, I'll talk to Teddy and arrange the whole thing. All you'll need to do is take the ferry and go. I'll take the,' I wanted to say goddamn but couldn't bring myself to do it, 'ferry with you, if you like. Now that's settled.'

It was a disastrous idea, the first of many which I was to have that year, especially about Lara and Jack.

Lara's parents were right. Boys could only lead to trouble, even boys who you yourself were not seeing. I wish I would have listened to them.

I know that now.

*

It went like this. Lara made it to Troy, without me by her side, thank God, where Jack met her with his car. They walked around for the night, there not being a wealth of things to do in Troy, and never kissed. Jack tried to hold Lara's hand. Or she thought he had until she dwelled on the moment for too long and convinced herself he hadn't. He drove her back to my house at nine o'clock, Lara hiding in the backseat the whole way. How Jack tolerated this behavior, neither of us could believe, but he asked for a second date and Lara agreed.

By that time we were coming into July and the Independence Day celebrations. I usually feel the summer dead after that, on the decline to autumn, the freshness of June gone. But that year I looked forward to the Island festivities as I had a boy to take me to the fireworks for once and was old enough to drink a beer with him at the Knights of Columbus table, something I used to envy the senior boys and girls of.

Lara did not feel the same. She declared the holiday a crisis.

'If I go with my parents, I'll be a baby. But if I don't go out, they'll think I'm sulking. And if I go with you and Teddy, I'll be third-wheeling for sure with Teddy giving me looks all evening of "ewww, go away."'

'Lara,' I sighed over my roast beef sandwich, the leftovers from Sunday's roast made by Hetty. Another lunchtime at my desk spent scheming Lara's future, the situation as seemingly hopeless as it had been the week and a half before.

'Why don't you both come with us again as a double-date? Your parents can't object to that – they'll be feet away. It's not like any of us are going to start at it in public.'

She dropped her sandwich. 'I can't eat this.'

'Don't be dramatic.' Rich coming from me, I know.

'They'll think we're starting something if they see that. And he'd have to pick me up at my house again, and this time my dad and he would start talking and you know my dad. I'm surprised he didn't bring up the Holy Ghost and the Virgin Mary before the dance, and he can't keep his mouth shut twice. And Jack doesn't go to church, and they'll find out that he's not even a Catholic, but Presbyterian, or probably an atheist, if he's honest about it. Did you know that?'

I hadn't, and it did make a difference.

'Do you want me to come along with you instead, as usual? I'm sure Teddy won't mind. He's not one for fireworks.'

'No, he'll hate me more. Taking away his date and his chance to be,' she searched for a word and came out with, 'sexy with you.'

'I swear he won't.' I stared down at my hands now finished with the sandwich, tempted to start playing with my cuticles. I didn't want a revisit of the last week's conversation with Lara over lunch.

'I make you pathetic by association,' she relented. 'You're sure you don't mind?'

I never got my fireworks with a boy or the beer either. Lara's watchful parents would not have approved, and I loved them too much to extend my right as a woman of age. I wasn't upset with Lara about it, not really. She was my best friend, and I couldn't begrudge time spent with her. I've never been like that, putting a boy first.

Besides, I snuck over to Teddy's the moment the Marcellis dropped me off, and that was the night my breasts were liberated from my bra. And Teddy allowed me to have a beer, and I smoked a cigarette with his head cradled between my naked breasts. It was like something out of a French painting. I was in love.

Anyway, the Marcellis found out about Jack and Lara the next night anyway, so everything really had been for naught. After that, the lunchtime chats stopped for a while, Lara being much too emotional to contain herself at an office desk, and we started walking home with each other after work instead.

On the afternoon of July sixth, I waited outside the A&P, jealous of Brandy Adams, former St. Luke's boy and now daytime manager, with his cigarette, chatting away to some girl I didn't know. She clearly wasn't St. Anne's. I thought of asking Brandy for one, but I couldn't get up the nerve. Lara hated the habit – she lived in fear of her parents finding out about my proclivity for nicotine and banning her from seeing me.

I waited and pushed back my cuticles instead.

Finally she emerged, her face flushed and her lip trembling. I did have to hand it to Lara. Despite being an ugly crier, she had mastered the lip tremble remarkably well.

Lara grabbed my hand, pulling me away from the eyes and smoke of Brandy Adams and his nameless girlfriend.

'We've got to go,' she whispered. 'I can't be late home.'

'Okay.'

I shook off her hand, and we started down the Island Boulevard, which was the closest thing we had to a main street. Everything was flat; there was little difference in height between the road and the curb, and grass seemed to grow through every available crack in the sidewalk. There were few shops left other than Delaney's and the A&P and the post office over on Staley Road. We did not like the town we came from. It looked abandoned even then, but we did not know anything else. Albany, Troy, and Rensselaer seemed no better, only bigger with cinemas and department stores. New York was the city of our dreams, I suppose, but it frightened us too. We knew we would not be together there as we were here.

'Where do I start?' shouted Lara over the buzz of the cars driving past us. There weren't many.

'At the beginning?' I suggested. I didn't want to have to sit through a whole lot of needless backstory to get to the meat and potatoes of the thing. I'd been tempted to say to start at the end and leave it like that. But I already knew the end. It was the only part I did. Lara had rung that morning to tell me.

Lara is a poor storyteller. It's a fact. She still is, actually, and she knows it too. I thought of the days at the lunch table when she'd wanted to tell a story to the other girls, she'd start but I'd finish it for her – at her request. That's the way things were. How she was going to get on without me come autumn, I didn't know. I wondered if she might stop speaking altogether.

It went like this.

Dejected from spending the holiday together, Lara and Jack carried out another rendezvous in Troy, this time daring to hold hands as they left the cinema.

After all the damn precaution of the time before, Lara huddling beneath a blanket on the rumble seat and not a peck goodnight, this one moment of hand holding was to determine their fate.

For there was Mr. Marcelli exiting old Mrs. Cerello's apartment block. A long-time parishioner of St. Luke's, Mrs. Cerello had moved across the Mohawk to live with her son and his wife in her later years. Damn Mrs. Cerello and her debilitating arthritis and damn Mr. Marcelli's good and gregarious nature. And damn me for knowing nothing of this and failing to calculate it into my schemes.

Lara tried to hide, but neither Jack nor Mr. Marcelli were of the type to back away from a hello. Mr. Marcelli did not cry out or bellow like he was some father in an opera. No, he shook Jack's hand and asked how he'd been enjoying his summer, and he thanked him again for taking his daughter to the dance and told him not to bother with driving Lara home. He'd take her.

Jack said all right and goodnight, and maybe he felt relieved. There was no need for him to worry about his parents receiving a phone call from the Marcellis questioning if they knew what their son had been up to. Not that they would have minded it, but it would have made a big stink about nothing. And, anyway, who knows what he thought of Lara then – not an easy lay, that's for sure. But what else, I don't know.

Lara knew what was coming, and she knew her father would make her wait until she was home and had consulted Mrs. Marcelli before he said another word about it. She was right about that. Mr. Marcelli did not speak to her on the drive home, and he did not wish her goodnight when they got in. She went straight to bed.

It was not until later after she heard the door of her parents' bedroom close that the conversation started. She crept from her bed and pressed her ear to their door.

There were no violent words, only tears and her mother gently muttering, 'Oh, Joe, she's a girl. She has to be expected to have boyfriends sometime. Nothing will come of this.'

'Nothing, Rose! Nothing. She sneaks around like a wolf in the night with him. She is ashamed to bring him home.'

Lara grew furious, her own tears falling madly. It was an easy sight for me to imagine when she told me of it.

'Ashamed, he said! Ashamed! As if we could do anything to be ashamed of! What else could I have done?' She paused but not long enough for me to answer, which suited me as I had no answer. After all, it had been my plan. 'They're the ones who forced me to sneak around. They could've been like other parents and let me have a date, but no, and now they say I was ashamed.'

This is what they wanted to do, she claimed – beat her back with guilt and ensure she never went with any boy again. I did feel for Lara, I really did.

Because she was right. If my mother had been alive, it wouldn't have been all 'boys don't think like girls but as long as you're safe and break it off at the end of the summer, I won't say another word' like Dads. Not my mother. She would have held my hand to her chest and asked me what I was doing with Teddy and did he drink and did he smoke and reminded me that nice girls only kissed boys with whom they were serious. But then perhaps she wouldn't have been like that. I didn't know. I couldn't know. My mother had a way of liking pretty clothes and of seeing me done up in them and hearing about potential romances, and I thought, yes, if she had been alive she would have been stricter than Dads, but she would have trusted me. I knew that. And she would have laughed about Lara's predicament and shaken her head. 'Our Lara,' she would have said. 'What has she done now?' She did love a gossip about my friends.

Our Lara. My Lara. What had she done now?

As we walked along the poorly paved roads of the Island, dusty and hot and each desperate for water, she confessed to me this.

'The thing is I don't even know if I like him, but he seems the only boy who will ever pay attention to me, and here my parents are getting mixed up in it and saying that I'm a wh–, well, you know what, for so much as holding his hand.'

She did laugh because it was funny. I laughed too.

'If only my parents knew what girls like Catherine Spence do, they'd be thankful to have a daughter like me.'

'Yes,' I said, 'but maybe they do know what girls like Catherine Spence do, and that's why they are so very concerned.'

'Lil, am I going to die a virgin?'

We laughed again, but this time it was not funny. This question weighed on each of our minds too heavily that summer.

It didn't help matters when the Marcellis learned Jack was Protestant.

A lapsed Irish Catholic would have been one thing perhaps, an obstacle to overcome, but with the strength lent by God through prayer, the Marcellis may have found it surmountable. But a mixed marriage? It could never be considered, not by Mr. Marcelli anyway.

'Lil, they want me to bring Jack to the house,' Lara told me on the walk home that Friday. It had been a long week. 'For dinner. My dad wants to have a long chat with him. What does he mean by that? If it wasn't bad enough having my parents forbid me to see Jack, they have to have him over for chicken marsala and broadcast to him how much of a freak I am.'

It was bad. I gave her that.

'Can't you come too?' she begged of me, but I did not agree. There is only so far you can go in orchestrating your friend's relationship. Especially when you don't know if you like the guy. And when she isn't sure either.

I did a lot for Jack and Lara, but of all the things I had done and would do, that was the only time the demand seemed too much. I don't know why.

'I can't, Lar. It would be strange if I did. I mean Jack would really start to think you were a freak then, always having to have your friend tag along.'

Her lips grew together. 'Yes, that's true.'

Here was Lara fighting for a boy she'd met little more than the month before. A boy she did not love. A boy who she admitted was slightly pudgy in the face and who, for as much as she could make out from a couple of dates, expressed no opinions of his own. Lara, who had fought for nothing in her life before, fought for him. A boy who would likely disappear with the summer – this was her cause. Oh well, at least it was something. Or, in the eyes of Lara, someone.

Jack was good humored about it too, or so Lara said later.

'He said he should have come over in jeans and with a pack of cigarettes rolled up under his sleeve and see how my father liked that. It would have given my dad a heart attack.' Her eyes danced. She was happy. Everything Jack said was funny to her now.

'But he was good. Very, very good. Lil, are you going to eat your sandwich or not?'

I stared down at the mustard on my thumb. I wasn't hungry anymore. It was too hot.

We'd resumed our lunches together in the week after the fights. I was happy to have my friend back, though I was sick of talk of Jack. It was bad of me. Whenever I told a story, Lara listened with rapt ears and added delicious comments throughout, making the reliving of the memory with her nearly as good as living it in the first place. I never felt the same about her stories, and I know I should have done. It may have saved us a lot of trouble if I had.

'You know my dad, well, he took my mother's hand and he said, "Rose and I have been married nearly thirty years, and, if the Lord will be so good, I hope another thirty still, but I would be a very foolish man if I thought that this marriage was about Rose and myself. You must have the Lord at the center of any marriage, I hope you know that." I thought I was going to die. Can you imagine my father saying that?'

I could.

'Jack deserves a sainthood for sitting through it and not running away. He's a saint. A real saint.'

'Well,' I said, 'He can't be a saint, really, because he's not a Catholic.'

'Very funny, Lil. You sound like my dad. He brought it up. I could have killed him, but he did it. He said, "You cannot marry my daughter unless you convert." And Jack, well, he said he understood! Am I engaged?'

'I don't know. Did he say he'd convert?'

'Not in so many words but…'

Lara laughed first, and I joined her, and we went on for a long time after that coming up with more preposterous marriage proposals until Lara said she'd have an accident if we didn't stop, and so we did.

'You know what sealed it?' said Lara after she'd recovered. 'It's because he's going to be a doctor. Money.'

'Yes,' I said. 'I thought it might be.'

It didn't bother Lara, though. She grinned and ate her sandwich and finished mine for me too.

'I'll be as fat as a pig if I keep eating like this. Ready in August for the county fair.'

'Yes,' I said. 'Yes.'

It was too hot to eat. Too hot to do anything but think of the evening when Teddy and I would be together again away from the eyes of parents. Who knew what would happen next.

Lara and I had boys for the first time, and our futures seemed secure, even if they weren't to be our future husbands. They would do. For the summer. That's probably all they wanted of us too.

And so began the happy days of our lives, together with our boys.

Chapter Eleven

Teddy first saw my breasts on Independence Day 1941. He made no comment upon them, which I didn't know at the time whether to take as a good thing or bad. Better nothing than an insult, but I thought they were nice enough. I knew they were small and when I laid flat on my back they disappeared, but I was eighteen. I had yet to grow.

We were in his living room, his parents out.

I knew he was going to have to see them. He'd been hinting around for the last week, kissing my neck and my décolletage, and once, daringly, grazing a hand underneath my right breast, feeling the weight of it.

No boy had taken this much time with me before. Hell, no boy had not gone from kissing to grabbing at me within ten minutes.

But Teddy wasn't a virgin. He wanted sex. I wasn't that naïve or so in love as not to see the blunt truth for what it was. Boys did not go with you for companionship. They wanted to see how far they could get you to go on a three-dollar date. And Teddy was no different.

He might take a few weeks to get to the point he wanted me at, but he was determined to get there just the same as all the others.

I didn't think I minded it. I knew happy endings didn't exist and that love did not and could not redeem you. It could make you happy enough for a while, and you might as well enjoy what you could get at the time. And I knew that if I was going to have to be offered up to men as a sexual creature for the next ten or twenty years, I wanted the entrance into that world to be as romantic as possible. I thought this was achievable with Teddy. He was as much myself as a boy could be, or so I thought.

What did I know of boys? I knew they got hard and rubbed their bulge against you and somehow expected to turn you on with that. As much as I loved Teddy and thought that he caressed me with the hands of a god, well, even he moved his harsh denim against my bare legs, grunting, groping at my breasts with boyish curiosity, and not saying a word.

'Lil,' he'd whisper, 'you don't have to, ahh, you don't have to do anything to me. Unless you want to.'

Other boys placed your hand directly on their penis. Teddy said things like, 'I don't want this to be about buying and selling, exchanging sexual favors. That's cheap. We'll have romance.'

And that was enough to woo me into reaching down my hand to fondle it over his jeans and then one day with the fly undone but his shorts remaining on. Touching the flesh itself appalled me more than the thought of penetration.

I tried to confess this to Lara, but at the end of it, she really was a prude. Something I hated her for. She was able to have her hand held without it being forced down to the crotch. What had I done wrong that meant I was never to have such respect? Wasn't I a good girl too?

I didn't feel one. All right, fine, I wasn't, considering the things I'd gone around doing. But it wasn't like I had been a good girl and then suddenly I dropped the bra for a few boys, and there went my virtue. No, there was something else to it.

There was some flaw in my character – a flaw I must still have because men take one look at me, and they figure they can dare a kiss and probably hit a home run while they're at it. And they're usually not too far from the truth, I hate to admit.

Lara, on the other hand, knew how to control a boy's wandering hands.

'You pick them up and put them on your shoulders. And if Jack doesn't stop with the funny business, I stop kissing him. It is very easy.'

'That's simple enough for you to say. But what if I don't want him to keep his hands on my shoulders?'

These sexier conversations were saved for our walks home. I was growing suspicious of Julia and Fran overhearing. Not that they would have said anything, but I didn't need anyone else chuckling at my naivety. I had some pride.

The walk took about fifteen minutes from the center of town to the water's edge where Lara lived on the east side of the Island. I'd have to curve back in slightly to get my own house, following the river to the north for a third of a mile or so. We didn't come home every day together – Lara only worked on Tuesdays, Wednesdays, and Fridays and didn't always finish at five as I did – but it was often enough that we did. This was the only time we could divulge properly, though my revelations were the more shocking. Lara's tended on the theme of, 'is kissing behind his ear going too far?'

Now that she had a boyfriend, or what she assumed was one, Lara had stopped voicing fears of never losing her own virginity and had instead turned her attention to ensuring I maintained mine.

'Lil, you can't. You have to wait until the morning after the wedding to do that,' she sighed as if to say, 'Don't you know anything?'

'What do you mean the morning after the wedding? Do you mean the wedding night?'

'No, it's the morning. No one has sex on the night after the wedding. You're too sleepy.'

'What? Who told you that?'

Lara tutted, pitying my ignorance. 'No one. I thought everyone knew that.'

'I've never heard of that in my life!'

'I don't know, but it's a fact. You want to go to sleep and you wake up and brush your teeth and then, well, it happens.'

'Come off of it. That's not how it happens. Besides, I'm not waiting for some wedding night or wedding morning.'

'Suit yourself. I am. Why buy the cow...'

'If you can get the milk for free, I know. But I don't want to be bought.'

'We'll see.'

'Don't you want to you, you know? With Jack?'

I thought she would blush, but she didn't. She was confident in her response.

'No. I can't think about that. If I do, then I'll get my thoughts trapped there, and I can't do that. You have to wait for your husband, that's what's right.' Seeing me turn my eyes down, she asked with some horror, 'Lil, what have you done?'

I grew defensive. 'Nothing.'

'It's not nothing! You haven't, have you?'

'No, but, I've umm...'

'Please don't tell me you've seen it, have you? His, well, his thingie?'

'No. Of course not, but I've, umm, I've felt it. Through his shorts, that is. When it's, umm, hard.'

'What? Lil, you can't do that. You'll have a baby!'

'For Christ's sake, you can't get pregnant from touching a boy's, well, you know what. Through his shorts.'

Her eyes were wide, her acne-scarred forehead wrinkled.

It was moments like these that I realized Lara had no chin.

'Did he touch you down there too?'

'No, only my breasts.'

'That's good. I mean you definitely can't have a baby if one of you has your underwear on. I know that for a fact. But he didn't, you know, did he?'

I could scarcely manage the word, but I was forced to be the sexually sophisticated one out of the two of us.

'Come,' I supplied, coolly.

I wanted a cigarette then, something to take the edge off of the conversation. I pressed my nails into the palm of my hand. I learned this as a trick to stop myself from pushing back on my cuticles. I never pressed hard enough to draw blood.

'He didn't,' I said.

'That's a relief. What does one do with that stuff?'

Lara had me there. I didn't really know either. I assumed take out your handkerchief, but then how to keep Hetty from seeing it in the laundry? And you couldn't exactly dispose of it in a trash can, what if someone spotted it when they were throwing away the remnants of a sandwich or something? Maybe the boy supplied his own handkerchief, but did you have to ask him for it, or did he know to hand it over when it happened?

That was the thing about sex. Once you worked out the basic mechanics of what bodies could do, there remained a lot of unanswered questions to which no one was too forthcoming with knowledgeable solutions. You'll know when it happens was not good enough for the inexperienced.

'Don't look at me like that. I've done nothing wrong. Come on, I've done worse with boys I've never seen again. And it's not like you're the Holy Virgin, either. You didn't want to be, remember? And don't you know what it does to Jack, all this kissing? It makes his pecker hard, dammit,

Lar! Christ, you're as bad of a tease as Madeleine Evans.'

Lara narrowed her eyes. We knew each other too well to fight fair.

'Sleeping with Teddy won't make him love you.'

'And Jack won't continue to go with you because you refuse to put out.'

I walked on, faster. Lara's legs couldn't keep up without her jogging beside me, which she did.

'Lil, stop.'

I didn't.

'Lillie. I'm sorry. Come on.'

I turned.

'What? Do you want to have a scene in the middle of the road?'

'Do you always have to be so dramatic?'

'I don't know, Lar. You're pretty good at that crap too, when you want to be. I just don't cry as easily as you.'

'Come on, Lil.' She took my hand and dragged me onto the curb of the road, out of the way of traffic, not that there was any. There never was on these back roads of the Island.

I saw she was close to tears, as if on cue, and relented.

'I'm sorry, Lil, it's … You have to promise me. You won't leave me behind, will you? You and Teddy, you're both, well, you'll go places I won't. You already do. But please don't leave me alone, promise me?'

I understood. And I told her so.

I promised.

I would remain a virgin until I was ready, and I would tell her first, that was the agreement we reached that afternoon.

It's funny, neither of us thought to have Lara make the same promise.

Would it have made a difference if we had?

*

Mid-August came. The big, fat spiders crept out in the evenings, spoiling our place on the porch, reminding me autumn would come. We were on the downward journey now, as happened every summer. We would abandon swimming suits and bare feet for collared shirts and cardigans once more. The thought of woolen socks in August made my skin itch, but the time would come soon enough.

I've never looked forward to autumn as some people do. How anyone could favor another season over summer is madness. Autumn with its crisp days and golden hues is a poor substitute for the brilliant greens and openness of summer. The possibilities close when autumn comes, or so I've always felt. But never did I dread its arrival more than that August of 1941.

I couldn't face going away from Teddy.

Because I knew Dads was right. It was a summer romance, an inevitable one perhaps, but nothing more. I had books to go off to, and Teddy had the city. I knew I could remain constant, studying by day and dreaming of my boy at night, choosing a different kiss to recall in minute detail in the moments before sleep came.

But it was no good. Teddy had black hair and hazel green eyes and a dead brother in his past. While I felt my prospects damaged by death, marking me out as inferior because I could not be happy and frivolous like others my age, for a young man this was a golden quality ensuring he could get laid anytime he brought the story up with the remotest of sensitivity. No, without a declaration of love, he wouldn't remain faithful to me.

He'd made no promises, and I knew he would not be pressed upon either. That was that. I could enjoy the summer – three months of having someone who understood me, as I thought he did then – lose my virginity to him, and leave for college as the dark sophisticated girl with first-hand experience of both death and sex.

It wasn't bound to make me friends, and I did have some reservations that it might attract the wrong sort of group of girls all together. I mean I didn't want to be leading the little Reds' literary circle or anything like that. It was fine enough for me to spend my time reading Lawrence and Kierkegaard and smoking until my eyes went sallow, convincing myself I'd discovered nuances in their works previously undetected by lesser readers, but, Jesus, listening to others prattle on in the same vein – it could not be endured.

Besides, I imagined those girls to be bores and drips who, no matter how much free love and socialism they preached at college, would, at the end of the four years, be married just the same as the ones on the Daisy Chain. Or, if they kept their independence, be living in some dingy basement apartment in Brooklyn, life forever the same and reeking of boiled potatoes and canned soup on the stove. There are few fates allowed to women, and they all sounded like hell at eighteen.

Lara was my only friend. Sure, there was Ellen who I liked, but she and I both knew we wouldn't keep in touch. I hated Madeline and Mary Elizabeth, and the other girls at St. Anne's were much the same – nice, friendly, good enough to get through the lunch table with for thirteen years, but I never exactly liked them, and they didn't really like me either. They thought I was odd.

But we had each other, Lara and I. We had since we were eight. But come September, we wouldn't any longer. Not as we had, anyway. After that summer, we wouldn't be able to recreate our friendship, even with each other. It wasn't so much we would grow apart but merely we would grow up. We wouldn't be everything for the other, not as we had been.

I'd spent eighteen years dreaming of leaving the Island and now … I wanted to remain where I was, on the cusp of growing up, anticipating what was to come next. It was better than living through it. Realities always seemed to disappoint me.

But not that summer.

I was happy. And I feared I mightn't be happy again.

It's difficult to leave the things and the places and the people that make us happy, and harder still when time makes those memories fade to sad ones, too painful to recollect with any sense of warm nostalgia.

My body felt heavy with the heat and humidity that August, and I was determined to go to Vassar very thin, as was the style. I could feel the water weight sitting heavy in my womb, and I believed myself to be ugly and fat and frizzy. A plain blob. I spent the waning afternoons stretched across my chintz bedspread, pushing my hands against my hips to make certain I could feel the bones protruding, that they hadn't been swallowed up by fat. They hadn't.

August is a horrible month, taunting us with every rain and whip of wind that winter is coming. September and Vassar and the days of loneliness were on their way. I laid there in my room, brooding, sucking in my stomach, dwelling on thoughts of unhappiness when I might have been out in the evenings, eating ice cream with Lara and laughing and happy. If the happiness had to be taken away from me in a month, I thought I might as well destroy it while I had the chance.

It's much worse when something you love is taken away

from you than when you violently abandon it. In the first instance, all you can do is grieve, which is awful and pathetic. In the latter, you can blame yourself, which is quite a productive activity, retracing every movement that may have led to your sin, deciding what to hate yourself for the most, imagining ways in which you might have behaved better while secretly always thankful you did not. Otherwise, there'd be grief instead of this. And that would be unbearable.

My mood darkened as the days shortened. Lara insisted on double dates more than I liked. Hers and Jack's conversation often bored me; but Jack was the only one of us with a car, and if we were to have any hope of going off the Island, we relied upon him.

We piled in the car one evening to go to a carnival in Troy, Lara insisting the boys both sit up front and we in the back. 'Otherwise you and Teddy might try some funny stuff,' was her reasoning.

Jack rolled down the windows, but even then it was hot and stuffy, my legs sticking together against the leather seat. I would have to peel myself from the car at the other end, leaving unpleasant sweat stains. I hadn't wanted to go out, much less with a pair of innocent gawkers.

Teddy said little. He didn't much care for these double dates. He resented anything that took him away from his beer and the possibility of sex.

'There better not be any clowns there, those things scare me,' said Jack as he drove.

'That's a circus, Jack. Not a carnival,' said Teddy. 'But yeah, those things scare the shit out of me too.'

I wasn't listening. It seemed to be wasted conversation made to fill the gaps. When had things become this damn awkward?

'I don't want to go on the Ferris wheel,' added Lara, 'That's what scares me.'

I didn't say anything. Too many things scared me.

'Do you want some ice cream or something?' Teddy asked once we got there and he'd paid for his ticket and everything. I'd paid my own way.

'I think ice cream sounds good,' said Jack, even though no one had asked him. It didn't matter. We ended up getting ice cream, and Lara took well over five minutes to decide on a flavor. I wasn't in the mood to tolerate her that night.

I never perked up, as my mother might have said. I could hear her voice, chirping away, saying, 'Now, Lillie, you are not a pretty girl when you frown.' Who cared about being pretty when you thought you might melt from the heat and your makeup was running, with the stench of fried potatoes and dough seeping into your pores? I was miserable, and I wanted to be.

Jack won a Kewpie Doll for Lara, but I told Teddy I would punch him if he tried to do the same. All too cutesy and apple pie for my taste. When Jack drove us all home, I had him drop me at my house first. I didn't want to be with Teddy that night. I didn't much feel like being kissed and acting romantic. I wanted to be alone. I wanted to sulk and lick my own wounds. And maybe inflict a few on others too.

The next morning, I woke early to a light rain. The worst of the heat had broken, and I felt lighter and resolved to be a good girl once more. Well, perhaps a good girl isn't the right way to describe it. Because what I aimed to be from then on wasn't the sort of girl Mary Elizabeth or Sister Margaret would consider to be good. I wasn't aiming for morality. What I meant to be was nice and agreeable. I wasn't going to go around picking any more fights. Or so I thought.

I wish I could say I stuck to this resolution, but I failed, as my nature was fated to insist on a method of attack. But before the hourglass emptied and I did smash it, I can attest that I did behave as kindly and generously towards Teddy as I could. It was our way to bicker, but, in those late August days, we were largely at peace with one another and had barely a harsh word between us.

And then September came.

Chapter Twelve

I can say, without a doubt, the happiest day I lived was August thirtieth, 1941. It was a perfect day and cannot be ruined by memory.

To know I lived it is enough, or so I used to think. For years I wouldn't so much as play it back in my mind, but I would will myself to relive the moment. I became particularly good at this while high and wrote some very pitiful poetry about it, all of which has since been burned.

I recounted the events of it once to my husband, laughing throughout, making a farce of it. It was our second or third date (I'd slept with him after the first), and I was explaining the furthest I'd been sexually before him. He found it quite precious, I think. But even that recounting couldn't spoil it. And now that that's all over, or nearly so it would seem, I've rather put that version out of my mind and returned to the original. Which I know is not true to life. How could it be?

It started early in the day. Teddy had stopped by the night before, Friday, after he'd returned from Albany where he had been clerking for his father, to ask if I might like to go on an expedition with him the next day, leaving after breakfast.

'Where to?' I asked, wondering what I was supposed to wear if I didn't know where we'd be off to.

'That's a surprise.'

Getting nothing else out of him, I wore a pale blue and white striped sundress and sandals, daringly deciding against wearing a slip. I felt deliciously naked as I sat next to Teddy in Mr. McCalman's Buick, which he'd been allowed to borrow for once. I'd so rarely driven with Teddy, and as I noted several months later on the drive back from New Jersey, he wasn't particularly good at it. He also had the nasty habit of smoking out the window.

But I didn't dwell on that then, nor did I consider my legs sticking to the seat. It was very early still with only a hint of the day's heat to come. I'd never been on a journey with a boy alone. Dads hadn't exactly been thrilled when I told him over breakfast, but he allowed me to go with his usual 'Okay,' the 'kay' harsh and drawn out. Only two weeks more of this nonsense, he must have thought.

We drove along for a while, out to the country. He hummed Bach, and I chatted on about Faulkner because I had finished reading *Light in August* the night before. Teddy liked Faulkner a lot more than I did, arrogantly claiming he understood him, which I went ahead and believed. I preferred Hemingway; there was something more immediate in his style that I took to reflect genuine feeling. Teddy liked Hemingway too, and he never judged the man for being a godless expatriate the way Mark Hamilton had ('Good art must be made by the moral' and all that crap). Except I don't think Teddy could have judged anyone for being wicked as he himself was about the least moral boy I knew. But I think I might have been mistaken. I think perhaps he was incredibly right-minded, much more so than I was or Lara. I would learn this very well in the months to come, but to an adolescent girl emerging from the nursery for the first time, a boy who smokes cigarettes and drinks can't be anything but bad. The world is too narrowly defined at eighteen.

'Where are we off to?' I asked as we neared an hour in the car. The day was heating up, and I was growing impatient.

'Nowhere in particular.'

'That's a lie. You know exactly.'

'Maybe. I thought we established this a long time ago. We're both pretty awful liars.'

He looked over at me and smiled. He remembered. And since there was no one else on the road, he took the cigarette out of his mouth and leaned over and kissed my cheek. I smiled too and said no more.

It must have been another hour. We passed Saratoga Falls where we'd spent our New Year's Eves until my mother died, and I figured we must be heading for the Finger Lakes. It seemed a long way to go. But I was content. Time ceased to matter, hell, even to exist, when I was with him.

Finally, he pulled over. We were in a forest outside Cedar Falls where the tumbling water flowed into the river and the rapids turned to soft rocks. Teddy took my hand. The day had wakened into its heat, and my sandals clung to my feet, forming the imprint of a cross. I shed them and ran towards the water, cooling my swollen ankles and whooping. Teddy followed behind, slowly.

I forgot about him, lost in my own reveries. In my own delight. The water was blessedly cool after such a drive. I raised the water to my face, forgetting I was wearing mascara and lipstick. It bled a little, but it didn't matter, not as it had before. For once, everything was wonderful.

When I turned, Teddy was standing on the bank, shirtless. God, was he beautiful. Tan and lean and boyish. And horribly, horribly young and beautiful. And mine. Yes, he was mine.

'Come in,' I beckoned to him.

'I like my view from here.'

'Come on. It feels lovely.'

'I can think of something else that would feel lovely.'

And I ran to him on the bank, and he pulled me up and kissed me.

'You next.' He smiled.

I took off my dress and dragged him backwards into the water, he in his old blue jeans and me in my panties and brassiere. I couldn't regret not wearing a slip now. It was shallow water, and he brought us back up to the bank. His shoes were thrown off, a belt tampered with, and pants fussed over. I stared at him, now only in his shorts and let out a laugh. It was the only thing I could think to do.

It was the first time I saw a naked boy. And it was the first time a boy saw me naked. I don't remember when the rest of the clothes went, and later we had a hard time retracing them because we weren't all that sure where they had gone either.

Sex had always perplexed me, scared me. But there, on that warm and waning summer afternoon, I wasn't frightened anymore. I looked at him frankly and allowed him to do the same to me. I knew I was thin, and I didn't have the biggest chest in the world or anything like that, but I thought I must have looked nice, at least to him. I've always thought that he was prettier than I. Maybe that's stupid, but God, did I think he was gorgeous.

We swam, and I giggled. And he teased me for giggling. We were Adam and Eve reborn. There was no such thing as sin. We hadn't created that yet.

It was the drive back when he asked, 'What do you want more than anything, Lil?'

'For the night to never end,' I answered, quickly. 'I wish some part of me might stay here forever, trapped in these hours and live through it again and again, with no future. And I think, or I mean I like to think, part of you does remain in moments where you feel like that. That I'll always be eighteen and it will be summer, and I'll be with you.'

It was the closest I ever came to telling him I loved him. He never said anything of the sort to me, but I think he knew what I meant.

'That's pretty,' he said.

And I don't know why but that was more of a compliment to me than if he had said 'you're pretty' because I knew he meant that too. He thought all of me was beautiful, including my thoughts. And that was better than sex.

'If all I could do was talk to you, that would be enough,' he said.

Other men have said the same to me many times over, cheapening the sentiment. Because I know now it's a roundabout way of getting me to cave in, but I think Teddy did mean it. I hope he did.

But it wasn't enough. Not for me. Maybe it could have been for him. Or maybe what he meant is it was enough to have me in that capacity, but he'd find some other girl to satisfy him in other ways in the Bronx, which I am sure he did. I never asked, later on, and he never said anything.

I did not allow my thoughts to turn to the future and our inevitable departures from the Island and each other on that night. I willed myself to absorb every detail as if I could press a memory between the pages of a book like a flower.

We didn't get home until after sunset, and I lied to Dads about having eaten. Hetty had left something out for me, but I didn't bother with it. Besides, I wasn't really hungry. I was hungry for life; I was hungry for him. But food, I couldn't have cared less about that right then.

We hadn't had sex. No, we hadn't gone that far. But as I stepped in front of the mirror and evaluated my girlish body, admiring what Teddy might admire in it, I knew I had to do it. Every other thought was muddled and jumbled, and I couldn't sort out how to feel. Not exactly. But that one thought kept pervading my mind. I wanted Teddy McCalman to make love to me, and I didn't care about Father Kavanaugh, or Dads, or Mama in purgatory, or even Lara and my promise. I was going to sin with full intention, and I wasn't going to go to confession after. I knew I would never go to confession again. I was going to let him make love to me, and damn, I was going to love him for it. I didn't know when or where or anything like that, I just knew it needed to happen. And before the end of the summer. Of that I was certain.

But it never happened. It fell apart, and it never happened. And it was my fault. Everything after that was my fault. I can say that now, almost without flinching, but not without guilt. No, never without guilt.

Chapter Thirteen

I went away two weeks later on the train to Poughkeepsie. Dads woke with a late summer cold and couldn't go with me as planned. My years of traveling alone began.

I had longed for this journey for years and then dreaded its approach for weeks. I had known I would be a sad passenger, but I did not imagine the extent of misery I would feel as I boarded the Amtrak from Albany. Dads had been up to dropping me there and Lara came along in the car. We said our goodbyes. I couldn't cry in front of Dads. I've never been able.

And perhaps that was for the best, the brave smile and all. I'd already confessed to Lara over breakfast when we had the room to ourselves, before Hetty came in to clear our plates and ask if I might like more coffee and Lara more tea.

I had no special attachment to Hetty and gave her no particularly fond farewell. She'd been with us on and off throughout my childhood, but Dads only took her on full time after my mother died. I'd soon learn many of the girls at Vassar doted terribly on their nannies and maids, and they thought it funny I'd never had much of one, only a hired woman to help my father get by as I was a student. I wondered what life might be like for Dads with me gone, but I didn't dwell on it. He had his friends and his golf, and he remarried the spring of my sophomore year.

But all the same, I never knew where Hetty's loyalties lay, and thought she might mention something to my father if I weren't careful. I only spoke when sure not to be interrupted.

It had happened like this.

Lara had wanted the final night for the four of us to be together. The three of them had another week to go before they went up. I'd been inclined to rebel against the whole plan. The last thing I wanted was an evening of Jack and Lara's insipid conversation, and I well knew that Lara would accompany me to the station the next day. But it did mean something to her to commemorate the end of it with one another and our 'boys of summer' as she called them. Lara and I had celebrated every last evening of summer together with a bonfire in her backyard, and she did not see why that year should be any different, other than that she insisted she could not host as usual due to her father's likelihood to spy on us. So, we went to Jack's.

Jack lived in one of the newer housing developments which, despite having thin walls, were much more stylish in appearance from the outside. He had a swimming pool like Catherine Spence. Jack was from money, well for Mohawk Island anyway, and he'd make more money still.

We spent the evening lounging in our swimsuits, Teddy chain smoking throughout. He would glance over at me lying on my stomach in my black suit, eyeing me up and down. His smile told me that his mind was similarly engaged as my own. Swimsuits and pools were overrated compared to nature.

'Let's light the bonfire,' Lara kept saying until one of the boys noticed. Teddy couldn't be bothered and Jack's attempt at one was rather half-hearted, I must say.

'My dad is out at a concert tonight with a lady friend,' I whispered as the other two fussed with the kindling. 'He said not to wait up for him which means at least eleven o'clock.'

Teddy nodded, absorbing my intent. 'Cigarette?'

'Yes, please.'

'Come on you two lovebirds, you're making me sick,' called Lara. 'Get over here.'

His eyes studied me to ensure I had meant what I said.

'Have Jack drive us back at nine, yeah?'

'Okay.'

My fate was settled. By eleven o'clock that night I would be a woman.

'Come on,' Lara yelled over to us. 'Jack is going to light it. Lil, you can recite some poetry to initiate it.' She turned to Jack to explain. 'She does that every year. We make a real ceremony out of it.'

I didn't quite know what Jack made of me. Teddy and Lara had had a lifetime to get used to my eccentric ways, and Jack hadn't, or so I thought. When I asked him about it that November morning as we lingered over coffee and stale conversation, watching the breakfast crowd turn into the lunch, he answered, 'It was easy getting to know you because I already did. You are Teddy, except a girl. I never knew two people could be the same like that.'

The same old Heathcliff and Cathy shit, as usual, but I was desperate for someone to speak of Teddy by then, and I drank in his words. *So he had noticed it too.*

But this was before all of that, when I was in my dubious of Jack phase. Well, maybe I've never quite grown out of that, but I've learned to think well enough of him. I've had to, I guess.

'Come on, Lil, you have to,' protested Lara when I told her I rather not. 'It's tradition.'

Lara the sentimentalist, a dominant trait in her, really. Gardenias at her wedding, bonfires and poetry at the end of summer, though not the next year. Of course neither of us knew it would be the last. We may have imagined we'd return the following September, back to us the original two, not daring to dream that the boys would maintain relationships across distance, but even that was impossible by then.

'Fine, if it means that much to you. "Ashes to ashes, dust to dust." There you are, now light the silly thing.'

'That's not good enough. It has to be something I don't know.'

I hadn't realized this was a rule. I rattled my brain for what I'd read recently, all a touch too precious, and I knew Teddy would gather my meaning.

When I spoke, it was for Teddy, but I meant it for Lara too. And not only because she had asked me to, but because I wanted her to understand somehow. Not the obscurity of the poetry – I knew well enough that would be beyond her – but I wanted her to know what was going to happen. She was my best friend, and I'd promised.

'Come slowly, Eden!
Lips unused to Thee –
Bashful – sip thy Jessamines
As the fainting Bee.'

I heard Lara give a cry of excitement and stopped. The moment was through.

'That's much better. I've no idea what it means.'

She hadn't understood. Oh well. I'd tried.

'Is that Emily Dickinson?' asked Jack. Who knew he was literate? Certainly not I.

'Oh, do go on, Lil.'

Teddy was growing impatient, I could tell. He'd had enough of our schoolgirl antics and lit another cigarette.

'Are we going to have this goddamn fire or not?' The light didn't catch from his match, and he tried again with a deep inhale. He had it. 'I've got to be home by nine.'

'Since when has Ted McCalman had a curfew?' laughed Jack.

'I don't, but Lillie here does. She has to go off to her finishing school in the morning and needs her beauty rest, you see.'

'All right,' relented Lara. 'Light the fire, Jack. We may as well get on it with it.'

I could tell the night was spoiled in a way, the joy and the fun had dissipated, but I didn't care. It had all seemed a trifle too forced anyway. I wanted Teddy to myself. Two more hours and I would have just that, and who knew how much longer until...?

At half past eight I went inside to change out of my wet suit and freshen my hair. Lara followed me into the house. She knew.

She waited until I'd emerged from the bathroom fully clothed to lay into me.

'How much longer 'til you take it all off again?'

'Shut up, Lar,' I said, trying to make my way through the bathroom door, but she wasn't having it. 'You know how it is.'

Her lips were pursed and eyes wide. 'I'm not kidding around here,' she said. 'Are you going to?'

Did she think she could stop this? What would she do, evoke my mother's ghost?

'Maybe,' I sighed. 'I don't know. It depends, I think. If he has anything, you know?'

Her stern face did not relax an inch. 'What things?'

'I don't want to end up with a baby, I know that much. And don't give me that crap about how Catholics don't use those things. They're supposed to wait until marriage too, and that's fine and well, but I'm not a Catholic any longer, you know that.'

'Oh, Lil.' I knew we were due for tears. 'It's not that, it isn't, I swear. It's, well, they say ... I don't know, it's ridiculous, I guess.'

I smiled. 'More ridiculous than waiting until your wedding morning?'

She smiled too. 'No, now that is not silly. That's practical. But, Lil, they say it makes you different after. You're chemically bound to the guy. It's science.'

I resumed my distance, collapsing my back against the frame of the door.

'First religion and now science. You won't let me escape from any angle, will you?'

Her anger did not return but was replaced with something sadder still – resignation. 'You two are already, well, eerily bound together or whatever that is between you, but you know he won't care.'

Was she in the right to speak these words, to allow the doubt to encroach? I'd feared much the same until the day by Cedar Falls. Hell, I didn't just fear it, I knew it was true.

'I swear, I want this. And isn't only to keep Teddy…'
Wasn't it?

'Lil, please don't if you don't want to, promise me, okay?'
'All right.'

She let me go.

But I knew it was coming, of that I was certain.

And Lara knew it too.

*

I hadn't wanted to give Jack much of a hug, but I did. He had driven me home and after all, he was the fourth member of our group. I knew already that if I was going to go around complaining about Teddy deserting me in the autumn, I'd have to tolerate much the same from Lara and listen to her wax lyrical about Jack's strong points. Maybe that's when I would learn what they were.

'Thanks for the summer,' I said.

'Ahh, you keep well now.'

How like a father his words were. Middle-aged at eighteen. But I didn't give it much thought.

'I'll see you in the morning, Lar. All right?'

Lara looked up at me from where she sat in the passenger's seat with the window down.

'You remember now.'

'I will. I said I promised, no?'

She scowled, her brows revealing their natural tendency to form together. 'Yes. Don't forget. I'll see you tomorrow morning. Goodnight.'

Goodnights and good lucks resounded all around, except from Teddy. He remained silent.

When at last they drove away, he said, 'Mind if I have a smoke before we go in?'

I wanted one too but didn't dare.

When we went in through the kitchen, my nerves started to get the best of me. I wished I had had that cigarette. To calm me down, though that's a load of nonsense. Nothing could have eased my thoughts at that moment. I was about to lose my virginity and the bravado of half past eight had gone.

'Do you, do you want some milk or some tea or something? I can't give you anything stronger because Dads...' I trailed off. I was rambling already.

Teddy stood up straight from where he'd been leaning against the door frame. He closed it and walk towards me. I thought he might take my hand, but he didn't. His eyes were sad.

'I think it's better that way,' he said, his mouth curving up on the side.

'Well, well,' I stumbled for words, 'do you want some milk

or something? Or I don't know what else we have. Hetty must've left something. Let me go and check the ice box.'

He tugged at my hand, and I felt the smoothness of his own. These fingers which held mine had been inside of me. They would soon be there again.

'Shh, you don't have to be nervous. Please don't be afraid.'

'I…' I didn't know what to say. The fingers would go inside me, then his pecker too. That was the way it happened. I'd be a virgin and then I wouldn't be anymore. That was it. 'I don't have any Shubert or Chopin or anything, but want to listen to some Frank Sinatra or something?'

He smiled and pulled me closer, raising my chin so that our eyes met one another. I shivered.

'Are you cold?'

'No, yes. I don't know.'

I gave a jerk. It wasn't right. Not yet. There needed to be something else, to put this awkwardness to rest first. It hadn't been like this at the lake. There I'd been free and easily assumed the role of a woman, confident to show my naked breasts and to see his … I couldn't form the word in my mind. I paced about the kitchen, pushing back a cuticle as I walked. I had wanted to keep my hands nice and lady-like. But I couldn't help it now.

'Lil…'

'We can go upstairs if you like. Dads won't be home until at least eleven.'

'Let's, let's listen to some records first.'

He was nervous too, and I was glad of it. I couldn't have stood to have had Teddy be his usual cocky self. I would have lost my temper a lot quicker on him if he had acted that way.

'All right,' I said, and I dashed off to the living room. He followed.

We sat on my sofa, and after a moment of agonizing hesitation, he placed his arm around my shoulder, and I leaned into it. He tipped my head backwards and kissed my lips. I thought I might cry it was so beautiful. I didn't know how many kisses we had left, and I wanted to savor them all. If I had only known…

When we did go upstairs, I forgot to stop the record. My legs were shaking, and my hands would only have muddled up the needle and scratched the thing.

'First door on the left,' I said.

Teddy sauntered in as if he'd done it every day. But it was funny to have Teddy in my room again, like this. He'd been in it years before when Adam died, and he spent the night at ours. Back when I thought that I was going to marry Clark Gable and had braces. Before I had developed any sort of a chest whatsoever. Back when we were nothing but kids, not even yet thinking of playing adults.

It was funnier still to have him kissing me as I leaned against the backboard of my bed. This was my room. This was where I'd been a girl and most alone. This is where I'd lie back at night and touch myself, slowly slipping in a finger the way Teddy taught me, breathing lightly, wishing to call his name. Sometimes I did when Dads wasn't home from work and Hetty had left for the day. I practiced my moans.

This had been my sanctuary of dreams. And now here was this boy. And when it was over? What was I going to do about the sheets and the thingie? Would he put it back it in his pocket and take it home to dispose? How did other girls manage it? I didn't know. I hadn't thought. The reality was coarse and smelled.

My eyes wandered to the crucifix hanging above my bed and the print of the Virgin Mary on my vanity. My mother had put those up, not me. They were her convictions, not mine. And yet they had borne witness to my growing up. They were part of the girl Lillie too.

'Teddy,' I whispered. He didn't answer but kept kissing my neck. I said his name again.

'Hmmm?'

'Do you think the Virgin is watching us?'

I could feel his chest expanding against mine. He was trying not to laugh.

'No, no it's only a print. Don't worry.'

'All right.' We kept kissing.

But then he stopped. 'Hey, Lil, what do you want?'

I stopped too.

What did I want? How could I answer what I wanted?

For night to never end. For kisses to continue forever. For there to be nothing beyond kissing because it is the only thing worth a damn, the rest of it nasty and horrible. To be able to take a pill or undergo a surgery to gain knowledge and not have to go through the whole rigmarole of deflowering and pain and being bound to a boy who'd forget. To have my mother to cry to after it was over, if she would listen. To make love. To keep you with me and not lose you. To never be abandoned again. To not have to feel the pain of fingers inside me. To never have to think of Tom Westerby again. To be loved. To be held. To fuck.

'I want…'

I couldn't think of a thing to say.

He waited.

'I don't know.'

It was the only thing of which I was sure.

'Maybe we better stop then.'

'No. No. That's not…'

'Lil, you don't know what comes next.'

And that was the start of it.

'I do too. It's…'

How dare Teddy McCalman tell me I didn't know what comes next. I wasn't some Mary Elizabeth thinking lovers rolled around, smooshed together and that was the epitome of love making, no real bodily exchange necessary. I hadn't spent the summer making myself sick over it only to come down to it and be told I was a virgin and would stay that way because I didn't understand what comes next. Bullshit.

'Shh.' He enveloped my thin shoulders against his own boyishly lithe frame. Child against child. 'I know you think you know stuff from novels and shit, but it's, come on, you don't, do you?'

'From novels? That's what you think of me? A little girl who reads books. That's all I'm good for, isn't it? Kiss me and talk to me, but you don't want me, do you? Don't you dare patronize me, Teddy. Don't you dare. Come on. I know that your pecker has to go inside of me and that it will hurt like hell, but that will be it. And I won't, well you know, because a girl never does on her first time, or so they say. And I don't mind, I … I … you have to do it.'

'And,' he spoke slowly as though measuring out each word, ignoring the lot of my insults, 'I'm glad you're not a little girl anymore, but,' he touched my breast and continued, 'I sort of wish, I sort of wish we were, kids again, that is.' And here he kissed my cheek, and I met his eyes, and I knew he loved me. He must have.

'Teddy…'

'Lil.'

He crushed me against his chest, but I was determined not to cry. That would be the end of it if I did. What a mess this was turning into! It wouldn't happen to other girls. When it came time for Ellen to do the deed, she'd have it over with nice and easy. Not some bedroom melodrama like this.

'Lil,' he sighed into my hair.

He didn't say the words, 'We shouldn't,' but I heard them in his voice.

In a fit of self-consciousness, I flew from him. I wrapped my arms about my body, covering my bare chest. I couldn't stand to have him evaluating or admiring me. Not then.

He swung his legs off the bed, as though preparing to rise, and stared at me. Waiting for what I might say next and already knowing he would have to be the one to speak with reason. I hated him, but I couldn't stop myself. I may have promised one thing to Lara, but I'd promised this to myself.

'Don't you have any scarlet letters or anything?'

'Sorry, I left Hawthorne at home for the night.'

There he was, mocking my innocence and stupidity, but I knew so very little of such things. How could I? I was a virgin, yes, but foremost I was a Catholic. I'd only learned of their existence thanks to Madeleine who remarked at the time, 'It comes down to this. Would you rather have a screaming brat hanging off your nipple or go to hell? Hmm?'

Go to hell, I thought, but not before Teddy. I wished him there now. He'd enjoy the place, I was sure of it, or at least he'd grin that cocky sonofabitch smirk of his and claim that he would, which was really just as bad.

But I wanted him. Despite every failing of his character, both real and imagined by me in my state of anger, I did love him. And I wanted him. Needed him to do this to me. Tonight. I couldn't wait until Thanksgiving, or whenever I'd see him next. I'd lose him by then to some New York girl. But it wasn't that alone. I knew that.

I was asking him, well, if you want to go and get deeply analytical about the whole thing, I think I was asking for him to come to bed to make up for not being able to ask him on that night years before, when all I'd wanted was an embrace and some love. A warm body to share my bed, to wrap his arms around me until I could pretend they weren't his but another's, my mother's. At least I think that's what I wanted. But who knows. Maybe all I did want was for him to make up for my loss of childhood or some bullshit, but I'd also spent most evenings there on the carpet touching myself and dreaming of how he might feel when he finally did it.

What did I want?

'French letters,' he said. 'Condoms.'

'Yes, those *things*. Do you have them? I mean, do you have any? I don't.'

'Yes, I do.'

Had I been expecting him to give that answer? Had I wanted him to?

'Okay, umm, should I, well, are you err, I mean, is it, you know … hard?'

'No, Lillie, I'm not.'

'Well…'

'Come here,' he said, reaching for my hand. But I couldn't. I moved further from him, my humiliation complete when he continued, 'This isn't exactly sexy, Lil. It's uhh, come on, can't we talk?'

And that was it. I could bear no more.

'Goddamnit!' I cried, throwing my hands up, my breasts revealed. I spat hair from my mouth, but there was too much of it. A mad Medusa I must have looked, but how could I be Medusa when at least she'd had sex?

'Goddamn you, Teddy, and goddamn this room and this night and me for being silly enough to think … Isn't this what you want? You and Tom Westerby and James Moore, and for Christ's sake, don't look at me like that, I barely did anything with James, but what if I had? Would you want me then? Do you only take sluts or something, Teddy? You and forty-year-old whores who fall for your cheesy lines because they can't read a book. Is that what you like? I mean, what is the matter with you? Why don't you … Here I am and I … I want you … I thought … I thought it's what you all wanted. This. I thought it would make me … it would make you … Why do you all do it? Why can't…'

The one time I wanted it, the one time I wouldn't have felt guilt or worried about sin. The one time I would have said yes with all of my heart, and he didn't want me. They only wanted me when I cried, when I was in pain. When I didn't want them. My lip quivered and my eyes burned. My chest ached. I was going to cry, the last bit of my pride lost.

'I need a cigarette,' he said.

It was over. He'd start fumbling for his clothes in a minute and he'd go. He might kiss me on the check like some sort of baby and tell me we could speak when I'd calmed down, but then he'd be gone. And what right had he to do that? I mean wasn't he the very one to insist Jack drive us back here at nine and to bring a condom. He'd wanted it too, I knew that. To play this moral high ground of it being best for all parties involved to keep my innocence intact, well, I wasn't buying that bullshit.

'You better light one for me too,' I said, still very much naked except for my thin panties. They were lacey and new.

He pulled on his trousers and buttoned his shirt.

'I don't think your father would like it too much if he came home to the smell of smoke coming from his daughter's bedroom, all right? I'm going out.'

'Don't you dare.'

He said nothing but slipped on his shoes and adjusted his belt.

'Where did I leave my sunglasses?' he muttered, absent-mindedly. He reached under the bed, but they weren't there. My stuffed puppy, Albert, was sitting on them. Teddy lifted him as if he were diseased. Probably thinking what a kid – she sleeps with stuffed animals and thinks she can have sex. What a joke. I bet he was going to have that cigarette alone so he could have a laugh about me.

'Fine, leave. Go away. Go smoke your damn cigarette and forget about me. I don't care.'

He threw a cigarette back to me, but I let it drop to the floor. I didn't want it, not really.

He paused at the door and gave me that look of his with the sympathetic eyes and smile screwed up to the left, the look only Teddy could give and that I used to like to think he could give only to me. 'Lil…'

I knew I needed him. I loved him. I knew sex didn't matter. I knew if all we did for the rest of the night was listen to some records or talk about Virginia Woolf who I was struggling through and Teddy was too afraid to approach, well, that would have been fine. It might have been better. Kissing Teddy, talking to Teddy, sitting with Teddy. It didn't matter. Everything was wonderful with him. I knew that.

My brow softened, and I nearly relented and went to him. I wanted his forgiveness but perhaps I was not ready to give him mine. I wish I knew myself better. I wish I knew myself as Teddy knew me.

He began to walk away. He needed his cigarette, but he'd come back. He wouldn't go ahead and leave me like this when we mightn't have a chance to see each other until Thanksgiving, if even then. Teddy usually went to his grandparents' in Boston. That meant Christmas. Surely he wouldn't leave me in this purgatory for three months. He could be cruel, or absent-minded and neglectful, but he wouldn't do that to me. He loved me. I had seen it in his eyes. No, he'd go and have that one cigarette, we'd both cool down a little but then he would come back and we'd make it up. And maybe the chance to do it had passed, but I could resign myself to that if only he would come back, and we could be in love again without saying the words.

But I couldn't bear it. I wanted him back so badly that I never wanted him to come back at all.

I ran out into the hall, my arm clutching at my breasts.

'Edward McCalman, go to hell!'

He turned, and he smiled, halfway down the stairs already. 'Already intending on it.'

'Oh God, Teddy!' I cried, collapsing at the head of the stairs, my eye nearly hitting against the banister as it had when I was a kid and needed stitches.

But it didn't stop him. I heard the door creak. He was smoking his cigarette, cool and calm. And I was left upstairs. Left with a cigarette but no lighter.

I should have run after him. I should have gone to him and kissed his face and apologized. It wouldn't have taken much. Teddy wasn't one for grudges, and I don't think he was that mad at me anyway. He knew how I fought. Rash and incoherent words spewing from my mouth, hurling insults which he'd later claim I never meant. Maybe I didn't, but I think I did. He with his back straight, his jaw set against my hurtful words, saying he needed a cigarette. Some air. A moment to forget what I bitch I could be.

Well, that might be fine for Teddy McCalman, but it wasn't good enough. How could he walk away from a scene? It should have ended in blood. It should have ended in sex. That was the way. But no, he walked away. Like some man exhausted after hours of entertaining a child living out her fantasies.

I crawled back to my bedroom, the wretched serpent that

I was. The room was in disarray with bedcovers on the floor and my clothes scattered. I wanted to tear at my pillows and pluck forth each feather. Instead I kicked at the cigarette resting on the floor, the paper splitting and the tobacco leaves spilling out.

'He couldn't even light it for me.'

It was hot, maddeningly so, and my skin, which hours before had glowed with the kiss of the summer sun, was now streaked with red. I pressed a hand to my temple. I was burning up.

My legs buckled, and I lowered myself to the ground, gently. I rested my head on the braided rug beneath my vanity set, my eyes lifted to the Virgin Mother. I longed to ask for forgiveness. To be consoled and comforted and cleansed. I thought to pray my Act of Contrition, but I couldn't form the words. Years and years of nothing but good Catholic education and I couldn't bring myself to remember the prayer.

Teddy never did come back. I'm glad he didn't, in a way. Maybe he was waiting for me to come out and fetch him. Maybe he decided to smoke a whole pack of cigarettes. I don't know.

But what would he have found if he had? Would I have forgiven him? I've never been sure. Probably not.

I wanted to be alone. I needed to sulk. I needed to find my own way out of this mood because I didn't have the comfort of a cigarette. Because I'd ruined the one he left for me, and goddamnit, I didn't have a match.

I cried until I couldn't make myself cry anymore. It hurt too much. I knew Dads had to come home at some time, and I couldn't have him find me like that. Curled up on my vanity rug without the decency of clothes, and with tobacco leaves scattered on the floor.

I struggled to where I had left the mess and cleaned it up with the last of my strength. I threw my dress, the simple frock I had once loved, onto a chair. I had bought it the week before up at Myers. It was pale green with an eyelet bodice because every girl knows you have to wear light colors to show off the best of a tan, and it had worked a wonder, or so I thought. Until now. Another dress wasted, bought with the earnings of my summer job at the *Dispatch*. I wore it for three more summers because I tried not to buy too many clothes during the war, but I never liked it.

I found my bra and my damp swimsuit and threw those up onto the chair too. I needed a nightgown. I couldn't think of anything else. I needed a nightgown. I needed to get myself to my bed. I needed to go to sleep. I needed to leave for Vassar in the morning. That was all.

And I needed Teddy. But he was gone, and I couldn't go to him. But I could have. The boy lived three doors down. I could have gone then or at three in the morning after Dads had put the house to bed. I could have gone over before breakfast or made Dads and Lara wait in the car when we left for the station. It would have taken a minute. I'm sorry, good-bye, a small kiss. That was it. That could have been the ending.

I could have gone, and I should have gone, but I didn't.

Though if I think about it, begging my mind to wander back and recall the series of events falling into place, lining them up neatly next to one another, each an individual tin soldier perfectly formed and standing to order, I wonder how differently things would have turned out. I think it might have been the same. The ending was the ending. That was it.

Still, I wish I had.

Chapter Fourteen

After that summer, what else mattered?

Lara was a sympathetic listener, but I knew she wasn't sorry for what happened, or what hadn't happened, really. I remained a virgin alongside her, and she was satisfied with that. I would live up to my word and take on a lover before marriage one day, but until then she and I were equals. Besides, she'd always hated Teddy, and I knew she couldn't stand the idea of him having more of me than her. She was a jealous girl.

It wasn't because of her I didn't lose it, and she knew that. But she didn't help matters by standing there in the hallway of Jack's house with her puppy-dog brown eyes, begging me not to go through with it, trying her best to restore a conscience in me.

Do you know, I'm not sure I've forgiven her. I don't think I have. I certainly hadn't by the following spring, I know that.

'Lil, he'll write, I know he will,' she said to me at the station while we waited for Dads to check my trunk. 'He's crazy about you.' Certain my cherry was safe from popping until Christmas, she could afford to be more generous in her estimation of Teddy.

'Lar, he won't come back.'

She pressed my hand. Each of us was shy in our feelings for the other, and we hesitated to show emotion through touch. Perhaps that explains why there are so few photos of us together from that time too. We loved each other, yes, but we were not intimate in the way other girls our age tended to be with their friends.

'We'll see about that,' she said with a weak smile.

The whistle blew.

My eyes burnt with the tears I was longing to shed but held back until I was safe to myself in the smoking car with a cup of black coffee.

I don't remember eating a thing from then until I came back for Christmas. I must have, but who can say. I never ate lunch. A cigarette and a coffee and maybe an orange. That was my first year at Vassar.

I lived in Strong in a room to myself that year. I was very lonely. The only friend I had was Mallory, and I met her the first night. Mallory lived in Strong too, but the floor below. Our jade green Samsonite luggage was mixed up by the porter unloading from the noon train. I barely noticed. The larger case held the same Claire McCardell dresses, two packs of Marlboros smuggled in at the bottom, and a bottle of Chanel No. 5 scent. But Mallory was two sizes bigger than I, mostly in the bust, and she had a monogrammed luggage tag. Mallory Sarah Jones.

I went to seek her out before supper with the idea that if we got along well enough, I might have someone to sit with for the meal. I've never had a talent for making friends.

I knocked on the door the luggage tag specified.

'Come in,' shouted a voice not tainted by nasal regional accent as most of the voices I had known until then were. It was the voice I imagined Daisy Buchanan might have had, sounding of money.

Mallory was from Manhattan. Her family were the sort who came over on the Mayflower or just there about. 'Not Pilgrims, of course, darling. None of us have an inch of religious spirit. But we've always been through and through patriots, or so Mommy claims. Who knows? The woman is bats. She'd lie about anything to get herself into her tight-assed little DAR society. I was one of their debs. Do you smoke, Lillie?'

I liked Mallory from the start. She was like Ellen but had actually had sex. She was the sort of girl I wished I could be but couldn't manage. I had too virginal of a face or something.

'Yes,' I said, stepping further into the room, closing the door. I didn't want anyone else to hear this girl saying words like ass. 'I mean, I've come because I think the porter mixed up our luggage. So really you have my cigarettes, and I have yours.'

She laughed, big and bawdy. Not refined in the least.

'I had wondered. Wishful thinking I was this size. Also these kid gloves are worn on the right hand, mine are the left. I'm left-handed. Like every goddamn criminal or artist, depends which way you look at it. Except I'm not an artist, so I must be a criminal. Don't get me wrong. I love to sleep with an artist, they say the most imaginative things about your body, calling you a Titian beauty instead of plain fat, but their, well, you know how it is, their pecker is never that big. I think that must be a sign of being an artist too. Inadequacy pushes you forward. All very Freudian. I'm studying psychology, by the way, or that's what I told Daddy when he signed the fat check to send me here. But that's why I'm such a scream or whatever those prudes like to say. Are you a prude? I'm sorry if you are, really, as much for my sake as yours.'

'No, I'm not a prude, or I don't think I am.'

She laughed again. 'You're blushing a teeny bit, so you must be a teeny bit of one. But I'll fix that. Drink?'

'Sure.'

Mallory invited me to sit on her bed. My mother had never let me have any friend sit on my bed as a kid. Friends were to be kept in the living room where they couldn't spread their germs as much. I could see that knowing Mallory would be an education.

'What do you like? I've brought it all.'

I peeked in the trunk she was rummaging through, and she was right. She'd brought a well-stocked bar. We weren't supposed to have booze in our rooms, I knew that. Beer or maybe a bottle of wine would be tolerated, but not liquor. I guessed with a surname like Jones, though, it didn't matter.

'What are you having?'

'Gin. It's all I drink. Stick to clear if you want to stay thin, or that's what Mommy always says. She's a vodka drinker, but I can't stand the stuff. Gin okay?'

'Sure.'

She mixed us two gimlets and passed one to me along with a Marlboro. She lit hers first and settled in next to me on the bed.

'You don't speak much, do you? Or is it that I am talking too much? I haven't given you a chance to say a word other than yes or no or sure. Or anything. Tell me something, Lillie, isn't it?'

'Yes.'

'There you go again with the yes. Say a sentence with at least five words. I'm dying to learn more about you, I swear. You're still here for instance and you've nearly finished your gin. Here, let me make you another one. I like you, you know that? You can drink. Help yourself to another cigarette, please.'

'Well,' I started, lighting another cigarette first for reassurance, 'I've come from the middle of nowhere, I guess, and I don't intend to go back. I'm here to study English literature.'

'I figured that much. You look the type. Either that or art history. Slender. Girls who do English are always slender and dark with tapering ankles, like you. But you're a lot prettier than other English majors. I confess this is based exclusively on observation of Chapin girls, and they all had something up their asses, that type. You don't strike me as that sort, Lillie. Do you mind if I call you L? I think it would suit you.'

I felt myself smiling. A friend made in less than an hour, and she'd done all of the work.

'No, not at all. I went to Catholic school and, well, you know, there were a lot of that sort of girl there too.'

She passed me a fresh drink which I drank faster than the first. Mallory did too.

'Well, well. You're a Catholic then. Irish? You look a pretty girl from the old country, a Cathleen ni Houlihan.'

My ears perked up.

'You've read Yeats?'

'Darling,' she said, settling herself back into her bed, bringing her pillow close to her face to snuggle, 'I've read simply everything, but I am not a literary type in the least. Don't mistake me for that. I just like literary people, like yourself. You have the best taste in alcohol, I find, and never the money to buy it. Or that's the case with the men. But I can buy it and you can keep me interesting, does that sound like a deal to you, L?'

'Sure.'

And that's how our friendship started, the only one I formed in A-term of my freshman year. There were other girls, mostly in the English major or who lived in Strong, but they were horrified when I decided to not go out for writing on *The Miscellany News* and refused to take part in sharing the short stories I was writing at the time. I never show my work to anyone and as for the paper, well, I figured it would have cut into my drinking time with

Mallory, which became the most important thing to me that A-term, next to studying.

I spent my days in lectures and the library and the nights with Mallory. It was a simple existence, and in memory I see myself as a happy girl enjoying freedom for the first time. But I wasn't. I was lonely, and I was sad.

*

Mallory lost her virginity to her deb date, or so she told me the third time we sat up drinking gin together.

'I swear, cross-my-heart-and-all, I thought that's what I was meant to do. They have you wearing this big white dress and he's in a tux, and hell, it cost as much as wedding. That's what Daddy said, but he's bitter. Three girls, no boys. Why, what was yours like?'

The question startled me. I choked on the ice in my drink. Did she mean…? Well, in any case, I hadn't had either.

'That's okay, I know you're a virgin. No need to lie. Have a ciggie?'

I took one. She lit it for me. My fingers were getting better at striking a match and clicking a lighter, but Mallory had a talent for it and always got it on the first go, even in the wind and rain.

'How'd you know?'

She reached for a cigarette of her own, giving her wrist a shake, the diamond tennis bracelet she'd received for her eighteenth birthday gleaming. She'd done that on purpose.

'Most girls here are, that's all. The only ones who've had their cherry popped *comme moi* are either a poor slut sticking a corn husk up her slit since the age of twelve or some daddy's girl rich enough not to have to give a shit about giving the milk away for free. But otherwise, for most girls, it ruins their stock value. That's what Daddy says anyway.'

'Your father said that?' I nearly blushed for her sake. The thought of Dads mentioning sex to me!

She shook her wrist as she tapped the ash from her cigarette. That meant yes.

'Does he know, well, about Tony?'

'I'd think so. He and Mommy walked in on us, you know, so unless they thought, hell, there's nothing else they could have thought, is there? You'd think they'd have had the decency to ring me and let me know they'd be in the city. All right, that's not fair. I imagine they go around telling their friends that they'd have thought their daughter would have enough decency not to be doing it with a dago in their apartment, in their bed, much the less.'

My eyes widened. Even after a week of knowing her, Mallory had the power to shock.

'Weren't they upset?'

'Mostly about the sheets. And the crystal. Mommy insisted on having a full inventory that night.'

'Oh.'

'Your parents are religious, aren't they? Mine aren't.'

I had to tell her. I hated that part of getting to know anyone. Having to reveal I didn't have parents as a plural but a parent in the singular. I expected a cliché stab at sympathy, which I resented. It was damn awkward to have a dead mother. It warranted comment.

Best to get it over with, though. That's the thing about the Island, most people knew. After the first few months of polite condolences people had minded their own business enough not to mention it, at least not to my face.

'It's just my father, actually. My mother died when I was younger. But she was very religious, yes.'

There, I'd done it. I wanted another drink.

'Jesus, help yourself to gin. You deserve it, all right. What shit. Can't say I didn't suspect something of the sort, though. You have an air of melancholy about you. Is that a literary enough turn of phrase?'

'I suppose so. It's a fairly poor one.'

She laughed her hardy, working woman's laugh.

'I'll make a fine psychiatrist, won't I? You can say that much. Diagnosing neuroses everywhere I go. Come on, L. Cheer up. We'll have another drink each and then we must go have something to eat.'

That was the thing about Mallory. She never liked to skip a meal as I did.

'You know,' she said, 'none of us are religious, we aren't of the Puritan stock. We must have deserted England for purely financial reasons. But that's not true. I have a cousin who is one of those, you know, born agains or whatever they call themselves. She found the Lord. Complete nut job. She had an abortion two summers ago and now she is leading baptisms, dunking heads in the river and all that shit. Did you ever know such a loony as that? Though madness does run in the Jones family.'

I liked listening to Mallory. She had a story about everything but not in that irritating way as some people do, trying to show off how experienced they are. That wasn't her style. She happened to have lived more life than I and to have come from a family where people spoke to one another.

I wanted to spill out my soul to Mallory, to make her my confessor. Tell her everything about the summer and Teddy. She'd understand – tell me I was naïve, and that she'd gotten over that puppy dog stuff years ago maybe – but understand nonetheless. She might have been able to offer an explanation for his behavior, though she'd probably have shrugged and said, 'Clear case of homosexuality.'

Mallory said that about any boy who didn't want to sleep with her. 'With these tits, come on, they must be. Even a bisexual would want these puppies.'

To this I could say nothing. What she might have said about me with my small breasts, I wasn't sure, but likely much the same. She'd just have employed different reasoning. 'You do have the most magnificent legs,' she told me once. 'And ass. Any man would love that. Did you ever notice some men are tits men and others like asses? I don't think it matters much. The poor slobs will take anything when you give it to them.'

I had only been able to nod in agreement. I hadn't known a thing about that. I wondered which Teddy preferred. He'd say mind if I put the question to him, but as Mallory taught me, that sort of talk is a bold-faced lie.

'Do you have a boyfriend?' That had been one of the first questions she'd asked me. Mallory was always to the point.

'No. Do you?'

That's when she told me about Tony. He wasn't her boyfriend, though. Don't go making that mistake. He was her lover, and a distant and causal one at that.

'I might see him over Thanksgiving, or I might not. I bet he's already knocked up some Brooklyn slut. We'll see.'

I wanted to ask Mallory how she avoided babies herself, but I was too scared. Once she attempted, rather drunkenly, to demonstrate how to slip a condom onto a phallus, using the neck of a bottle of champagne as her object. But it snapped.

She collapsed in a fit of hysterics. 'Look, L, it's jizzing! Ha! I'll die!'

I remained ignorant.

Chapter Fifteen

Lara and I spoke every Saturday evening for ten minutes on the telephone. Other girls used their phone privilege to ring home or their sweetheart. I called Dads some weeks but not most. He had his lady friend and was happy enough without me.

Lara was the closest thing I had to a sweetheart. She was the only person I had left.

We spent the ten minutes hurriedly reviewing those final days of summer, scrambling to find meaning behind every word and action of our young men. Jack hadn't rung her either since they'd said goodbye. He'd sent her a total of three letters which hadn't said much and promised less.

'I don't get it, Lil. How does a boy go from being so hot to nothing? I thought … I nearly let him see my … I'm glad I didn't. I wouldn't be able to look at them myself now if I had.'

'Oh, Lara.' I had to watch my language. The phone was situated in the parlor for the communal use of Strong House. The other girls were scattered about on sofas and chairs, chatting quietly with a friend or sewing, or, worst of all, studying. All lonely creatures, really. The best girls, like Mallory, had dates on Saturday nights.

That's where she was, getting ready to go out. Sometimes she set me up with some ridiculous man, but I hated it. I preferred to stay in and read my book and wash my hair. I rather enjoyed Saturday evenings to myself. I'd drink cocoa and try to work on a story, if I could muster the energy. Most of the time I moped around, wondering if this might be the week I'd get a letter from Teddy. Early in the evening, after supper, I'd phone Lara.

She had to make confession every Saturday afternoon. Of that I did not envy her. Otherwise, she spent her evenings much the same as I did – dateless.

'I can't help but feel that that cannot be the end to your story. It can't be,' said Lara. It was an agreed rule that we devoted the first five minutes to analyzing where Jack's and her relationship may have gone wrong and the last five minutes to Teddy's and mine. 'How could two such beautiful people – yes, I will recognize that Teddy is beautiful, all right – how can that be it? No, he'll come back. He has to. You're a gem.'

Lara lived in a room in a middle-class Victorian house owned by Saint Rose's. They had a private study in the house where the girls were allowed to make their phone calls. She could never be certain of who was eavesdropping outside the room, eagerly awaiting her turn, but for the most part, Lara could be more colorful in her language than I.

'I don't know,' I sighed. I could never give too much away in these conversations. 'He must have found another girl by now. A New York type. He didn't, we weren't … I'll write it in a letter to you, Lar, and send it in the first post Monday. Okay? I have to go.'

It was in our letters that we could expose ourselves to the other. I was better at it, writing down my feelings. Lara wasn't so much, but I only skimmed her letters. They bored me.

Lara was lonely too. I knew that. But Lara's loneliness was the common alienation of youth, and she'd find comfort in a nice boy someday, Jack or not.

But me, I knew I couldn't be fixed like that. I thought Teddy could do it, and perhaps he could have helped. I believed us to suffer the same sort of loneliness, and I think he thought that too. And if you suffer the same sort of loneliness as someone else, well then, you can't be envious of the other's loneliness, but instead can rest in it together and learn not to struggle against it. Lara and I could never do that.

Sometimes I did wish for a nice boy and a nice, little, common life. To have some version of happiness, even if it were an artificial one at that. Lara could have it and certainly would. And I hated her for that. Her loneliness was to be cured and her dependency on me was sure to decline, and I was to be left with no one to cling to or to cling to me.

I often went to bed miserable on a Saturday night. I'd try to work on a story, but all I could concentrate on was another letter to Lara.

Once I got drunk on the whiskey Mallory had bought as a consolation for the date she'd arranged for me canceling at the last minute. That was a bad time. I wrote a letter to Teddy, angry and quoting *Paradise Lost* for Lord knows what reason other than I was reading the latter books for the first time and resented that we couldn't speak of them together.

I posted it that night and had to beg the postmistress first thing Monday morning to open up the letter box and let me have it back. She explained it was a federal offense to do so as technically once posted, the letter became the property of the recipient. I had to dig up the messy bits of my story, explaining to her I'd rather rashly written a hateful letter to an old flame, and I'd die if he received it. Thankfully, she had a heart or perhaps a similar tale in her own past and gave the letter back to me with a warning not to be so impetuous in the future.

I wasn't.

*

It was around mid-October that Mallory began to cook up her scheme for a weekend out in New York.

'You mean to tell me, L, all you've had of a time in New York is a couple of Broadway plays and a pathetic fraternity party? You've barely lived! That's the trouble with you, do you know that? I'm not saying you have to hand it over to a boy on a plate or anything, don't get me wrong. But come on, you deserve some fun. It'll make you less neurotic, I swear. Look at me. I used to be a bottle filled to the brim with neuroses, or whatever the expression is. I don't care. All I know is I was ready to burst. And so, you know what I did?'

'What?' I asked as I took a drag on my eleventh cigarette of the evening. I'd been in Mallory's room for a little less than an hour. When we got started, we got started, Mallory and me.

'I started touching myself. It helped a hell of a lot. I recommend you try it.'

I wondered what Mallory would say if I told her I did that too and it didn't help. It made things worse, not only because it was racking up another sin I wasn't going to confess, but it made me lonelier still.

She lit her twelfth and waved her right hand to blow the smoke from her face, the tennis bracelet twinkling.

'I know you Catholics. Classic repression cases the lot of you.'

'Not exactly, Mal. It's more like, well, I don't know. I've gotten up to some stuff, but it never feels worth the sin or I don't know, the risk of a rabbit dying, you know. A few times it has, but a lot of the time it just hurts. Does that happen to you?'

'It did. Not after I started touching myself though, I'm telling you. It changes your world. Now I tell the guy how I want it, that's it. If he doesn't like that, then fine. I get up and go my own way. Simple as that.'

'Really?'

'Really.'

God, how I wished to be like Mallory at eighteen. Hell, I still do. Maybe Teddy wouldn't have left me then. Maybe my husband wouldn't have either. But maybe not. I think they liked my weakness; it hid their own.

'Now come on, let's have a think. We've got to get up to New York. I'll fix it with my parents some weekend when they're away in the Hamptons, and you and I can go up and have a time of it. How does that sound? Would your father permit it?'

There was no question of that. I knew he would. Dads loved to hear I had a Protestant friend, an old money family one at that.

'I guess so. What would we do?'

Mallory got up to open a window. The room was stuffy with smoke and the radiators had turned on a few weeks before, though we didn't need them. It was the last of Indian summer. Other girls were making the most of it, spending their evenings out on the lawn. Not Mallory and me.

'Deb season is coming, of course. My sister, Olive, is up for hers this year. We could go to that, I suppose. No, that's no good. Deb balls are only good for one thing and that's finding out where the best party afterwards will be. No, that won't do. Besides you'd hate the whole scene. Strictly no Jews or Catholics.'

If Mallory was my rich Protestant friend, I was her Catholic and middle-class one.

'Couldn't we go up and have dinner someplace and find a nightclub? I'd like that.' I thought I might have too. I'd never been to a bar before.

'No,' decided Mallory. 'Too risky. You have to wait on finding men that way. You know how it goes. You sit at some table howling away with laughter, just trying to convince some dumb bastard that you and your friend are having a whale of a time and he and his dumber bastard of a friend should buy you drinks. Nah, I'm not one for that scene. I prefer a real party.'

Based on Mallory's description, I was certain she was right. I'd hate the nightclub scene. But I already knew I hated the world of parties, and I was reluctant to re-enter it.

'Do you know of any parties in New York?' I asked.

'No,' she admitted, reaching for her thirteenth and offering me my twelfth, 'but I can find out easily enough. I'll write to my friend Joey. He's at the New School. One of those artists I was telling you about. Except that Joey isn't really an artist. I mean he is, in a way, I guess. He's good enough at painting to get a girl in bed because of it.' She didn't have to admit she had been one of those girls. I knew it already. 'But he is also Joseph Alexander Campbell III. Joey my ass. He'll be a banker like his father by twenty-five.'

'He sounds like a stuffed shirt. How would he know a good party?'

'He is and he isn't. He's an artist enough to live in the Village and have artist friends, or least other New School types, you know. That would work well enough. I'll write him a letter.'

I'd never been bohemian before, and I told Mallory as much.

'You don't say, L.'

'Well, I mean, what would I wear?'

Mallory had to have a think on that. And another drink first. I had one too.

'I know,' she said. 'I can give you my black smock dress. It's from when I wanted to be an actress, darling. Thank God that phase passed, as Mommy would say. But seriously, that would do well enough. Of course it will be too big and shapeless but black is your color, I know it. Can you sew?'

I couldn't.

'Do you know any girls who can? I sure can't.'

The thing was I hadn't bothered to get to know many of the other girls, and so far no one had proffered herself up as a seamstress.

Who did I know?

Jesus Christ, I thought. Mary Elizabeth. Poor, sad, obscure Mary Elizabeth. She'd been making her own clothes since she was twelve and, as much as I disliked her, I had to admit she knew what she was doing with a needle and thread. She managed to make her lumpy figure look suitable enough. She must be a miracle worker.

'Mary Elizabeth could do it,' I said.

'The nun? Won't she make it into a habit?'

I took a sip from my drink. Mallory had recently started to make gin martinis. They were delicious.

'No, she's good at it. She used to make the costumes for the drama department back at St. Anne's. Her mother is a seamstress. She taught her.'

'Well, glory be. Ask the nun to sew you something up out of this. There must be plenty of material. Go grab that *Vogue* off my desk. We'll find something out of there for her to copy. I'll wear my burgundy, I think. That will look fine. You in black and me in burgundy. It accentuates the puppies. That will do us both well.'

*

Mary Elizabeth was delighted to fix up the dress for me.

And Mallory found us a party to go to at the last minute, the first weekend of November. 'It's for Guy Fawkes, you know. These New England types looking down their noses at other New Englanders from New York. What a laugh. It doesn't matter. There'll be some shoddy bonfire in the apartment, but as long as the police aren't called down, it'll be fine.'

Mary Elizabeth finished the dress within a day of me having commissioned it. She was very quick and thorough with a needle. She hadn't been able to bring her mother's sewing machine with her – it was needed at home – and this she did regret.

'I never think hand sewn things as nice as machine, but it's the best I can do.' The best she could do was pretty good, and I told her so.

'Now, have her make it up like this. She won't want to give you cleavage because she's a nun,' said Mallory as we flipped through the *Vogue* together, 'not that with your tits it would be anything but modest anyway. Don't give me that look, L. You're lucky, I swear. You'll be able to wear low-cut dresses and never be branded a slut. Trust me. But not this party. Okay?

'I think have her cut it low in the back and keep the collar high as it is. You're skinny, your back will look nice. Like a prized greyhound. Cut it just above the knee, don't you think?'

I nodded. I had thought I knew something of clothes until I met Mallory. She knew best for every woman and shape. It was her genius.

'Then this is the important part. Have your nunny take the fabric she's cut from the bottom and make that into a sash which will tie in the back and cinch in your waist. If she does it like how I'm imagining it, it will look effortless and *très chic*, no?'

I agreed.

Mary Elizabeth did it like how Mallory imagined, and it turned out well. But I knew as I slipped it on for Mary Elizabeth in her room that lonely, grey Sunday afternoon in late October that it would be for naught. I'd never had a dress I loved bring me luck. It always brought rather the opposite fate. I was right on that.

'You look like a movie star,' sighed Mary Elizabeth. She might be able to sew a dress fit for a woman, but her thoughts remained those of a schoolgirl.

'Thanks.'

'You look frailer than ever, though. Gosh darn, I don't know how you do it.'

Mary Elizabeth lived in Main, and I in Strong. We never took our meals together for which I was thankful. I didn't want a return to the St. Anne's lunch days.

'I haven't seen anything of you since we've been here. I'm so glad you came over to say hello about this dress. How's it all been treating you? Would you like some cocoa? Mother sent it in a care package for me specially for entertaining.'

I remembered her saying how she would do that. I thought it must be nice to have a mother to pack you cocoa and think about the nice things you could serve your friends when they dropped in to say hello. I had packed my own chocolate and soda crackers with money Dads had given me for such a purpose, but it wasn't the same as having a mother do it for you.

I said I would like a cup of it very much.

'Good. Take a seat please, it won't take a minute. I'll go warm the kettle downstairs and be back.'

I don't know why I stayed to visit with Mary Elizabeth. I had always hated her, and she was well on my nerves already that afternoon. But I was lonely for my own people and to be the girl I once was. The girl I was in Mary Elizabeth's eyes. Clean and good and pretty.

Maybe we could have been friends. She wasn't that awful if I thought about it. Mary Elizabeth liked to read, and I knew her favorite book was *Jane Eyre* too. She'd read most of Shakespeare, and I'd never heard her say the ridiculous nonsense Mark Hamilton did about good art needing to be moral or anything like that. She had a Van Gogh print on her wall above her bed, so I knew she couldn't believe in such bullshit.

Mary Elizabeth liked to draw cartoons of dogs and cats, and she was quite good at it. Although when she tried to take a drawing class, she learned she'd have to draw a naked man.

'And while that might be all right for some girls, I don't want to see that until my wedding night,' she told me over our cocoa. 'Do you know what the art teacher told me when I asked if I might take the class but be excused from that?'

'No.'

'She said think of *it* as a teapot. A teapot with the spout sticking out!'

Her eyes danced with an almost wicked pleasure while waiting for my reaction, and then she laughed and I laughed too. I never knew her capable of such mirth. It almost made me like her.

But then she went and spoiled it all by asking, 'Which Mass do you go to?'

This had been a question of some concern to my Aunt Claire, but Dads had said, 'I'd go to the Episcopalian chapel. It'll be easier on you. Just mind you do go.'

I wondered if Dads would turn to playing golf of a Sunday morning when the spring came, or if Aunt Claire would keep him in line too.

Because Aunt Claire did not approve. She rang my Aunt Jo to ask where she and my mother managed to get to every Sunday when they were Vassar girls. She knew my mother would never have dared to substitute an Episcopalian service for a Catholic and declare it the same thing anyhow.

Aunt Jo remembered there'd been a choir mistress who took them in her father's automobile of a Sunday when the weather held to a church in Newburgh. 'It was a long drive, though,' she admitted, 'and Lord knows if the woman is even alive. She was fairly ancient twenty years ago. What was her name?'

Hazel Bartley was dug up from the recesses of Aunt Jo's memory, and I'd been instructed to look her up when I arrived at Vassar to see if she might be willing to take the daughter of Mary LeFevre to Mass, or know of a good Catholic with a car who might.

'Tomorrow's Sunday,' Dads reminded me on the platform as we waited for the train, 'I don't know, but if I were you, I'd go to the chapel on campus and forget this whole business of Miss Bartley. But I'll leave that to you. You are eighteen.'

It was the first and last time Dads willingly left a decision to me. When I married, I didn't tell him 'til after.

Nor did I tell him I never stepped inside the chapel in my three years at Vassar and Hazel Bartley was long deceased. Besides, I couldn't have brought myself to suddenly become a Protestant any more than my mother could have done it. At heart I knew I'd rather be a bad Catholic than anything else in the world, and that seemed less offensive to God too. You can't go around picking a religion to suit your timetable and circumstances. I was born a Catholic and that was that. I didn't have to be born one; I could as easily have been born an Episcopalian.

But how to explain this to Mary Elizabeth with her cow eyes and earnest smile?

'I haven't been able to, I'm afraid. The woman my aunt suggested from years ago has died and, well, you know how it is. This place isn't exactly teeming with Catholics.'

'You poor thing,' cried Mary Elizabeth, grabbing my hand in sympathy. 'Why, our Lord will understand. You've had exceptional circumstances. But I'm so glad you've come to see me because I can help.

'Mr. Walsh, the Latin instructor, he's a Catholic, and he takes me and a few of the other girls to the Church of the Holy Trinity in Arlington every Sunday, and his wife treats us to Sunday dinner at their little house, and it is divine. I was there earlier today, and it's the happiest part of my whole week. You'd love it. Would you like for me to ask Mr. Walsh tomorrow after class if you might join us next week? It'll be a bit of a squeeze in the car but you're tiny and...'

I had to stop her before she got ahead of herself. Or more like before the Catholic guilt rose up far enough in my throat that I agreed. I'm not a natural liar. While I do tend to exaggerate at the truth a lot of the time, I'm actually a fairly honest person. But I couldn't tell Mary Elizabeth the truth and so I lied. It was for her own good.

'I've decided to go to the chapel here on campus, as a matter of fact. You know my father's mother was an Episcopalian and...'

Her brown eyes dropped to her lap.

'Oh.'

That's the good thing about Catholics. They never actively try to convert. It's not their way. They just pray for you. I knew Mary Elizabeth would do that for me, but it's not such a bad thing to have an extra person praying for you, I thought, even if I hated the person doing it.

I finished my cocoa as quickly as was polite and thanked

her. She made me promise to come by again soon, but I never did.

I asked what I owed her for altering the dress. It only seemed right to pay her, but she wouldn't hear of it.

I gave her the five dollars I had intended to anyway but told her to give it to the Church of the Holy Trinity the next Sunday, and she took the money eagerly and smiled in her obnoxious way with the bottom set of teeth jutting out, reminding me why we couldn't be friends.

I know very well what she used that money for. A month's worth of candles praying for my soul. Oh well. It didn't work, but I don't have the sin of not paying Mary Elizabeth to carry around on my conscience. And that counts for something.

Chapter Sixteen

On Friday, November seventh, 1941, after we finished our classes, Mallory and I caught the four o'clock train to New York. We sat in the smoking carriage with our Marlboros and ate sandwiches and marshmallows and drank black coffee. It was a happy journey, and I took it for a good omen.

I asked Mallory what sort of people she thought might be there. She shrugged and answered, 'I don't know, L. It's always a smorgasbord. Some roughs but mostly college kids like you and me trying to play it rough for a weekend. Greenwich Village types, you know.'

I didn't.

'Which colleges do Greenwich Village types go to?'

Here Mallory shrugged again and stuffed a pretty pink and white marshmallow in her mouth. 'The New School like Joey, I guess. Maybe Columbia? Probably some Chapin girls too. I don't know. What does it matter?'

I hadn't told Mallory about Teddy, and I wasn't sure whether to take her into confidence and see if she might know a way to get in touch with a Fordham freshman and get him to the party. But I couldn't do it.

Instead I said, 'I don't know. I knew some boys from St. Luke's who ended up at Columbia and Fordham, that's all. I thought they might be there.'

'Fat chance but then again, small world. Who knows! Have a cigarette, L, you're looking nervy.'

I took one gladly. It helped.

When we got into Grand Central, Mallory knew what to do. She hailed a taxi without hesitation and announced her

Park Avenue address. I remembered how shy I'd been that March with Aunt Jo and Uncle Bill and was ashamed. Look at Mallory, I thought. The same age as I, and she knows herself and her own power while I don't.

Mallory's parents' apartment was similar to Aunt Jo's, but nicer. Aunt Jo had the economy version aspiring to look like it, which looked cheap once I'd seen the real thing.

The elevator man was friendly to Mallory and asked who her pretty friend might be, and if I'd been with Lara, let's say, we would have giggled. Mallory wasn't one for giggling. She told him my name and that was it.

'We'll be here all weekend,' she added as we exited the lift.

'That way he knows what's what,' she explained in a whisper. 'I should have told him not to be shocked at what hours we come and go, but it might not be the same guy next time. We'll see.'

Mallory had a casual way of dismissing most people. I don't think she really liked anyone.

But we had a grand time of it that evening.

Mallory collapsed on a plush sofa and lit a Marlboro. She wasn't one for tours.

'Now, darling, what shall we do? The party is tomorrow, so we have all evening to ourselves. Let's have our hair set in the afternoon; I'll ring the salon now. Whatever you like *except* some corny Broadway show. You're not some country bumpkin in the city for the first time, and I won't tolerate it.'

I was a country bumpkin though, and it was my first time in the city, really. The other times, as Mallory had said before, didn't count.

'Can we go for some chop suey?' I ventured, carefully. I wasn't sure if that was something a real New Yorker ate or only a tourist. 'I've never had Chinese food.'

Mallory jumped.

'For Christ's sake, are you kidding me? Never had Chinese? You really are a country bumpkin. Come on. Let's get dressed and we'll go out. We'll start at the Plaza for cocktails. We might as well. You'll get a kick out of it and you brought that pink dress of yours, didn't you?'

I nodded.

'Okay, fine. We'll start there. And then if it's chop suey you want, that's what you'll get. Next thing you'll want to do is go to the Automat!'

Mallory laughed heartily at her own joke. I didn't know what the Automat was, but I didn't ask. I thought it must be a bowling alley or the dry cleaners or something.

We curled our own hair and painted our nails and doused ourselves in Chanel. We must have smoked a thousand cigarettes between us before we left the apartment. Mallory's parents didn't mind that she smoked inside the apartment. They did the same.

Mallory made us several gin martinis each, and by the time we left I knew my eyes betrayed me as a drunkard. But I didn't care. The chop suey would sort me out when we came to have it.

It was a happy night. We jumped in a taxi to the Plaza and had two drinks each, refusing offers from men. That was fun in its own way too. From there we took a taxi down to Chinatown where we ate plates full of chop suey. I ordered a second – the first time in my life I had dared to be so greedy – and ate every morsel. I was very drunk by that time but also very happy.

We looked silly sitting in that tiny basement shack in our evening dresses, trying not to lick our fingers. Neither of us could manage chopsticks. We howled and cackled, and my old laugh returned. Not the fake little mousy one I'd been hiding behind for months.

On the cab ride home, Mallory fell asleep, lipstick smeared and drooling. She curled up in the backseat like a kitten, and I knew she mightn't admit it, but it was the best time she'd had in ages too.

*

That was the only night I spent in the Jones' apartment that weekend. The next night was the party, and I never did make it back from that. I don't think Mallory did either.

I was set up in her sister Olive's room. She was a failed ballerina. Her feet turned out to be the wrong shape, or so Mallory said. She didn't buy it, though. 'It's because of her tits. Ballerinas can't have an inch of fat on them. But they're not allowed to say that.'

The room was filled with Degas prints, sadly no originals (though there was a real Matisse in the living room), and dance competition trophies. The girl who usually slept there seemed much younger than sixteen to me, but I suppose if you'd gone into my room with the religious iconography plastered about and Albert plopped down on the bedspread, you might think I was ten. No wonder Teddy left after seeing it.

In the morning we had the light hangovers that only eighteen-year-olds can, but which they mistake for suffering nonetheless. The Jones' maid came in around nine to tidy up and empty the ashtrays. Mallory had her fix us a breakfast of bacon and eggs with toast. By ten o'clock, with a cup of coffee and cigarette in hand, we were feeling fine.

'I've booked us in for three o'clock hair,' said Mallory over breakfast. 'I don't know what you want to do until then. Go shopping? I don't know. Darling, you know I'm hopeless at deciding how to spend my time, especially the afternoons. It's such a lonely time.'

I didn't know Mallory felt lonely at times like that, but I said no more about it.

We decided against shopping and stayed in. Another happy day spent talking and drinking coffee. I began to like Mallory. The apartment was much nicer than a stuffy dormitory room where we might be caught out smoking, and she seemed softer here in her own environment. I had never thought before that her whole tough attitude might be an act. I'd been too jealous to consider.

*

'Bring that ashtray over here, L.'

It was quarter to nine and we'd been getting ready since three. We'd spent a lot of the time mixing drinks and putting on records, but any way you looked at it, it was six hours.

'We'll get there for ten,' Mallory decided. 'I say that's still too early, but we'll go mad in here otherwise. Pass me that red lipstick, won't you, darling?'

Mallory decided that for this sort of party I ought to take advantage of how young I looked. She shrugged in her usual way and said, 'Some men are into that crap.'

I wore nothing on my face but mascara and red lipstick. I thought I looked underdone, especially next to the likes of Mallory, but she said it was perfect and I believed her.

She was right in the end. The less makeup one wears, the less there is to run.

Was I excited? I suppose so. I thought I might meet the sort of people I'd always wanted to get on with but hadn't yet known. Artists and writers, and really just a lot of other lonely kids who liked to drink too much and speak pretentious thoughts, and didn't give a damn about society's expectations of them. It's nice to meet someone and say, 'You too? I thought I was the only one.'

I wanted what I'd had with Teddy in other people. I hoped it would ease my heart and the loneliness, but suspected it might only multiply it. I couldn't be sure. Really, I wanted Teddy. And I stupidly thought that though the chance was small, he might be there.

And so, with my hair curled and rolled and my face plain, I dressed with heavy expectation. I gave a long look at myself in the mirror. What girl would return to this apartment later? I wouldn't quite be the girl I saw before me; somehow I'd be changed. And I hoped. I am ashamed to admit I hoped.

At ten o'clock, we hailed a taxi and started on our way.

It was to be a long night.

*

I knew we would separate after we arrived. Mallory might introduce me to a few people, a boy perhaps, and she'd be off to find her own fun.

The party was on the top floor of a three-story red brick block on West Twelfth and Greenwich. I know because when I moved to the East Village in the last year of the war, I often thought about crossing Washington Square Park to see it again. I never did.

But I longed to know the apartment in daylight and without the smell of alcohol and marijuana. To end my fear that that night was continuous, a purgatory I was damned to live repeatedly without end. I had once spoken to Teddy of my desire to have a part of me trapped in a moment always. The problem with that is you can't choose which moments you get trapped in and they usually aren't the happy ones.

Half hateful and half sentimental, I'd wonder how I could have been that girl that night. I thought I was better then, stronger, in the spring of '45. But I wasn't. Nor am I now.

How could I once have been that drunken fool of a girl found curled up behind the garbage can in the second-floor hallway, reeking of vomit and smoke? But the thing is, I still am that girl, though now I am over ten years older and simply called an eccentric. Or I guess it depends who is speaking of me. Some would probably call me a drunk and be done with it.

But I've never really been a drunk, you see. It's only that it's a far easier and more interesting thing to be rather than a grief-stricken girl from the middle of nowhere. Alcoholism is a standard enough illness to understand, and it's all good fun while the party is going. And when you are young and gay and pretty, plenty of others are drunks too and that's okay. To have a drink is normal at eighteen. To be the girl who succumbs to severe bouts of melancholy and tears every Saturday night, well, that's not. And it gets tedious and it gets boring to listen to that girl. Because most people just don't know what to do with the tears. It's awkward for everyone, really.

The war made it easier to be sad. Losing one's lover was commonplace and to have a drink and a cry about it was too. But then the war ended, and it became unpatriotic to be so sad and that's when the trouble started over again.

The girl who entered the party that night would continue to enter the same party for years to come. Even if that particular night ended and that particular apartment looks normal enough to a pedestrian of a Sunday morning, I am damned to live it again and again, though the location has certainly changed several times, and the reasons for crying vary.

But I did not know that then.

*

The stench of marijuana met us at the door. Mallory explained to me what it was. I had not smelled it before.

Nor had I encountered this type of poverty.

We were buzzed in, a novelty in itself, but there was no hall light to be found, so Mallory used her Zippo. I felt myself transported to an earlier era of speakeasies and secret dens of depravity. The superintendent had neglected to install a light fixture. We stumbled up the staircase, making our way across the crinkled linoleum in our heels as carefully as we could. It didn't help that each of us had had three gin fizzes before we left. Or I think we'd had three gin fizzes each. It may have been more.

We knew the third floor was our destination. We could hear the music.

'Who else do you know who will be here? I mean, besides Joey,' I asked when we made it to the second floor. If I'd been with Lara, though I never would have been with Lara at this sort of thing, but if I had, I would have asked if we could go home. I'd lost my nerve. But I knew Mallory wouldn't stand for that even if she could see well enough too that another night of staying up drinking together and eating in a cheap restaurant would be a hell of a lot more fun than this dump.

'We'll see. I'll probably know more than I like. Stick by me, darling. You'll be fine. But Jesus, get that innocent bird look out of your eyes. You're bound to be raped with a look like that.'

'But, Mal…'

'I'm serious, a girl knows what she's talking about. Now come on.'

I followed her lead up the last flight and into the party.

'The first thing we do,' Mallory whispered to me, 'is we go and we freshen our lipstick before the john stinks of shit. And hold onto your coat. A fur like that will be gone if you so much as turn your eyes. Trust me.'

I thought I'd been to parties before, but I hadn't. Those evenings on the Island had been nothing more than a couple of backwards hicks having a few beers and grinding their bits together for a laugh.

This was life, or so Mallory claimed.

But she'd been right about one thing. It was just a bunch of kids playing rough.

It was nothing but candles. Apparently the electricity had been shut off earlier in the week.

The other girls in that ill-lit room wore their hair long and stringy. I felt very silly with my curls and rolled bangs. But I was glad I'd worn little makeup as these girls didn't appear to be wearing any. Mallory looked completely out of place with her full skirted-burgundy dress and garishly painted face. But I got it. That had been her intention.

These girls with their dirty hair, pale skin, and fingers yellowed from too many cigarettes had Claire McCardell dresses in their closets the same as Mallory and me and their daddies had plenty in the bank too. They weren't poor. Not in the least.

I wasn't stupid. I knew what poverty looked like and now I learned what the fantasy of it looked like too. It was kids with fine cheek bones and expensive educations dressing up and yelling at each other about Spain and Franco and Stalin and Mussolini. There were a few who had come to Trotsky-ism five years too late and there were others who were convinced that Stalin winning the war and spreading communism to the world was the only way forward. Roosevelt was nothing to them. He was a conservative old aunt.

The heat of the room was overwhelming, and the sweetness of the marijuana clogged my nostrils. In the musky air lay a hint of beer mixed with vodka and cheap aftershave. I had smelled it before. I felt sick. There were too many bodies, and I could scarcely make any of them out in the poor light.

I followed Mallory to the bathroom. Blessedly the apartment had its own and not a shared one in the hall. And the light worked which meant it was all a lie about the electricity being shut off. A small luxury to celebrate.

'It's pretty quiet, but it will liven up in an hour or two,' said Mallory as she lined her lips with red. 'Here you go.' She passed the tube of lipstick to me. 'Do you think it's sanitary to use the t.p. to blot? Hell, what am I thinking? Come on, L, cheer up.'

I pinched at my cheeks. I didn't want to be pale like those cadavers outside. 'Is this what these things are usually like?'

'More or less. I can tell you don't like it, but you will once you get talking to people. Avoid the politicos. They're the worst.'

'Okay.'

'Let's get a drink.'

'Okay.'

A drink did make it better. I had a whiskey and ginger followed quickly by another. Mallory passed me a cigarette.

'Come on, there's Joey over there. I'll introduce you.'

We wound our way through the bodies to where Joey was crouched in the corner, alone, with a typewriter on his lap.

'He gets drunk and tries to write poetry,' whispered Mallory with a malicious twang to her voice. I wonder if she suspected that I used to do much the same.

It was a two-bed apartment with a large reception room between the two, the bathroom running to the side on the right. Then a long corridor led to the kitchen where we'd come in. Every surface seemed to be covered by a person. Couples monopolized the sofas to kiss and pet. I didn't want to know what was going on in the bedrooms, and I was hoping I wouldn't find out like I had at Ned's last party. I had sworn to myself to keep my lips pure for Teddy. After him, well, how could I go back to meaningless kisses? I couldn't, but I did. Just not that night. I was good, for once.

'Joey!' screeched Mallory. He didn't look up. 'Joey!'

He heard her that time.

'Hi, Mal.'

He remained seated on the floor and made no effort to shake our hands or really to show any interest in either of us. I wondered how Mallory could have slept with him. Even from his position stooped there on the ground I could tell he was fairly short. Shorter than Mallory who wasn't as tall as I. He had dark hair, which was already beginning to thin on the crown, and gold-rimmed spectacles. He too looked his part.

Mallory whispered to me, 'We never came to a thing. He couldn't get it hard when we, well, you know how it is. There's nothing worse than that. Getting your tits out for a guy and shoving your puss at him for nada.'

If only she knew.

'Do you have drinks?' He directed the question at me without interest.

'Yes.'

'That's good.'

He said no more and continued his typing.

'For Christ's sake, Joe, we came all the way up here to see you and this is the reaction we get? Barely a hello and not a don't you look nice. What's the deal?'

'Nothing,' he said, allowing the briskness of his tone to

convey his annoyance. In case we didn't get the hint, he added, 'I'm trying to work, can't you see?'

I didn't blame Joey for wanting to be alone. I did too.

'Work? In this zoo? What's the point of coming to a party if you're going to sit in a corner writing all night?'

'I'm observing the animals in their natural habitat.'

'Jesus, Joe, I thought you wanted to be a painter.'

He adjusted his glasses. 'That was last summer. I've since discovered my real talent. The short story.'

'Christ almighty. All right then, I get it. But I better not be in any of those, do you hear me? And if I am, well, if you make my breasts even one inch smaller and my waist larger, I'll never forgive you.'

Mallory laughed, but Joey did not. I reverted to the mouse laugh of the past several months.

'We'll leave you too it then, Mr. Hemingway.'

'Thank you.'

And I heard the keys of the typewriter going again.

'Jesus, L, some people! Ciggie?'

Mallory offered one to me lit, and I took it from her mouth.

'Where are the ashtrays?' I asked.

'This place is an ashtray.'

I don't think she was that upset by Joey, but it did shake her. That had been her ticket. Oh well, she must have thought, I'm the sexiest girl here, the only one worth having, I may as well try my luck.

'L,' she said, 'whatever you do, don't leave without me, okay?'

I nodded.

'I mean it. I know you think we can't get separated in here, but trust me, we can and we will. Now, let's go talk to that boy over there with the mustache. Doesn't he think he's Clark Gable?'

'You go, Mal. I want to, ahh,' I looked to the two windows

in the room where the smokers huddled, 'get some air.'

'Suit yourself. Remember what I said, okay?'

'Okay.'

Mallory turned her back to me and returned to the far wall of the room where the makeshift bar stood along with the Clark Gable doppelganger. I thought she could have done better than him, but it wasn't nice to say so.

As for myself, I thought I might try my own luck in the kitchen. I needed air.

And that's where I found him.

Chapter Seventeen

But it wasn't Teddy. Only Jack.

But someone I knew, and from the Island, was better than nothing. Besides, I thought he might have news of Teddy and that was something.

The kitchen was less crowded than the main room, but that wasn't saying much. It stank worse in there too with the added flavor of rancid cheese. I wondered if the supposed electricity failure had stopped the refrigerator.

But there was Jack at the table between the window and the stovetop, lighting a cigarette. I noticed he only took a few drags before he passed it to the boy on his left. I thought it was a funny practice but then I learned it was a funny cigarette too. There was a crowd of six or seven boys at the table and others lingering about, hoping for a drag. The girls stuck mainly to the walls, slumping their backs and laughing hoarsely.

I made my way to Jack.

'Hey, watch out there, sister,' said one particularly ragged looking youth. His checkered shirt was filthy and frayed, and he had a rather amateur beard coming in. I wondered if his father was a banker, lawyer, or doctor.

'Hey,' I said, but it came out meeker than I'd hoped, 'I want to speak to someone at the table.'

'Whatever, cherry.'

I took no notice.

'Jack.'

He looked up at once. His eyes were merry and bloodshot, but they recognized me, and he smiled.

'Lillie Carrigan!'

He got up from his place at the table to come around and hug me. I didn't like hugging Jack. I don't like hugging anyone.

'Lillie, how are you? Here, have a seat.' He offered me his own. Always the gentleman, Jack, even when tight.

I had not known Jack to drink nor had I mistaken him for a Red bohemian. But then I remembered Catherine Spence and thought, well, maybe he isn't but he likes the type. That was Jack for you. He couldn't say anything of interest himself, so he surrounded himself with people who could.

I sat, turning to the boys on my left and my right as though to say how do you do. They ignored me.

'I'm okay,' I said. 'I wish I'd grabbed another drink before I left the main room.'

'We've got plenty here,' said Jack. He moved his hands to the back of my chair protectively. I rather wondered if this would be one of those scenes where he tried to make it with me, and I'd either have to defend Lara's honor or get drunk enough, or really just sad enough, and go along with it. 'What do you want?'

I tilted my head back to have a look at him. 'Whiskey, please.'

'Right,' he slammed his hands against the chair, 'I'll be back.'

I wished I hadn't sent him away. Now I had to make small talk with these boys. Except they said nothing to me and so I sat there quietly sipping the dregs of the drink I had until Jack returned.

'Here you go, Lillie.' He passed me a paper cup. I touched the soggy bottom, tapping it up with my fingers.

'Thanks.'

'Leo, do you mind moving over? I want to talk to my friend Lillie here.'

'Sure.'

Leo seemed a complacent fellow. He got up and gave his seat to Jack, looking me over. Evaluating me, I knew. Probably thinking, well, good enough.

Go to hell, I thought. At least I look clean.

Jack settled himself in, placing his body perpendicular to mine and resting his arms with their casual rolled-up sleeves (I noted they were clean too) on his knees. 'Tell me, what brings you to this hellhole?'

I had never heard Jack speak this way. Is this the boy he was without Lara? I didn't like him any better for it. Besides, I was every bit as nice of a girl as Lara and deserved to be talked to properly and without swearing. But then that wasn't true. I was at this nasty party and the likes of Lara was not. I deserved it, but what infuriated me was that Jack knew it too. I wondered what Teddy had told him of me.

'I thought it would be fun,' I answered, lamely.

'And?'

'It isn't.'

'Poor Lillie,' laughed Jack, shaking his head back and forth.

'Is Teddy here?' I nearly shouted it.

'No.' He continued to shake his head.

'Do you see much of him these days?'

'Yeah, I'm up near Harlem, you know, and he's in the Bronx, so yeah, we see each other.'

'But he didn't want to come tonight?'

He didn't answer at first. I knew what it meant. Teddy wasn't there because he was preoccupied. He had a date. He had a date with a girl who he thought would put out, so he couldn't risk it by bringing her to a party where the bedrooms might be previously occupied. Jack didn't need to say a thing. I knew it already.

'Look, Lillie...'

'Look, Jack, you don't need to say anything.' I tried to

muster a laugh but couldn't. 'That's all over with the summer. I wondered how he might be doing is all. Good. Well, how are you?'

Jack's face relaxed. Whether he bought it or not, I don't know. I guess he didn't after the next morning.

'I'm okay, I'm okay. Jeez, it's great to see you here.'

'Hey, Jack,' said the boy to my left, 'can you roll another?'

'Yeah, yeah. Hey, Pete, this is my friend, Lillie. Remember that girl I said I was seeing over the summer? This is her best friend.'

Pete nodded along. He didn't care. He wanted another funny little cigarette.

'You mean the dago?'

'Yeah, yeah,' answered Jack between licking the paper.

Dago!

Was this Jack then? Was this how he spoke of Lara to his friends? The girl he had gently courted throughout the summer? Who he'd patiently waited for in Troy to take to the cinema without the hope of holding her hand? This was Jack, the fourth in our quartet. My least favorite, but still.

And what might he say of me when I left the table?

'That's my friend's ex-girl. She was all right, she's got a nice ass, can't you tell, yeah, yeah, but she's crazy as hell. She begged my friend, Teddy McCalman, you know him, yeah, yeah. She begged him to have sex with her because she's a virgin you see, and you know how it is for a guy. Jeez, you don't want to mess with that kind of girl. When she's already crazy like that you don't know what she might do if you…'

I looked Peter over as I noticed he was doing the same to me. I hoped his conclusion was kinder than my own.

'Hey, you want some of this?' He held up the cigarette Jack had rolled.

Teddy was crazy for it, I knew that, and I thought if the

first taste of a cigarette could bring back the taste of his mouth, hell, this might do the same.

'Sure, thanks.'

'Lillie, don't…'

But Jack was too late. I'd inhaled. I was sick, almost at once.

'Shit,' I heard Pete say.

I dared not lift my head for shame.

'I've got to, I've got…'

'Lil…'

I couldn't wait for Jack to finish his sentence. I was going to cry. I had sick in the curls of my hair and I was going to cry.

'Get out of my way, get out of my way,' I mumbled, pushing my way through the small crowd.

'Hey!'

'Shit, you spilled my drink!'

'Shit, man, I've never seen that before.'

Go to hell! Go to hell!

In the corridor, where it was darkest, I felt my way through the bodies, careless of what I touched. If I could only make it to the bathroom before the tears came, I'd be safe. Then I'd wash my face, have a cigarette to calm my nerves, drink some water (though perhaps best not to drink the water?) and find Mallory. We'd be in a cab in fifteen minutes.

I pounded on the door but no one answered. I peeked beneath it. There was no light, but that meant nothing in this apartment. I risked it and went in. There was no one.

I sat on the cool porcelain bowl of the toilet. It didn't have a seat. Of course not. I bet whoever rented this damned apartment removed it on purpose.

There was a knock at the door and then a gentle easing of it open. I heard the lock click. I looked up, too tired to feel panic. Now would come the inevitable rape. I sighed.

'Lillie Carrigan?'

But it wasn't Jack's voice and it wasn't Mallory's.

It was Mark Hamilton's.

Mark Hamilton. The very one who'd gone and abandoned me and started this whole mess, if I thought about it. But it wasn't his fault. Not really. I'd been messed up in the head long before that March evening. Since I was fifteen and living with Dads and Aunt Claire after … But it wasn't that either. It was the Hail Marys and the bleeding hearts and the devil and the terrible conclusion of learning I didn't have a vocation after all when I was twelve and I felt a twinge … And it was Mark Hamilton and his belief that I was the lost, a black sheep to be found … Baa, baa, black sheep … But it wasn't that either. I was not a lost sheep, or a black one or a … I was a girl who had lost her mother … But she'd never understood me, either. She worried about me and the girl I was becoming, did become, and she would spend hours praying for my soul like Mary Elizabeth and Mark, just sitting there in the Lady Chapel, nothing of herself, for herself, nothing but loneliness too … It was Teddy with his cigarettes and his whiskey and his kisses and his boyish grief and anger at the world … It was me with too many novels and … But, then again, maybe there was nothing the matter with me.

I had seen very little of Mark since the disaster of Easter Sunday. There had been Mass over the summer when he was back from Yale, but nothing more than a polite hello, how's it treating you? When do you go up to Vassar? Etc.

'Is it as good as Fitzgerald?'

The mole winked at me. I nearly fancied myself in love with him again. I was drunk enough for it.

'Beg your pardon?'

He came closer. With another boy I might have felt in danger and screamed. But not with Mark.

'This, is it like a scene in one of your novels? Isn't this what they do in them?'

'What, live in filthy little apartments with toilets that don't have seats and pretend to have the electricity shut off because it's glamorous to be poor?'

He smiled. 'Yes.'

I let my head hang down, allowing it to rock back and forth. I wondered if he could smell the vomit on me.

'No, but I guess that's the point in the books too. No one has a good time at the parties. They usually end up doing something stupid. But you wouldn't know, would you? You don't read modern trash.'

'But I do. I very much like Huxley.'

'Oh.'

I had not read Huxley.

'Have you come for inspiration?'

'What?'

'Will this scene be in one of your novels? One you write, I mean.'

'Oh.'

That was rather nice of him. Had he intended to flatter?

'No, I mean, I'm not like Joey in the corner with the typewriter. I'm not here to watch the animals in the zoo or anything like that. I guess I'm here because I'm bored. My friend from Vassar brought me. She thought I needed an education, I guess. Maybe she's right.'

Mark laughed. 'It's some education. I came up here to see a play some of the guys are in and after they knew some people here, so here I am.'

I noticed a beer bottle in his hand.

'Have you taken to drink?'

'No, but even our Lord drank.'

Almost human and then always a prick.

'Mark,' I said, shyly, slowly, rising from the porcelain bowl to make my way to him, 'I'm not doing very well.'

I thought he might hug me, but he didn't. Thank God.

'What do you mean?'

'I mean…'

What did I mean? Why was it that when people asked me to explain myself, I never could? You'd think I'd have been able to, given how much time I spent thinking about myself and how I felt and all.

'Goddamnit, why didn't…'

But I couldn't get the words out. I couldn't tell him what had happened to me that night. I could not accuse him of what he had done to me. Leaving me alone, open prey. And he wouldn't have bought it. Not with his Aquinas and his St. Augustine. The woman is always the sinner. After all, it was Eve who led Adam astray and that bullshit.

'I'd like to be … Please go.'

I saw the mole and the beautiful hazel eyes and the lanky, boyish build and the brilliant mind. My ideal of so many months back. And I remembered his hollow character which he'd given up to Christ and the Church, and now I knew why. He hated us women.

'I don't think you should be left alone, Lillie. You don't look very well. Listen, I'll get you a taxi.'

But I remembered Mallory's words, and I did not want to be alone with Mark. I wanted to be alone with myself. I wouldn't be so lonely then.

'I … I…'

I didn't want to speak anymore. I got up to leave without a goodbye, and I didn't feel bad about it. How was I supposed to know I'd never see Mark Hamilton again? That I'd miss Mass that Christmas and that the war would start and he'd be one of the first to enlist? How could I possibly have known he'd never see another November eighth in his short life? None of us really know what days we'll see or which people for that matter. So that's not something I carry around on my conscience, and I suspect Mark wouldn't expect me to.

I couldn't think about Mark or Jack or Teddy on his date getting laid because it's dangerous to have sentimental thoughts when you're as far gone as I was. What I needed was a glass of champagne. A glass of champagne, I find, fixes most evils, particularly drunken ones. It is the best hangover cure I know of too.

But I didn't suppose anyone would have a bottle at a party like this, but perhaps it would be the sort of the thing they would. A 'we spend our money on champagne rather than electricity' sort of philosophy. I don't know. I couldn't figure those kids out.

I thought if I made my way to the bar, I might find Mallory and we could go home and have a glass of champagne there. And maybe she'd run a bubble bath for me in her parents' room and sit by my side as I bathed and washed my hair and chatter on about how shit she'd found the night.

But she wasn't there. And I did not know where I was. I recognized no person from earlier in the night. I mean I know I thought they all pretty much looked the same but … Was I that drunk? Had there been a swap of bodies? Had a new crowd arrived while the old one moved on to another party at another apartment?

But there was Joey in the corner, typing. I was reliant on him. 'Joey!'

He glanced up from the paper. His eyes had acquired a glazed-over look in the hour since I'd seen him. I wondered what he'd been hitting. It was something strong.

'Joey,' I said again.

'Yes? What do you want?'

I crouched down to his level, hoping to make it easier to speak, but Joey hardly wanted to carry on a conversation with me. He wanted to get back to his typing. I guess he must have thought he was onto something, but I mean in the ten years from that night, I've certainly never seen the product of his labor published.

'Do you know where Mallory's gone?'

He gave no sign of life and no reply.

'Come on, you're supposed to be sitting here studying your animals and you mean to tell me that you didn't keep your eye on Mallory?'

'I didn't say I haven't seen her. I have. But I simply do not know where she went from there. I saw her leave this room with that Clark Gable doppelganger. Rather *gauche*, I think…'

'You saw her leave this room with him?'

'Do you not have ears? Yes, that's what I saw, but that is all. I have no more for you.'

'Go to hell.'

I stood up. Another person I didn't say goodbye to, but I don't know if Joey died in the war or a drunk driving accident or maybe he's alive and he did publish that short story, only in a place where I've never found it. I probably wasn't his audience.

It was no good, though. I couldn't face the thought of searching for Mallory. There were five rooms she could be in. Two I could rule out, but I'd never be able to spot her in the corridor, I dared not try the bedrooms for fear of what I might see, and I could not bear to return to the scene of my humiliation in the kitchen.

And suddenly, I was very tired. I needed to go to sleep.

But I couldn't sit on the sofa and close my eyes. I'd wake up to being petted or worse.

I didn't have a key to Mallory's apartment, and I wasn't sure the concierge would trust my story enough to let me in.

I could go to Aunt Jo, I thought, but I'd promised Mallory and even if she didn't intend to keep her half of the bargain to me, I couldn't betray her. Besides, Aunt Jo would holler and ring Dads if I showed up in this state. No, I couldn't do that. I must stay here, somewhere.

I made my way back through the corridor like a sleepwalker damned to repeat the same night terror, but one which she has become so long acquainted with that it no longer has the power to frighten her, only annoy. A trial to be borne again and again.

When I reached the kitchen, I stuck to the wall, easing my body to the door, silently praying no one would notice or remember me. One prayer which was answered.

I'd sit on the stairs until Mallory came out, I decided. That would be best because she'd be sure to see me. I plopped my weary body down outside the door, resting my head against the wall, removing my heels. It was no good. The music was too loud, the smell too foul. I picked myself up and went down a flight, where I settled my back against the empty garbage can.

How have I come to this?

But my thoughts didn't last long.

I fell asleep at once.

*

It was Jack who found me in the early hours of the morning before the rising of the faint November sun.

'Lillie, Lillie, wake up. Are you okay?'

I refocused my eyes to understand that Jack Allen, my best friend's former beau, was kneeling beside me in a dirty Greenwich Village apartment building, shaking me awake. My head banged back against the trash can.

'Ow!'

'Jeez, Lillie, are you all right?'

I hung my head. My mouth was dry and tasted of burnt toast with jam that was too sweet.

'Where's Mallory?' I managed to ask.

'Mallory? Who's Mallory?'

'Mallory Jones. Busty blonde with burgundy dress. No one else looks like her. She went off with Clark Gable and … Jesus, I'm going to be sick.'

But I wasn't. I wished I had been. A spike of pain shot across the frontal lobe, pounding in my temples. I'd had this particular headache before, once a month at least, and I knew there was only one cure. To be sick helped.

But unless I made myself, I couldn't. I had to get back to the bathroom and…

'Most everyone has left. I don't think she's here, your friend. I haven't seen her.'

'Goddamnit.'

'Come on, this is no place to stay.'

Jack helped me to my feet, but I immediately collapsed.

'Must sleep. Can't get up.'

'Get up, Lillie.'

This time he didn't so much as help but force me to stand. He picked up my fur from the floor and stuck my arms through it in succession. 'There. Come on. Where are you going?'

Back to Mallory on Park Avenue? My suitcase and my makeup, a change of clothes … I needed those things. But the thought of making it uptown then back to midtown and then to Vassar … God, it would be hours, and I needed sleep. Either you've got to be sick or you need to sleep when you feel as I did. I know.

'Vassar,' I croaked.

'And how do you get to Vassar? Don't answer train. I know that. Which train and which station would be more useful?'

'Grand Central. I don't know the times. I left that up to Mallory but…'

All right, it should be frequent enough. Come on, we'll get on the subway uptown.'

'Jesus, I can't get on the subway, Jack. I'll be sick if we do.'

Jack paused and nearly dropped me. 'Woah, hold steady there. All right, I think I have enough cash on me for a taxi…'

'No, no, no. No good. Will be sick if we move. I need to sleep or…'

'Lillie, we've got to go, do you understand?'

I nodded, then doubled back. The pain was too much.

'Can we walk?' I asked. 'I think, I think I could walk, and the clean air would sort me out.'

'Fine, if you think you can make it, let's walk. Put your shoes on.'

*

It was a funny morning. The only time I spent alone with Jack, and I think perhaps I ever will. I see no reason why I might again.

We spoke little on the walk. This did not strike me as odd at the time, though given Jack's natural verbosity, I suppose it was. I couldn't think to speak, and what could I have said? How can you be so goddamn chipper when you must have drunk as much as I? Why are you unkind to Lara when you know she loves you? Do I smell of sick? It was better to remain silent and concentrate on my steps, counting the streets in accession.

But when we reached Forty-second Street, I knew I could not get on that train. Not yet.

There are times when even I know I cannot be alone.

And Jack, well, he was better than no one. Hell, he was better than Mark Hamilton, and that was something.

'Jack?' I asked, 'What are, I mean are you in a hurry to get back? Do you want to get some breakfast or something?'

'Sure, I could eat.'

We watched the sun rise, as it did late in the morning in early November, from the window of a diner on West Forty-fourth Street. I excused myself to the bathroom when we arrived, requesting for Jack to order a black coffee and an orange in my absence. I spent five minutes with my finger down my throat. When that didn't do the trick, and it usually doesn't for me, I spun in circles until I retched in the bowl. It wasn't much more than spittle, but as I washed my hands, I felt a violent push and was sick. There, much better, as I knew I would be if I could manage it.

'Is that all you're going to eat?' Jack asked when I returned to the table and saw my coffee and orange waiting for me. Jack was waiting for his. He'd ordered a cooked breakfast.

'I can never eat much when I feel like this.'

'I know you're, ahh, all right. I'll say it. I remember you being thin and all but are you eating anything?'

I shrugged because that's what Mallory would do. 'Enough. My stomach's pretty weak at the moment.'

'Fine. I hope you don't mind waiting while I eat, do you? I've got a lot coming.'

'I like to watch other people eat.'

That was a bold-faced lie. I hate watching other people eat almost as much I hate having others watch me. It's the listening to it that I find unbearable.

But I was desperate for company, and I was going to have to take it.

'So, how are you liking Vassar?'

How are you liking Vassar?

What kind of question was that? Here I was hungover out of my panties with smudged mascara, faintly smelling of sick and probably piss too, and Jack could see how pale and skinny I'd become in the past two months, and he wondered how I might be liking college?

'I like the classes and lectures,' I answered, truthfully. 'It's better than St. Anne's. How's Columbia?'

'You know,' and he here he smiled, 'I really like it. I wasn't sure I'd like New York – do you know I'd never been – but it's great.'

I attempted a weak smile. It's nice when someone's happy.

'And do you go to parties like that a lot?'

'Sometimes, you know how it is. But I guess you must find this too. A lot of time you have to be with the books.'

'I do.'

'But yeah, when there's a chance and a good party like last night, it's good to let off steam. You know, Lillie, I don't think you're smoking that correctly?'

He stared at me with my lit cigarette.

'That's funny. You inhaled the one last night, but you don't...'

'I can't inhale when I'm hungover,' I said. Which was and wasn't true. I never really inhaled much in those days. I wasn't a real smoker, yet.

'I'm sorry you're hungover. Sometimes I think the first time when you smoke like that, it can make you sick. I don't blame you.'

'Thanks.'

Jack, always the conversationalist. He could speak to drying plaster, or whatever it was Lara used to say of him and her father both.

'Why'd you do it, Jack? Why'd you let them make fun of Lara like that?' I thought I might as well ask it. I wanted to, so I did.

'Woah, what do you mean there? I never said...'

'You let those boys call her a dago, and I know that some people say things like that and all, but it's not a nice way to describe the girl you used to go with, or I don't think so anyway. I used to think you were in love with her, but that's probably pretty dumb. I used to think Teddy loved me too.'

Jack wasn't one for playing the defensive. He accepted what I said.

He sighed. 'You know how it is...'

'I'm afraid I don't. I only know how Lara feels because I feel the same. I have a fairly good imagination, I'll admit, but somehow I can't imagine how freshman year of college goes straight to boys' heads and allows them to think it's well within their rights to ignore girls they might have loved and who definitely loved them.'

'Jes – jeez, I don't know. Well, you know how Lara is. She's, Christ, how to say it without offending you?'

I met his eyes, forcing him to go on.

'You might as well.'

'Jeez,' he said, running a hand through his light brown bangs which had a tendency to stand up straight. 'She's the type of girl you marry. And I wasn't ready for that. I've only just turned nineteen. We'll see, maybe someday.'

'I see.' I took out another cigarette and lit it. This time I tried to inhale, but without much success. 'And what type of girl am I then, Jack?'

'Ahh, come on, Lillie.'

'I want to know.'

Now both hands were in his hair, and I could tell he had a hangover too, but not as bad as my own.

'What did you think of me this summer?'

'It was easy getting to know you because I already did. You are Teddy, except a girl. I never knew two people could be the same like that.'

It was enough to do me in in my fragile state.

'I ... I, Jack, why doesn't he write to me? Or call me? Or, I mean, do you know what happened?'

He shook his head. I believed him.

'That's probably for the best then, and I won't tell you. I miss him, though. Jack, I love him. I really do. And, well, was he on a date last night? Tell me that.'

This time he nodded.

'Thank you.'

'Come on, don't take it to heart. Teddy's a special case. I hardly understand the guy myself.'

I lit a third cigarette. I wasn't really smoking them, just allowing them to burn and ash in my fingers. It gave me a purpose, something to do.

'Get the bill, if you will. I'm leaving.'

'Look, Lillie, sit down,' Jack commanded. I didn't know him capable of it. 'I haven't gotten my breakfast. Sit down. We'll go soon.'

'Fine.'

And I took a drag.

*

But we didn't go soon. We stayed through to the lunch crowd, lingering over cups of half-drunk coffee. Jack finally broke down and ordered a slice of pie so they wouldn't turn us out.

Jack's a talker, and I suppose I can be one too. But what we spoke of for five hours, I cannot recall. We'd digress at times to the topics of literature, we liked the same books, and politics, both of us fearful pinks, and speculations of war. He didn't want to fight, and he guaranteed me he wouldn't enlist if it came. It's the only lie I've ever known Jack to tell me, but he didn't know it was a lie then.

He spoke of his former relationship with Catherine Spence and confessed that he, as I had long suspected, slept with her. The last time, in fact, had been after the Spring Formal, but that's when he knew for sure it was over.

'You see, I do like Lara. I knew that after I'd, well, you know, with Catherine.'

I've never told Lara. I wonder if it would have made a difference if I had. Oh well, maybe one day I'll be drunk enough and will. You never can tell what I'm inclined to do when I drink, though I am a fairly good secret keeper. As this story will attest.

But I did not mind him telling me about Catherine Spence. It made me like him more. I could try to understand him this way. See him as a person rather than as the fourth member of that summer, the only one who happened to have a car.

We spoke little more of Teddy. I knew he did not want to, and it would only give me the shakes.

When we could stave off the waitress no longer with refills of coffee and a promise of a fair tip, Jack settled up and we left.

He walked me to Forty-second and waited with me for a while at the station, until I told him he might go. I was ready to be alone.

I allowed him to hug me this time with a genuine affection which I returned.

'Ring up Lara, if you can. It would mean a lot to her. And to me.'

'Sure, I'll do that.'

And he went away, shuffling his feet through the station, never turning to wave goodbye. He and I were not friends like that.

Maybe I shouldn't have talked to Jack like that that day. I should never have meddled in Jack and Lara's affairs, playing the matchmaker who brings off the happy ending. But I knew Lara would have wanted me to, though I never mentioned to her I had. Only that I'd seen Jack at a party.

I suppose, what I did that day, by telling him to pursue her again, I suppose I innocently set into motion the events which would follow, events in which I would have to do wrong against Lara. Because that was the only way.

I knew none of that then. And maybe I think I understand it looking back, but maybe I don't. Perhaps it was inevitable. Perhaps they would have fallen together without my pushing. Or perhaps not. But I can't think like that. Because I did what I did, and they did what they did, and then we all had to do what we had to do.

But that morning, I was hungover, and I knew not what I did.

Chapter Eighteen

The November rains came, and then the snow. I was very lonely. Lonelier still than I had been in September. I had Mallory, but I no longer trusted her.

I phoned her that Sunday afternoon from Grand Central. I was not expecting her to answer.

'L,' a groggy voice croaked down the phone, 'what the hell was I thinking last night? Darling, I am horrified, cross my heart and say a prayer, or whatever the lousy expression is. Did you make it? Goddamnit, where did you make it to? I am simply dying today. I should have myself cooked up for Sunday dinner, I feel *that* awful.'

'I'm fine, Mal. I only wanted to let you know I'm at the station and heading back. I'll stop by this evening for my valise, if that's all right?'

'We'll need the hair of the dog tonight, I'll tell you that much, L. Come around, I don't know, I'll be back by supper, I imagine. I have to be, that's all there is to it.'

'I have to go,' I said. 'They've announced my train. I'll see you tonight.'

I hung up the phone. I was not furious and I was not sad. I was only tired.

I reached Vassar by three o'clock in the afternoon, a mere forty-eight hours away, but I was right. I'd come back a different girl.

No more parties, I resolved. Cut back on drinking. Must cut out smoking. I don't even like it that much. The taste of a cigarette can't bring back Teddy. He's not sitting up dreaming of me. He's in bed with a girl. I hope she has a thin mustache or thick thighs. Some abnormality.

I fell asleep quickly and slept fitfully through to supper.

*

I went to see Mallory after supper as planned. She was late back and missed the meal itself.

'L, come in. I've brought us up a whole new stockpile of gin. This will see us through to Christmas.'

'Thanks,' I said, weakly.

'Darling, I know you must be fuming. I have no excuse. I went off with a boy who couldn't even get it up. He was too drunk. That must be humiliating for a guy. But I didn't mind. I fell right asleep in his bed and that was that. He only lived a few blocks over and I had every intention of coming back for you, but once my head hit the pillow, I swear on my grandfather's grave, I didn't so much as twitch until nine this morning. And what do you think I wake to? A reedy mustached, sunken-chest pervert rubbing his pecker against my leg, practically getting off. Anyway, darling, here have a cigarette?' I shook my head. I was determined to keep my resolutions for a day. 'Suit yourself. I suppose you wouldn't like a tiny drink?'

'No thanks.'

'L,' Mallory said, purposefully drawing out the one letter of her name for me, hoping forgiveness lay at the end of it. She threw her weary hungover body on the bed. 'Don't hold a grudge against me. I did wrong. I know it. I'm so ashamed of myself that I can't help but make light of it. I've got nothing else I can do except apologize profusely, which I am. Can you forgive me, darling? Did something awful happen?'

'Not much,' I said, aiming to sound indifferent, but my

face betrayed me. 'I tried some tea and threw up. And I ran into two boys I knew from the Island. One got me to the train this morning.'

'Poor darling. You must forgive me.'

I said I forgave her but I was exhausted and must get on with some studying before bed.

'Of course, of course. Here's your suitcase. I had everything pressed for you before it was packed.'

'Thanks,' I said, swinging my legs from the bed to the floor. They ached. It was the first hangover of my life to last past eleven in the morning.

Mallory walked me to her door. She really was sorry.

'Are you sure this changes nothing between us? If you can forgive me, maybe I can one day think to forgive myself.'

'It's all right, Mal. I know how it is. It happens at a party like that.'

But things had changed. I didn't like to say it, but we both knew it. I didn't go around in the evening for a while after that, despite Mallory inviting me. A few times she came to me, and we drank cocoa and snacked on soda crackers, but neither of us particularly liked the arrangement. Mallory was simply one of those friends you can get on with when drinking but not so well when sober.

Things with Lara were poor too. For Jack had gone to her. He wrote to her and the following weekend went home to visit her by way of Albany. She relayed this to me during our usual Saturday evening chat. He was picking her up in an hour and she didn't know what to wear.

'I've become a pork chop,' she admitted. 'What do I have that fits and won't repulse him?'

'Well, where are you going?' I asked, bored with my own question before I finished it.

'For dinner. Jack's found some Italian restaurant and

wants my opinion on it. We might even have wine.'

'That's nice.'

I could think of little else to say. Lara's and my relationship, for as much as we do love each other, only works in two scenarios – when we are both happy or when we are both miserable. It's at its worst when we have contrary emotions. Lara would say the very worst is when I'm happy and she is not because she's a far more jealous person than I and turns her sadness into hatred for me. It's happened before, and it might have been the story of that summer if she had not found Jack. When it is the other way around, I listen to her talk without taking in a word of it and cry myself to sleep. I never punished Lara for it, or at least I thought I never would. I did in the end, but I don't think it was motivated by jealousy. I maintain that. But who knows?

I began to dread our Saturday evening chats. Lara would be getting ready for her date and scarcely bother to ask about me. I was grateful for that, in a way, because I no longer had to reveal myself or the inner workings of my heart to anyone. The letters continued, and as I never paid much attention to Lara's response, nothing changed there.

I allowed Mallory to set me up with a boy from Iona for a Saturday night date the week before Thanksgiving, but we had little in common. He later reported back to Mallory's date that I was a pampered brat.

'It's only because you didn't put out,' Mallory told me as we had our last evening of gin before breaking up for the holiday. 'He can go pull his own off if that's going to be his attitude to the whole thing. But Christ, L, did you have to give him a handshake at the end?' Mallory cackled. 'I bet that lazy sonofabitch never had that before.'

'Well, I was hardly going to shake hands with his pecker.' And I laughed too. I had learned something from Mallory in those months. Cynicism.

I went home the day before Thanksgiving, taking the train to Albany and feeling younger than eighteen. I knew Teddy would not be there. He went to Boston every year to see his father's family. I dreaded Lara and her girlish happiness. I made up lies to tell Aunt Claire when she asked about Mass, and I carefully considered which would be the most appropriate stories to share with Dads. Thanksgiving dinner, as usual, would rely on my conversational contributions. It was exhausting.

I saw Lara but once that break. We went to Delaney's for a milkshake and hamburger on the Friday, but the night was a failure, and we did not try to see each other again before I left Sunday morning.

Lara was all news of Jack. I did not speak of myself. She'd grown tired of listening to my woes over Teddy, and she would have been horrified to learn of my recent escapades.

'Are you living on a diet of coffee and cigarettes?' she asked when we met. 'You look unhealthy.'

'Thanks,' I mumbled. 'I can't keep food down at the moment.'

'Well, you should try.'

I had nothing to reply.

We ordered our hamburgers, and I tried to get it down. It tasted good, and I was hungry. But I couldn't finish it. My stomach had shrunk.

Lara wolfed hers down between storytelling. Who was this new Lara, confident to speak and believe in her story enough to tell it without hesitation?

'Jack wants me to go see him in New York the weekend after next,' she confessed. 'The fraternity he's pledging is throwing a Christmas party, and I'm to be his date, can you believe that? Me at a New York party.'

I thought of the spring when it had been I venturing into

the new waters of New York. The novelty was gone.

'It's not in the Village, is it?'

'No, it's uptown, in their house, I think. And I'll get to wear my red and green tartan dress I had made up last Christmas for the Salvation Army dance my dad decided against the day before. Remember that?'

'Yes.' I had not gone either.

'Jack wants me to come Friday after classes let out, but I don't know. My parents know nothing about it. They wouldn't allow it. I have one aunt in Brooklyn, but she wouldn't let me leave the house after five, I'm sure, so I can't possibly stay with her.'

'Better to ask forgiveness than permission.'

'That's what I think. But Friday night too? I'd have to stay with Jack, and I don't know what funny business he might try.'

I gave Lara a sad smile. It should have been I who was saying the things coming out of her mouth, only about Teddy. But here she was with her boy, and I alone.

'I don't know about that. Jack respects you.'

I couldn't tell her what he'd said to me about her being the marrying type. It would be revealing too much.

'I don't know.' Her eyes grew wide and she pinched in her cheeks. I thought of this as Lara's inquisitive monkey look.

'I'll think about it. I won't ask what you would do because I know.'

I might have let that hurt me, once. But all I did was shrug. I didn't care much anymore.

*

The news was heralded in by telegram. I'd never received a telegram before that, and in the days before the war it didn't carry the same connotation as it would in the months to come.

Uncle Rory must be dead, I thought, and Dads won't mind if I don't come home for the funeral, and I won't. But it's nice to know. That was my immediate conclusion when Louise Anderson knocked on my door that Saturday morning of December sixth to let me know there was a telegram boy for me down in the parlor.

'Thanks, Louise,' I said. I had no intention of running down the stairs dramatically to sign for it. I thought I'd take my time to find my loafers and cardigan first, which I did.

'Aren't you curious?' asked Louise. She was from Michigan and when she spoke her mouth opened sideways instead of up and down like most people.

'It's probably nothing more than a death in the family. Where's my other slipper?'

'I'd be curious is all.'

'Well, come on, I'm ready to go.'

I walked with Louise down to the parlor. We saw some of each other, and I didn't hate her which is as much of a recommendation for a girl as anything else I can possibly say. She studied history and economics and, like me, was middle class, tediously teetering towards the Left but with a staunch Republican streak branded into her from birth.

'Are you going to the talent review at Joss tonight? Dotty and I might go over after supper, if you want to come?'

'Sure,' I said and meant it. It sounded as good a plan as any. I needed to make more friends.

'That's the boy over there.' She pointed to a youth near the piano. He'd positioned himself in such a way as to guarantee himself a glimpse of Trixie Everett's cleavage as she practiced her Schubert. I hadn't left him waiting for nothing.

'Are you Lillie Carrigan?' he asked.

'I am.'

'Please sign.'

I signed for it, and he was off without so much as a final glance at Trixie's breasts. He must have been in a hurry.

Uncle Rory passed last night – Stop – Aunt Claire with me – Stop – Funeral Tuesday – Stop – Don't worry if can't come – Stop – Love Dad.

I was certain it would say that.

But then, what if … No, Teddy was too cheap to think of it. There was no hope of that.

I opened it. But it wasn't Dads and it wasn't Teddy.

In NY – Stop – Big news – Stop – Come if can – Stop – Send reply – Sigma Nu – one hundred thirteen – Stop – Lara.

New York. Lara. Why would Lara be in New York? I looked to the grandfather clock to see it wasn't yet half past ten. What was she doing…?

Then it struck. Lara. New York. Jack.

If she's gone ahead and…

I saw red. And then I saw my bank account with the funds Dads generously provided each month. Did I have enough? I had to. I never spent much of it. Mallory and I rarely left campus and when we did, she paid. I'd stopped buying clothes too. There was no reason to.

Louise peaked her head up from her Gibbon. She must've been considering how much time would suffice until she could ask, 'Is anything the matter?'

'No, but I'm not sure I can go to the review anymore. I've got to catch a train to New York for the day.'

'Oh?'

'It's nothing serious,' I lied.

Louise nodded along. Who knows where her imagination leapt? 'Come along if you make it back in time,' she said with a feigned nonchalance. 'We won't head over until after supper. There'll be sherry.'

'I'll try.'

But I knew I'd never go. I might make it back in time, but I'd be sure to be in tears when I did.

Because Lara had done it. I was certain. She'd beaten me back and now beaten me to the punch.

I took along my fur and *Middlemarch* and set off for Poughkeepsie on Mallory's bicycle.

*

I resented the money I spent on a reply telegram from Poughkeepsie station. With that and tickets all to go and be miserable. Six hours, I thought. I'll try to be back in my room within six hours. And I'll get as drunk as I like. I'll have Mallory lend me a bottle when she goes out. She won't mind.

I sent the following message:

Meet at one – Stop – Grand Central – Stop – Lil.

Six words. And even that was too much.

I boarded the train and tried to read of Ludlow and Rosamond and Dorothea and Will, but my stomach was eating itself with nerves. I'd been sick on the train journey home from New York a few weeks' previous, and I had no intention of doing that again.

Go to hell, Lara!

What was I to say when we met? The stern look did not suit my face as it did hers, as it would have done if things had happened the way they were supposed to. This was meant to be my conversation! I was destined to lose it first and knowingly smile as I related the events to her. And now…

I knew I shouldn't think about it, but it was impossible not to imagine Lara naked and moaning and Jack with his heavy man's face huffing and puffing. Or would Lara have worn her tight-lipped expression waiting for him to get on with it? No, I didn't think so. She had admitted to me in the past she was capable of passion.

Lara looked haggard when I saw her and that was something. All that nonsense about a girl glowing after, well, I was glad to see it was nonsense. She was wearing her black felt coat, waist-length. Underneath she wore a grey wool skirt (thankfully not her uniform skirt from St. Anne's as I feared it might be), a maroon sweater, and thick black tights. On her feet she wore flat oxfords. Lara did not start wearing heels until much later, towards the end of the war, I believe. Her face had not been touched by makeup.

She met my train, but she did not rush forward to greet me. Neither of us particularly wanted to live through this encounter, I could see that much. Lara must've awoken in Jack's bed with a dilemma. Should she risk telling me and face my anger or wait, in which case I'd hold it against her for not telling me? She'd decided the former but likely only because she needed to tell someone, and I knew Lara had few other girlfriends.

'Hi, Lar,' I said. We did not embrace. We rarely did.

'Hello, Lil. Do you,' and here her eyes went wide, 'want to get a drink?'

'A drink?'

She nodded with her lips pursed.

'Okay.'

We went to the Oyster Bar in the station because that seemed as good of a place as any. Besides, I wanted to get back as soon as I could manage.

Lara looked over the menu, curiously. I was sure she hadn't tasted liquor before, but who knew. I'd thought she was waiting until the morning after her wedding too.

'What's in a Manhattan?' she asked.

'You wouldn't like it. Stick to vodka or gin.' I took out a cigarette. I knew Lara hated the habit, but she would just have to put up with it. It wasn't like she was going home to her parents. 'I might have one, though. You can try it.'

'Let's do that. I'll have a gin rickey, whatever that is.'

Once the drinks were ordered, we had nothing to hide behind.

'So,' I ventured.

Lara made her monkey face, and I hated the ugly bitch. She gave nothing away.

'Lar,' I said. 'Did you?'

'Yes.'

I thought I might cry. I wasn't sure why.

'With Jack?'

'Yes.'

'Are we going to have to play twenty questions or can you tell me about it?'

She sighed. 'I knew you'd get upset and…'

'And I thought you were a good girl.'

'Being a good girl has nothing to do with it!'

I inhaled.

'It had plenty to do with it this summer.'

'That's not fair. Jack and I aren't Teddy and you. Teddy would have…'

'What? Fucked me and left me?' I stubbed out my cigarette.

'Don't say words like that. If you have to be like this…'

I lit another.

'Like what? Honest? You went around all summer preaching to me about how I'd disturb the ghost of my mother if I so much as touched a boy, and you go and do this? How could you, Lar? You said it yourself. Sleeping with a boy won't make him love you.'

The drinks arrived, interrupting.

'Thank you very much. No, nothing else for now,' I said, my voice deepening to assume a mature air.

She waited until the waiter left before she hissed, 'It wasn't like that, Lil.'

'Wasn't like what? You can't believe…'

'I do! He, Jack, he said he'd marry me. He said I was the girl he wanted to marry but four more years was an awful long time to wait and it wouldn't be a sin…'

'Where's the ring then?' I asked. It's what Mallory would have said.

'Why do you have to be so horrible? Listen, I'm sorry about Teddy, but if he was … Lil, you have to admit it was probably for the best, don't you?'

I narrowed my eyes and took a sip of my drink. Lara had yet to taste hers.

'You think I'm not the type of girl a boy marries, don't you?'

'I swear that's not what I meant.' She raised the glass to her lips. 'That's disgusting.'

'I'll drink it if you won't. That's what you think of me anyway, isn't it?'

'Stop it, Lil, stop it. I was going to tell you that Jack said he loved me, and he wants to marry me, and it was the happiest night of my life and … I knew you couldn't be happy for me. You're incapable of being happy for others'

'Pot and kettle.'

'I don't understand.'

'Pot calling the kettle black. That's rich coming from you. You have never once been happy for me.'

'Lil, it was different.'

'I don't see that.' I finished my drink and flagged down the waiter. If I had money in my account I might as well use it to get drunk.

Lara was closing in on the typical tears. I knew I should stop. Concede. Listen in awe of her womanly knowledge. But I couldn't do it.

At last, I said, 'Lar, it's, well…' I nearly cried myself. 'I loved Teddy and … It isn't only that. I've had this albatross around my neck. It's difficult to be a child virgin when you don't feel like a child anymore. I have to lose it, but I can't do it. And Teddy wouldn't do it to me. And I feel pretty silly and … You're a good girl. I'm not. We both know that. I had to lose it, and I can't. But you, I mean, did you even want to? Did he force you? Did he say he'd only marry you if … Jesus, tell me what happened.'

'I wanted to. It's just I never told you I did. I was afraid.'

I understood.

'And he was nice about it and everything?'

She could not speak but only nod.

'And did he use…?'

Here she blushed, the tomato red hue returning. 'No, he, umm, well, you know. He pulled it out in time.'

Mallory had told me that was never a good idea, and I shared what I knew with Lara.

'I don't know. He says it works.'

'Okay.'

Who was I to doubt her? I said no more.

I sat there, toying with the cherry stem in my second drink. I didn't want it anymore. I wanted my friend back.

'Lar, I'm sorry.'

'I'm sorry too.'

I knew she meant it, but I don't think I did.

She went on to reveal in hushed tones how the evening had gone. How he had persuaded her to come down, taken her to see *Macbeth* at the National Theatre (another thing I envied her – I had yet to see a production of Shakespeare myself at that time), dinner in the Village with a taxi back uptown, where Lara admitted he held her hand tightly against his chest and whispered, 'I lied. There isn't really a separate bedroom.'

'I knew then. But I thought, oh, Lillie. It wasn't very nice. Jack says it gets better for a girl, and we have the rest of our lives together now. Aren't you going to be happy for me?'

I had known since we'd turned eighteen that I likely only had three or four years left of her being my friend rather than some man's wife. So here we were. I wasn't shocked. But I was sad. I had lost my friend.

'We might as well get champagne in that case,' I said. It was the best I could do. If I couldn't be happy for her, I might as well order her champagne. Ring in the advent of her womanhood while I remained in the nursery with a cigarette I couldn't inhale.

I couldn't afford a bottle, but I ordered us each a champagne cocktail which was sweet, and Lara liked it.

'You wouldn't think it to look at him but he's very passionate,' Lara admitted after her second drink. She was tipsy and she was happy, and she was my best friend. I had to be happy for her or pretend to be. My sadness could wait for the train journey home.

I left her at half past three, claiming I really had to be back in time for supper, though I knew I wouldn't go because I would not eat a thing.

Lara did hug me goodbye, I remember that. 'Thank you, Lil,' she whispered. And she squeezed my hand.

'Have fun at your party,' I said.

'I will. Are you sure you don't want me to ask Jack if there's a spare date going?'

I shook my head and smiled as best I could.

How long ago May felt.

Chapter Nineteen

Who was I going to get to sleep with me? This was the predominant question on my mind throughout the train ride back to Poughkeepsie.

What boys did I know?

How could Lara with her angelic goodness and fear of her father go ahead and lose her virginity to a boy I knew to be less than serious in his intentions? I had seen the other side of the curtain and presumed to know his character.

All right, time did reveal Jack's intentions to be true. He married Lara in June 1947. I was bridesmaid with Charlie Vaughn as best man. Another Columbia man. He tried to sleep with me, as I recall, but I was engaged and said no. Never have I lost sleep over that decision.

But I did not know that then, and I assumed in two months' time, or perhaps even by Christmas, I would be comforting Lara's tears.

'And I had sex with him,' she would cry. 'I was a virgin! What will I give my husband now?'

I was so certain of it that I went ahead and imagined myself in my living room before the electric fireplace, patting her back as she cried, denouncing Jack an ass, and Hetty coming in when beckoned with cocoa and marble cake.

But the alternative happened. She married Jack. Thanks to Teddy and to me she married a buffoon who said 'jeez' and called her a dago. Whoopee. I might have been jealous of her non-virgin status, but never did I envy her Jack.

I was pale and thin and unlikely to attract a stranger to bed, but I did consider it. How easy it would have been to waltz into Mallory's room and ask if she could find me a date last minute. She would have been elated. But I didn't. Instead I asked her for whiskey, which she was glad enough to provide.

As I review this scene, my thoughts are near laughable. When you are eighteen and have yet to experience the world, or what I mean to say is that when you are a virgin, you believe, falsely, that great knowledge lies on the other side of the bend. It doesn't. I guess Lara had learned that, but I read her unwillingness to divulge details as a selfish pact amongst experienced people not to reveal their secrets.

Writing this I know that there is no spiritual change or epiphany. If anything, the epiphany lies not in the brilliant loss of innocence, but rather it is the realization that the loss of innocence is meaningless. There is nothing gained, nor anything lost except the belief that it would be significant.

Sex is a mundane feature of life, that's the truth of it. But parents and the priests go around making it a taboo and creating the obsession. You have to try it and be disappointed; that's the only solution to unraveling and essentially devaluing the mystery.

Five years later, I would sleep with a man, a man I now call my husband and who I married eight months after the first time; I owe that to my conscience. I awoke that morning much the same as any other except that I was in a foreign bed and worried about how I might manage to brush my teeth and fix my face before he wakened. His arms were covered in dark fur and mercifully were not wrapped around me. I felt no change, other than that I felt some discomfort and soreness and desperately needed the bathroom.

Had Lara felt grown up that morning? No, I doubt it. But I thought she had; and I couldn't reconcile myself either to the thought that Lara, the more immature and weaker of us, had managed to grow up first, or that everything I was anticipating was false.

Here I was, nothing more than an eighteen-year-old virgin with curlers in her hair, night cream on her face, and a tumbler full of whiskey next to her as she wept her heart out to the Virgin Mother.

But what really got me, and I mean it, is that Lara had lived up to my ideal – she had lost it to her first love. That's something I never did.

*

Mallory came and got me for brunch.

Should I apologize for the stink and decay?

I took out a cigarette.

That should cover up the stench.

I hated Sundays, brunch most of all. I never took much to eat. An orange and a coffee.

We were fortunate in that Strong had its own dining room and thus did not have to bundle up of a Sunday morning to face the snow. There were about one hundred of us at every meal, and while I realize this was quite a small number, it felt overwhelming to me that morning. Everyone was talking, mouths full, grey sausages half-eaten and abandoned on plates alongside runny eggs, Veronica Jacobs sporting a hickey, and Carolyn Jenkins relating the plot of *The Wolf Man*. She'd gone to see it the night before with Robert Anderson, practically her steady, and 'I had to grab for his hand, gosh, I was frightened. The fangs and everything. I know it's Hollywood makeup, but they do make it look scary. And then, oh, Robert, he put his arm around me, and I died. I swear it. I died. And goodness, if that weren't enough, he whispered to me – gosh, Peggy, cross my heart I'm not lying – he whispered, "Don't be frightened, darling. It's only a kid's film." He called me darling. He's never done that before.'

I didn't think anyone had called me darling before other than Mallory. We were rather affectionate about names with each other. Teddy never had been that way with me. Dads called me honey sometimes.

'That's awfully fresh, Carrie, don't you think?' asked Peggy Peterson. She was a fellow English major and an absolute prude. Worse than Mary Elizabeth I would say, because she was also an atheist. I had the childish idea that all atheists would be in favor of looser morals and sex in general, but Vassar taught me elsewise.

'Well,' Carolyn blushed. She was proud of her conquest, but that prig Peggy wasn't going to allow it. 'I did. But it was so scary that I lost my mind a little. Besides,' she huffed, picking up her fork, 'we are practically going steady, you know.'

'Well,' said Peggy, she too picking up her cutlery, a signal that she would have the last word on the matter, 'practically going steady isn't going steady and it certainly is not engaged.'

Mallory was oblivious to this. She stared at her fresh manicure, examining her pointer and middle fingers for signs of discoloration.

'Bitches,' she mumbled.

I laughed. I was glad to have Mallory.

'L,' she whispered so our neighbors could not hear, 'I don't think I can bear the parlor for coffee, do you? Let's grab a cup each and go to my room. We can listen to the wireless there.'

The one appeal of spending a Sunday afternoon lounged in the parlor was the wireless with a coffee, but Mallory went and acquired her own radio, so by mid-October we had foregone this tradition of student life as well.

'Okay,' I said, 'but I can't smoke too much. I think I'm coming down with a sore throat or something. And I have to write an essay on *Middlemarch* for Friday, and I'm only on page three hundred.'

'Baby, there'll be plenty of time for that.'

Why I trusted Mallory when I knew exactly how the afternoon would end, I don't know. I guess I wanted it to end that way was all.

'All right. But I'm not drinking anything other than coffee.'

Mallory was unphased. 'Suit yourself.'

As it turned out, Mallory and I for once had an occasion to drink that afternoon other than out of boredom. When the news came over the wireless about Pearl Harbor, Mallory rose from her bed and went without a word to her trunk to start mixing us a drink.

When she passed me the gin cocktail with a cigarette, she shook her head with the emotion closest to despair I ever saw in her. 'We might as well. There's nothing else to do now.'

'But I've got to write my essay on *Middlemarch*!' I protested.

'Do you think anyone is going to give a damn about the most boring novel written in the English language after this? Trust me, you'll never have to write that essay.'

She was right, but not for the reason she thought.

'Do you think we should go downstairs? There might be an announcement.'

Mallory lit her cigarette.

'You really want to go down into that pool of bullshit? No thank you. I think we'll be just fine up here.'

Everyone has a story about that day. Some young American in the Balliol Junior Common Room was hearing the news late that Sunday afternoon, the sun already set, and he'd head up to London on the first train Monday morning only to return by midday via Paddington. He could not enlist. His eyesight was too poor. I'd hear this story nearly five years later, while I myself sat in Balliol with a neat scotch in hand, falling in love with this shy boy with the bad eyes – my husband.

And what did I tell him in turn? I said I was drunk, and he laughed, and I think that may have been when he fell in love with me, or so he would claim later when he fell out of love.

What I had done specifically was to drink six gins, smoke twenty-seven cigarettes, and collapse in bed next to Mallory, her feet kicking me to move over. The single bed was too small for both of our asses.

The day to live in infamy is a blur and really wasn't much different from other Sundays that A-term, other than that it was probably my worst offense. It is perhaps most notable in my personal biography as being the last Sunday I spent at Vassar that term.

I woke about three in the morning, my head splitting, mouth foul, and breasts swelling with fever. I don't know why, but my breasts seem to enlarge when I'm hungover. It started that year, and I get it just the same now. The fever also tends to concentrate in my ass. What this is about, I do not know.

But I do know that I was scared. Not because of some daft fear of the Japanese bombing us in our beds, or of the Nazis crossing the Atlantic to invade Boston or New York. No, I was afraid for the same reason I always was, war or no war. Teddy would go away from me without a goodbye and if the Japanese or the Nazis did end up bombing us to smithereens, I'd be bound to die a virgin.

Chapter Twenty

I was sent home from school three days later after being discovered on the bathroom floor, violently ill and with a fever. A rash had set in the night before, beginning on my genitals before spreading with the rapidity of a forest fire to my legs and creeping up my belly.

I was too nervous to ask Mallory how long it might take for a venereal disease to reveal itself. I hadn't kissed a boy since Teddy, and I didn't think him the sort to pick up bugs. But if he had? My neck went clammy with fear. How could I, a virgin, have contracted a venereal disease? Dads could never know, but he would have to if there were any hope of a cure.

This was worse than pregnancy. At least that I knew how you could and could not come by and had an idea of how one might fix it quickly enough.

But no. I somehow had contracted a venereal disease from touching a boy's pecker with my hands. What were my other offences? Fingers allowed, or not allowed for that matter, inside of me? A tongue in the mouth?

I knew very little of such diseases in those days, but I had heard that there were a large variety, most of which I was unaware. I only knew for sure of syphilis, which could end in the asylum if not treated, and something called crabs, which gave you a rash and an itch down there. I assumed it was the latter.

Perhaps it was the harsh detergent of the laundry at Vassar. Maybe my panties had come in contact with a naughtier girl's, and the crabs had crawled on over onto mine. Like headlice. Had they come from Mallory? I doubted it. Mallory couldn't possibly have come down with crabs and not told me about it.

There was nothing else for me to do but to try to sleep early, which I surrendered to easily enough. I awoke in the night, my throat swollen. I'd had scarlet fever as a kid, but it wasn't like that. There was a taste of bile sat in my throat. I tried to contract my throat to push the bile up and swallow it, the way one might do with mucus, but it wouldn't budge and the pain of trying again was excruciating.

Was this what the plague had been like? I had never come over ill so suddenly in my life. Admittedly I had been dragging my feet since the weekend, but I attributed that to the double-whammy of shocking news. And the mild sore throat to winter, too many cigarettes, and ineffective radiators.

I was going to be sick. I dragged myself from the bed. My legs felt like those of a newborn lamb. I thought I might faint. I steadied myself against the frame of the bed, moving my feet into their slippers.

Somehow I made it to the bathroom where I was discovered in a semi-conscious state. I was later told by Veronica Jacobs, who found me, 'At first I just thought you were drunk as a skunk, passed out like that. I tried to cover you up decently and get you back to your room before someone else found you and reported you. But you couldn't speak when I asked you what the matter was. It came out in a whisper. Your throat had closed up or something. And goodness, Lillie, there was a golf ball on the side of your throat there. I'd never seen anything like it in my life.'

Veronica was right. A small lump, or small compared to what it had been, the size of a marble, remained on both sides of my neck underneath my chin for six months. I can feel the tenderness today, and if I touch them, I choke up the same metallic taste of bile. This has never really gone away, but I've grown used to it. My glands swell up whenever I come down with the slightest of colds, a reminder of that extended illness that came to dominate the winter of my freshman year.

My spleen did not return to its normal size until March. That's when the doctor deemed it safe for me to resume playing sports, not that I cared about that. I will admit, though, I didn't dare touch myself during that time. Nor did I drink. I was scared. If it burst, I died, or so I was told.

Mononucleosis is perhaps better known by its colloquial name, the 'kissing disease.' I guess it was a venereal disease I had, in a way, but I couldn't have caught it from kissing. How I came to pick it up, I don't know, but Dr. Burke told me it was the worst case he'd seen. Dads rang for him when we arrived home from Vassar that Wednesday afternoon. He'd left work as soon as the infirmary called. They didn't like the idea of putting me on a train with that rash.

I remember little of the journey except of how Dads bundled me up in my fur and his own coat too. I thought he looked very worried, but I didn't pause to consider it. I slept.

'We'll fix you, don't you worry about that,' I seem to recall Dr. Burke saying to me several times as he examined my rash. He had never said a thing like that to me before. I knew it meant I really ought to panic, but I didn't have the strength.

I learned later they had feared the worst – meningitis. A sadly common disease to pick up in communal living. But it wasn't. So as long as I watched my spleen and didn't laugh too hard or run or bump into anything or take a tumble, I'd be fine. I slept for the next seventeen hours and did not wake until Friday morning. I was ravenous when I did and found I could swallow again.

I did not leave the bed for longer than a few hours of

permitted sitting in the living room until the New Year. There was a great deal of talk about the necessity of me missing the B-term and perhaps the rest of the year. I managed somehow to be signed off to return by the end of January, though I never could burn the candle at both ends, as the saying goes, again.

Lara came to see me over the holidays. But we did not bow our heads together before the electric fireplace gorging on cookies and popcorn, as I had envisioned us weeks before. I had no broken heart to soothe, well other than my own. Rather, I'd a girl in love to endure.

Jack had gone along with the Marcelli family to Midnight Mass, as I learned. I'd not gone that year. Dr. Burke advised I leave the house as little as possible, something I gladly complied to when it came to Mass.

'Did you take the Eucharist?' I asked. I was being a bitch. I knew it and, worse, Lara knew it too.

'Yes,' she answered, her lips puckering, 'why wouldn't I?'

'You committed a mortal sin, Lar. Come on, we've known that since before our First Holy Communion.'

'You never seemed to mind the thought of mortal sin before,' she snapped.

'I'm an atheist.'

'Since when?'

'Since Easter.'

Lara waved off my comment; she refused to be troubled by it.

'That's because of your, what's his name, Nietzsche.' She pronounced the name as is common amongst Americans, with a harsh 'che' as in cheese at the end. 'You want some boy to sleep with you because you've read him.'

'I have a mind of my own. I don't rely on reading books to get me into bed.'

This wasn't exactly true.

Lara straightened her red flannel skirt and folded her lips together, biting through the skin with her teeth.

'Lillie, we don't have very much time together. I don't want to fight. Please.'

I relented.

Our interactions continued on a similar course throughout those late December and early January days. Still she came to see me. Our friendship had undergone other such periods of tribulation and prevailed. Both of us were confident that once I regained my strength and fixed my mind to a goal other than winning back Teddy, our relations would improve too. Jack showed no signs of leaving anytime soon so I'd simply have to find a way to tolerate him.

On the day before New Year's Eve, the deepest wish of my girlish heart was granted. Teddy came to see me.

Dads knocked on my door that morning with news of a visitor.

'Are you up to seeing anyone, honey?'

I thought it was only Lara again or perhaps Mary Elizabeth. She'd come a few times to see me which was nice of her. She hoped I wouldn't be absent from Vassar for long.

'Yes, but who is it?'

'It's Ted, honey.'

All Dads knew of our romance was that it had, thankfully, fizzled out and that was by sheer observation. He never asked me any questions about it. He must've thought there was no longer the threat of seduction from that quarter because he let Teddy into my room and left us alone. Dads wasn't one for eavesdropping.

'Hello, Lillie,' he said. I saw him there standing behind Dads, an inch or two taller, his black hair sticking up. He must've just showered. It had grown long.

'I'll leave you two to visit,' said Dads as he widened the opening of the door, allowing Teddy to enter. 'If you need anything, I'll be downstairs.'

'Thanks.'

Then we were alone, as I'd feared we mightn't be again.

He had called me Lillie. He never called me Lillie. I was Lil to him. I knew from his greeting alone that our fight had not ended. And that was my fault.

'Hello, Teddy.'

I sat up in bed and spread the covers over me. Though he had seen me naked, had seen me naked in that very bed before, I felt self-conscious about him seeing me in my nightgown with its rosettes embroidered on a lace collar. No longer were we lovers or friends. We were acquaintances, childhood neighbors. And seeing a girl in her nightgown is far too intimate for an acquaintance.

'You feeling better?' He ran his hand through his unruly hair and attempted a smile, but all that came out was a glimpse of three teeth on the left side of his mouth. He was nervous.

'You can sit down,' I said.

I didn't like him standing. Not because it made me uncomfortable to see him uncomfortable, but because I didn't like how tall he stood next to my bed. He looked around the room and the only chair was my vanity bench. He could hardly sit on such a delicate and feminine stool.

'You can sit on my bed if you like.'

That would have felt like the most natural thing in the world for the old Teddy and Lillie, but now ... Everything was strange and strained. It was nice of him to visit, though. I have to say that in his favor.

'Okay.'

He sat.

We'd never encountered this problem before. This problem of silence. We had always had something to talk about, or, if we were silent, it wasn't due to a lack of conversation.

I spoke.

'I've been reading *Mrs. Dalloway*. Have you read it?'

'No, I can't seem to get through Woolf.'

Yes, I remembered that about Teddy.

'You should try it. It's very good. And it's a comfort to read about other people going mad when you are yourself.'

He stared straight ahead and bit his inner cheek. 'Is that what's the matter with you?'

I pulled my covers close. 'No. It's mono, but I suspect it wasn't helped by the way I've been behaving these last few months.'

Teddy did not reply at first. I saw the gleam in his eyes and knew him to be thinking out his words, a habit of his which in itself had the power to drive me crazy. When he spoke, his voice soft and light, he said, 'We're all a little mad, I think. I sure know I am. Lil, I...'

I perked up at the sound of this familiar name.

'Yes?'

He paused, biting his inner cheek again, screwing his mouth up to the left corner.

'I think, I think I like my messed-up mind too much. I wouldn't know how to get on without it.'

Teddy and I may have hated ourselves, but behind the self-loathing lay an egotism that smirked at anyone destined to have a nice life, like Lara or Jack. They could not have much talent or purpose. We loved being damned if genius was to be our reward.

'You don't think I'm nutty?'

He smiled. 'I've always known you were nutty. Didn't need a doctor to tell me that.'

We settled into our comfortable silence of old.

A couple more minutes passed, a few comments here and there, but mostly we sat on staring, our eyes searching over the other. I loved him still. Very much. And I can't help but to think he loved me. Very much too.

At last he made a movement, signaling his intention to rise. 'I've got to get going. But it was good to see you, Lil.'

I smiled though I wanted to cry. I did not want my Teddy to leave me again.

'Teddy?'

He stayed seated, his eyes intently studying mine.

'Yeah, what is it?'

I sat up and took a deep breath, bracing myself. I was scared to ask the question, but I was a hell of a lot more scared to hear his reply.

'Teddy, have you enlisted?'

And praise to be to the Father, and to the Son, and to the Holy Ghost for he blessedly shook his head.

'Nah, I can't.'

My eyes grew closer together, asking why.

'Adam. You know my mother. She doesn't want me enlisting. She's says it's enough to have lost one son. If they call me up, I'll have to go, but until then…'

I was going to ask him if he were disappointed, but I didn't. That would have been a stupid question. I already knew the answer.

'Oh.'

'Yeah.'

'I'm sorry.'

I wasn't really.

'Yeah, it's all right. I'll have to go back to Fordham and putter about a while longer. I'll find something to do.'

Despite being friends and lovers with Edward Mc-

Calman for years and years and years, I'd no idea what he wanted to do when he graduated from school. But he didn't know either. That's the thing. I assumed he'd be a writer. I used to imagine us heading off to Paris together, and we'd each write during the day, and at night we'd come together and drink our wine and make love. I wish we could have had that life. Even if it hadn't lasted, even if it were to have ended with us hating one another, I wish we could have had it. If only for a little while.

The thing is I would have that life. Just not with Teddy.

'Right,' he slapped his hands together, 'I should get going. You probably need to rest or something anyway.'

'Yes, I probably should rest.'

'All right.'

He stood up.

I wanted him to kiss me. If it were only on the cheek, I would have been content. I thought I could be bold and tell him I loved him and how much I wanted him. I could kiss him. But I couldn't; I had mono. A good excuse for my cowardice.

'Take care, Lil.'

'Thanks.'

He was gone.

I didn't see Teddy again until April, when I needed him not for my own purposes but for Lara's.

But so goes life.

*

I saw less of Mallory after Christmas. Dr. Burke warned me, outside of Dads' earshot thankfully, that I shouldn't smoke so much. 'It's bad for your nerves and your figure,' he said. I took his advice for a few months. The metallic taste in my mouth put me off it. I struggled to reacquaint myself to the taste of coffee too. I ate little, as always.

When I returned to Vassar at the end of January 1942, it was very much to the same world. Oh, certainly some girls thought the study of Greek and of music was frivolous and removed of its former purpose. What could it do to end the war, they argued, while others, mostly the crew at the *Misc*, which I fell in with that B-term, defended the humanities as being virtuous not only for their own sakes but because they upheld the very values for which our boys sacrificed their lives. It was a whole lot of bullshit, I guess, but we believed it well enough.

I took to working in the message center and learned to clean my own room. Some of the other girls volunteered for kitchen duty, but I wasn't going near food. It was bad enough having to eat the stuff, which I did rarely.

Mallory, I seem to recall, did nothing. She could scarcely muster the energy to keep her room tidy.

'For Christ's sake,' she'd say, 'is me darning socks and emptying my own ashtray really going to see off Hitler?'

The truth of the matter was that the one thing Mallory enjoyed was when we went on a group venture down to the Dutch to meet servicemen and attempt to raise their spirits. I hated this activity and usually refrained.

'L, you always say you want to do more for the war effort and here we have it,' was her argument.

'Come off of it,' I'd reply. 'I don't want to go down and flirt with a lot of West Point boys. I didn't want to do it before the war started, and I'm sure as hell not going now.'

Though sometimes I did go. It was better than speaking to Lara on the telephone of a Saturday night.

But those were not lonely days. There was plenty to do and idle hands were deemed unpatriotic. The most significant thing that happened to me during the war, in regard to my education at Vassar, was I left in December 1944, rather than in the spring. It was part of the college's temporary initiative to graduate us early to make us available for the use of our country. I went to New York and smoked. I also attempted my first novel and failed.

When the war came, it was the hour in which I could act, but I did nothing. There was the matter of my recent illness to consider. Dads never would have permitted me to go abroad as a nurse or a journalist as I may have dreamed, even if I'd been in the best of health, which I wasn't. And I did not want to go. So I did not fight. Instead I did the usual things. I went to Red Cross dances, another favorite activity of Mallory's, and I gave up wearing silk stockings.

Dads had not fought in the last war. He'd been finishing his law degree and did not enlist. My mother spoke of the Great War as a great inconvenience because Aunt Jo hadn't been able to have a proper deb ball. How I had listened to those stories when I was growing up and glibly thought, if only I'd been alive, I would've acted. Useless Mama, I thought, terribly feminine.

But I did no better.

I sometimes wonder if it was the inactivity which is to blame. Perhaps it was my overarching guilt for not taking on the burden of my generation that led me to meddle in Lara's affairs the way I did. I suppose it's what the analysts might say, the ones my husband threatens me with. I can hear them now (I assume there'd be a series of them; I'd never be able to stick with one). Corrupted by religion, a case of misplaced Catholic guilt, a girlhood stunted by the war and by death. Not a classic case, but a fairly neat one in its arch, if you thought about it.

Or maybe I just wanted for Lara to feel pain as I had felt

pain. To destroy the last of her innocence, swiftly. To make us equals on new terms. But the reasons for why I did what I did, they don't matter. There are no justifications. I knew that then, and I'm certain of it now.

I was selfish. I always have been. That's all.

Chapter Twenty-one

The news of death arrived by telegram. The second I'd received.

Again I was called down to the parlor to sign for it of a Saturday morning. It was early April, and we'd returned from our Easter holidays earlier in the week. I'd not gone home that year, but instead went to New York with Mallory and spent a blissful three days amongst fellow heathens. Her parents tempered our drinking, but only slightly, and they took me to see *Porgy and Bess* at the Majestic. It was my first opera.

I awoke that morning not unhappy. The spring beckoned, I'd slept well, and I'd a date for the evening with the older brother of one of the girls on the *Misc*, a senior at Cornell who'd had a collection of poetry brought out. It was hardly the life I would have chosen, perhaps, but it seemed fairly compatible to a life I may have once imagined for myself.

I could not guess at the meaning of the telegram. I knew few boys who'd enlisted, the predominant one being Jack, but I knew from my latest conversation with Lara, a fortnight previous, that he was at Fort Bragg down in North Carolina and would not ship out for some time.

Maybe Uncle Rory really had died. It couldn't be Lara again throwing away her pocket money on telegrams to report frivolous stories of hers and Jack's relations. Maybe it was about Jack, though. Maybe he'd been in a jeep accident or his gun kicked back at him or something. I spent the next three years of the war thinking each time I signed for a telegram, it was only Lara writing to let me know of

Jack's demise. Would I have been upset? I wonder.

In fact, it was Lara, more cryptic than before.

Emergency – Stop – Come – Stop – Albany – Stop – Lara.

It seemed an odd message. *Emergency* rather than *tragedy*. Or *horrible news*. Surely she would have written that if it were Jack.

I sighed.

I looked at the clock. It was later in the day than it had been in December. Quarter to twelve. If I went now, borrowing Mallory's bicycle to get to the station, I might be able to make it back for my date. I hoped.

Why I didn't place a call to Lara at Saint Rose's first, I don't know. I didn't think of it. I read the telegram and resigned myself to the duty of undertaking a back and forth journey to Albany. I went to my room, took out my spring mackintosh, picked up *Madame Bovary* and my handbag, and wondered how quickly I could cycle. Would there be a half past noon train I could make?

I was not anxious throughout the journey. I read my book, which I enjoyed, and chalked up the telegram to being nothing more than Lara's usual hysterics.

I sent no reply. I thought I'd go to her housing and knock on. That seemed the simplest, or rather the cheapest, thing to do. I was tired of spending money on Jack and Lara's affairs.

The weather was mild, but I took a taxi from the station to the college. It felt a rare treat.

When I arrived on Madison Ave. to the house I knew Lara lived in from her letters, I was yet an untroubled girl. That's not to say I wasn't dreading the encounter, as I certainly was, and I felt the outbreak of a fight to be inevitable. They seemed to be when Lara and I met.

Lara anticipated my knock, but she did not welcome me in.

'Let me grab my coat,' she said, hurriedly. 'We better go out.'

I did not mind. The weather was that of early spring, and Lara and I were fond of walking together. I thought of our summer treks along suburban roads, me running ahead of her, jumping and twirling, exclaiming the preposterous and sickening sentiment of 'A girl in love can't be anything other than a girl in love.' How young eighteen seemed even to my then more cynical nineteen-year-old self. I would never again be the girl of the previous spring, but neither did I want to be.

Once we were outside and a good fifty yards away from the house, Lara spoke.

'Let's go to the park,' she said.

'Okay.'

It was not like Lara to withhold information, but I knew she struggled to narrate stories and perhaps she needed to be settled before she could begin.

But she did not speak when we reached Washington Park, except to say, 'Let's make it to the pond. We can sit there.'

'Okay.'

When we reached the pond and a bench of which Lara approved, there being no persons on the benches to either side, she continued her silence.

I was annoyed. Here I'd rushed down to Albany to sit on a damp bench with a friend I didn't like very much anymore. I was tired of her beckoning me at her whim, mandating my behavior but following her own course without consulting me. This was not the friendship of our childhood. She was the woman now, and I the inexperienced girl, and I reeled from the knowledge of it each time I saw her.

'Lar, come on,' I said, 'I have a date in a few hours, I've got to make it back to Poughkeepsie. Can we get the show on the road here?'

She raised her eyes to me, and it was then I saw these were not my Lara's eyes. These eyes were stones; they were dead and revealed no secrets.

'Is that all you can think about? Your stupid date?' she asked, her voice acidic. Only I knew of what bitterness and hatred Lara was capable. I don't think even now Jack can be fully aware. I knew her first and loved her best.

'Lar,' I cried more from exasperation than genuine concern. 'Please tell me, what is it?'

'It's ... it's ... oh, Lillie!'

With the tremble of a lip, the hysterics took over. I hugged her to my breast, smoothing her unclean hair from her brow.

'Shh, shh.'

I waited for my Lara. I'd grown patience. I do not know for how long she cried. She choked on her tears and bile, mucus staining the front of my pale blue mackintosh. Another expense for the sake of Jack and Lara. It would need to be dry cleaned. It mattered little.

When at last she pulled her head up from my breast to meet my gaze, she was ready to confide.

'Lillie, it happened.'

'What happened?'

I nearly shook her. She would not speak.

'What is it, Lar? Please tell me.'

But she did not need to. I guessed at the conclusion of the conversation before she said it. It was obvious enough.

'Are you...?' I asked, softly. I did not need her to answer. I did not want her to.

But she nodded and confirmed what we both knew already.

'Are you certain?'

'Yes.'

'Really? I didn't bleed for a month last winter because I'd lost too much weight and the stress and everything. If ever

I'm the least bit anxious, I'm a week late.'

'No. It's not that.'

'It can't be…'

'Lillie!' Her voice was shrill. I stopped.

'I know, okay. It's been two months – two months! And this,' she grabbed at the fat of her abdomen not tucked into its usual girdle. 'What is it but a baby?'

'I don't know, Lar.'

I'd lost my patience. I returned to being no more than a scared girl. But I could not cry. I had to allow her to spill her tears and not add to their number with my own. Besides, my tears would not have been for her. They would have been, well, for something else. Not quite for myself. Out of relief, really, I suppose, that this had not happened to me. And then there was that terrible, horrible thought creeping in, flashing across my mind's eye, blood red like murder. She deserved it. Yes, she deserved it. After everything she said to me, and here she was the one. No, I could not speak of that.

Lara was my best friend – is my best friend, still, or so we tell each other. And so I was kind, or behaved with what I thought to be kindness, however mistaken I may have been. I told her to do as I would have done. As I had long thought out on those summer evenings with Teddy's lips on my breast, fearing what might happen if we slept together. But it wouldn't have happened to me. I was too clever for that.

'Lar.' I spoke very slowly. 'You do know…'

What could I say? I knew I would need to tell her, that I would need to make her listen. There was only one solution to the problem, I could see that.

It was like when I was fourteen and tore my first pair of silk stockings ahead of the eighth-grade commencement ceremony. I'd been wearing them too much around my room, undressing before my mirror, pretending a man's eyes were watching me rather than my own. And just like that a ladder appeared, and when I tried to smooth it out, my nail caught, and they tore. I couldn't tell my mother. Not so much because she would have been upset about the stockings themselves, but I couldn't think to explain what had happened. She would not have approved of my striptease. And so I took my small birthday savings and went to Delaney's after school the next day and purchased another pair. I threw the others in an industrial garbage can behind the drugstore. I never told a soul. Some things we must do on our own.

'Lar,' I started again, but she interrupted me.

'My dad! Lillie, he'll kill me. And it will kill my mother, after Jimmy. This is why they said don't go with boys. They knew, they knew!'

'Lara, stop,' I said, perhaps too loudly. I took a look at our surroundings. No one had as of yet sat upon the two empty benches. The pond was, for the most part, deserted. The mild day had grown grey, promising rain within the hour. Only those desperate for exercise or fresh air ventured into the park that afternoon. We were safe.

'Why?' she continued. 'This is why I told you not to do it, I knew too. I knew this would happen. God doesn't allow you to sin and not punish. He's a vengeful God and…'

I could've slapped her. I would listen to her cry, I would hear her tirades against her parents. That I could understand. But I would not tolerate this confusion with the Holy Father getting all mixed in.

'Shut up, Lar.'

It was as good as a slap.

'Now,' I said, 'you're pregnant and you're sure?'

She nodded. I could see she couldn't bring herself to say the words.

'Well, then you're pregnant.'

'But…'

'Lar, if you're pregnant, you're pregnant. There is nothing you can do to change the fact that you will have once been pregnant.'

Her eyes awakened. Did she understand? I don't think she did.

'You say you can't tell your parents, which I know as well as you is true. But they would love you even if you did, I know that too. See what they did for Jimmy?'

'But Jimmy is a boy. They've never forgiven his wife. She's a slut.'

'That's true,' I admitted. 'They've never forgiven her, but I think they would you. Look how they love little Peter.'

'Jack won't marry me,' she blurted out.

That was it. Now I knew the truth of it. The fear of her father was only part of it, a significant part perhaps, but not the critical one. Jack might not marry her if he knew. He had loved Catherine Spence, he'd as good as admitted that to me, but he could not follow her to England. He said he loved Lara but who knew for how long. He'd also told me he wouldn't enlist, but he did in February. That must have been when the baby was made. I could not trust what he said. I did not know him, and I wonder if Lara did, if she does.

Would Teddy have married me if the worst had happened? I doubted it. But we with our dark heads buried in books knew how to avoid such things. Jack had been selfish and Lara too trusting. And this was the conclusion.

The April wind whipped at our hair, which we both wore loose. I tasted it catching in my mouth. Rain threatened. I suggested we find a café for a coffee, but Lara refused.

'No one can hear,' she said, her lips forming a thin determined line. Lara had the sort of lips that could transform from full to thin with a look. Mine were always thin.

'All right.'

Neither of us spoke until a young father with his toddler passed, ready with crumbs to feed the ducks. They were to remember this as a happy April day, how different from us.

'Lil,' whispered Lara, returning my thoughts to the matter on hand, 'I can't go and have a child. Jack would...'

I must act. That I knew. Here was my Lara, my bosom friend of childhood, with whom I had shared a bed, divulging secrets under covers with breath of cookies and chocolate milk.

It was not I who had committed her sin, but I felt the guilt of it. Yet Lara had acted of her own free will, I did not force her to fall in love. All right, yes, I was responsible for playing matchmaker twice, but I hadn't forced her to have sex. Neither had I warned her against it. I had not thought to nor would I have if I dreamt it a possibility. I was not Lara.

If I objected to Lara and Jack sleeping together on any count other than one of jealousy, it was that I did not think their love great enough, but she said it was, and I believed her.

No, I could not be responsible for this, but I was. Somehow I must be. Because I could not accept Lara as her own free agent. She would not have made this choice without having been led astray.

And what of Jack? Surely the blame lay with him, he was the man and the one with the penis. I bet he used the same trite lines on her too about blue balling with a hint thrown in of love because good girls can't be bought by guilt of blue balling alone. He knew of the world of sex before we guessed at it. Protection would have been easy for him to come by, but he refused and did not educate Lara of its likely necessity. It was his fault, if it were any or ours, and I knew that, but Jack to me was a useless figure. He wasn't capable of action.

But I was. I always had been.

I was the Eve. I introduced the apple to Lara. Of that I was guilty, if nothing else. And so, in a way, it was my sin too.

But I wasn't like Lara, tearing myself up over the Holy Father and the Holy Ghost. I knew how to go about removing the consequence of love. The consequences of sin were to be worried of later.

'Lar,' I said. I waited until she met my eyes to continue. 'You know there are ways to, well, you know, to get rid of it.'

'No. Lillie, that's a sin. You can't.'

'You already sinned. You're living in mortal sin, I mean, if you want to believe in all that bullshit. And you've been taking Communion which makes the sin worse. Again, if you believe it. But, Lar, you don't believe it. And neither do I. And neither does Jack.'

'You can't get rid of a baby. That's not possible.'

'Of course it's possible. You go to a doctor and he fixes you up. That's all there is to it.'

'Lil, that's murder and you know it, and I won't hear another word about it.'

But I could not allow her to terminate the conversation. I knew what was right and persevered.

'It's illegal,' I said, 'I'll give you that. But plenty of girls do it. I'll ask around.'

'Don't you dare,' she snapped.

I raised myself from the bench, sitting back down fast on my hands. Now I couldn't slap her.

'Lara, listen. You cannot and will not have this child. Or you can if you like, but we both know you do not like the thought of that. You want to close your eyes and wish it away and return to your virginal self, but it isn't going to happen. If you want to tell your parents fine, go ahead. If you want to see if Jack will marry you right away, fine. He very well might. But he also might die. You will be left with a baby, without your education, and back at home with your parents who sure as hell are never going to let you go around with boys again because once the cow is sold every man knows the milk is free.'

I'm surprised she didn't hit me. Oh well, it was hardly worse than what she'd said to me that summer.

'Now, I can ask a girl back at Vassar. She'll know who to see, and you and I will go and see that man. No one will ever know. Not Jack and not your parents.'

Lara furrowed her brow, her lips coming together in a pout.

'Has, has she had one?'

'No. But her cousin has. And they're very rich people so she would have gone to a good doctor and not some back-alley butcher. I'll make certain of that. I'll not have you killed. You can trust me.'

'Yes.'

It was then that the rain began to fall. But we had made our decisions and needed to speak of it no more.

The plan was set into action, but it was I who must be the first mover. This was agreed.

I caught the train back and went on my date. I had a nice time too, and I continued to see that boy for some time, but that part of my history bears no relevance on this story and so I will say no more of it.

The next day I asked Mallory.

And then I called Teddy.

Chapter Twenty-two

When my mother died, I refused to look on the corpse. Though we kept the body in the house for two days of grieving, I did not enter the living room. I retreated to the kitchen, brewing coffee and refilling platters of cheese with Hetty. She kept me in with her.

Dads never spoke of it except to say I could suit myself as I liked. He understood.

I knew Aunt Claire did not entirely approve, but she said nothing of it. That's the benefit of descending from a line of quiet people.

I did not like sleeping in the house and I knew neither did Dads, not while she was there. Slyly lying dead in the same room where she died. Suddenly. A slight sickness in her stomach, a pounding in her head. An hour of lie down before breakfast would see her right, said Hetty. It was Dads who found her. I was in bed.

I did not attend the funeral. I refused to do my duty. I could not see my mother dead. I accepted the fact without the sight, the antithesis of Thomas the Doubter. I said I would not go from the start, and I remember Aunt Jo knocking on the door of my room asking which dress I would like for Hetty to press for me, and I told her it did not matter. I would not go. She sent for Dads who gently pressed upon me that I should dress and go. It's what my mother would have wanted he said, but I claimed other-wise. I knew her better; I loved her more. Dads hugged me and said he loved me, and there was almost a scene, but there wasn't. I loved him very much, but I could not bring myself to say so.

I sought refuge in the kitchen, cutting the crusts from thin slices of brown bread which Hetty would use for the salmon sandwiches. Never had Hetty and I been close, and this did not form a bond of any sort between us. She'd been my mother's temporary help through the years, and she started to come every day once my mother died, but that was it. We did not speak.

Aunt Jo insisted on telling me how beautiful my mother had been made up to look. 'She was on the Daisy Chain, you know.' Yes, I knew. Aunt Jo had not been. She was fat where my mother had been slender, like my own figure promised to be at fifteen. 'You should have seen her.'

I was glad I hadn't, but I did not say so. I gave a sad but encouraging smile. It was her grief too. But we could not share in it.

I remember little else of the day, except for when Teddy came to me and clasped my hand. I could see he had been crying too. I wondered why, or really for whom, but I did not ask. I wished to take him to the backyard where the overspill of guests gathered, strewn sulkily across the lawn, women's heels sinking into the soft March earth, and to find a secret corner where he might kiss me. To me, kisses came with death. But he did not, and I went to bed that night crying over it. Not for my mother. That I could not do.

When Dads knocked on my door that morning, just as I was waking, and he told me Dr. Burke was downstairs but there was no hope, I knew my mother was dead and I have thought of her forever in the past tense since. It is difficult to see the dead as alive, even in our memories.

*

255

Mallory had never had an abortion, but her cousin Coralie had.

I joined Mallory in her room after brunch for a gin fizz. It was the first I had since my illness. And the cigarette too. Both tasted rotten. I finished neither.

I flopped down on Mallory's bed as she mixed the drinks from her steamer trunk. I had missed the ritual.

'Mal,' I began, 'do you, I mean, well, how does one go about getting an abortion, say?'

Mallory dropped an ice cube in the glass, making a violent plunk. She turned. The drinks remained unfinished.

'Goddamn, L, when did you give it up? Didn't I tell you to use condoms? I would have taken you to get fitted for a diaphragm if you'd have let me know.'

'No,' I protested, 'it isn't me. I'm very much, well, intact. It doesn't matter. It's for a friend.'

'Sure,' said Mallory. She returned to her mixing. 'Well,' she continued, handing me my glass and snuggling in next to me on the bed, 'I'd have to dig up my little black book.'

'You keep the name of a doctor in your little black book?'

'Yes,' she said with the rise of an eyebrow, 'and it's one number I hope never to use for myself. Let me get it for you.'

It took her some time to find it. First the stockings drawer was searched, then her handbag. Finally she located it on top of her nightstand beneath her copy of *Rebecca*. She tapped on the cover. 'It's good that. I'll let you borrow it when I finish.'

'Thanks.'

'Now let me see ... It's some foreign name. It's the man Cousin Coralie went to when she was up the duff, not that she mentions it now. Jesus. Who's this friend of yours, L?'

I didn't wish to speak of the matter to Mallory, though I knew she'd understand. I almost confessed, but I stopped myself. If I'd been in a cattier mood I might have done, and the night would have ended with the usual several gins, mocking Lara with her dowdy school uniform skirts for maternity clothes and her pathetic boyfriend Jack who was to be none the wiser of the whole affair.

But instead I said, 'A friend from home. I went to see her yesterday in Albany. Her boyfriend is about to ship out, and she can't have it. That's all.'

Mallory's interest waned. 'Okay, sure. His name is Trodoski. Is that Russian? Polish? Who knows. He's good, though. My friend Dorothy Neill went to him last year, I think. Now that was *quite* the scandal. She was carrying her father's partner's baby, or so she claimed. If you ask me, Dorothy was no great catch for an older man. She wasn't the type. Now, you're the type. You have that dopey virgin look older men get a hard-on just imagining. They'll say they won't want to deflower you, but shit, they would pay money at auction for a shot at your cherry.'

'Thanks, Mal.' I did not tell her it was one of my secret fantasies to have an older lover. 'He's good? He won't, you know, kill her by accident?'

'I mean,' said Mallory, pausing to light a cigarette, 'you never know with these things. That's why I say wrap it up. Much safer in the long run. But, yes.' Again she paused, taking a drag. 'I know two, no wait, three girls who have gone to him, and none of them have died yet. He's a real gynecologist. He practices this on the side.'

'Right. Can I have one?'

Mallory passed me the pack and her Zippo.

'Do you know how much he costs?'

'I haven't a clue,' she answered, tapping the ash with a shake of her wrist. She wasn't wearing the tennis bracelet. 'When you call, say you were recommended to him by Coralie Featherstone, that's my cousin. You have to say someone recommended you, otherwise he'll think you're a snitch.'

'Thanks, I'll do that.'

I flicked the Zippo to my cigarette, catching the flame instantly. I did not like it, though, and stubbed it out quickly.

*

I cycled to the station the following evening to place two phone calls. They could not be made in the parlor of Strong.

I acted as Mallory said. I spoke to a tired receptionist who readily accepted the name of Coralie Featherstone and recommended that I come on Friday afternoon, around four, if I could. It would be quieter then. I knew she didn't believe me when I said it wasn't for me but for my friend. Still, I gave the name as Angela Allen.

I knew the price would be extortionate. I'd read about this before. And I knew no doctor would take pity on Lara and I with our clean fingernails and clear diction. Even then, I was shocked by the fee the receptionist mentioned, requesting for it to be paid in full in cash on the day. I had nothing to pawn, except my mother's fur and her engagement ring, but these things I could not part with. And so I made my next phone call. To Teddy.

I figured if I was going to bear the responsibility on Lara's side, he could for Jack. After all, he'd been the one to set them up. But I could not blame him for it. He knew less than I what the consequences might be.

I rang Mrs. McCalman first for his number at the boarding house. She knew nothing of our fight and was kind. I sensed she was drunk.

I dialed the number before I could regret it. My heart quickened. I'd forgotten the low softness of his voice, the gentle twang of it.

'Hello, this is Ted.'

'Teddy?' I squeaked.

'Lil?' I could feel his smile through the phone. I was glad he wasn't annoyed to hear from me as I'd feared.

'Teddy, I'm so sorry to call like this, but I haven't very long, and so I've just got to come out and say it. But first, swear you won't tell a soul, especially not Jack, okay?'

'Okay.'

It was the time to be blunt. I could not play Lara's coy act of making him guess at the truth as I had had to do with her.

'Teddy, it's very bad. I know you think I am exaggerating, but Lara is pregnant. There, I've said it.'

'Jesus. Wow. Right. I'm guessing it's Jack's?'

'Of course, who else? I mean, yes.' This was not the moment to defend her virtue. 'But not for long. I've fixed that. I've found a doctor who will, well, you know.'

'Yes.'

'And I've got some money but ... I'm paying what I can for Lara, but it's $400, and I only have $250 in my account, you see and ... I'll ask Lara how much she can swing, but I don't think it will be much. Her parents don't give her the allowance I get from Dads and...'

'Lil, you need, what, $150?'

'Yes.'

'Fine. When do you need it?'

'By Friday.'

'All right. Can you get to New York?'

'Yes, can you meet me at Grand Central? I'll come down in the morning before we go to Princeton. That's where the doctor is, and we'll catch the train from there, Lara and I.'

'I can drive from New York to Princeton.'

I did not know what he was on about. I hardly expected his company. Only his money.

'But you don't have a car. And what about the gasoline?'

'I'll get it from one of the guys. There're ways.'

'Don't use the black market.'

He chuckled in his soft way. Everything about Teddy was soft, especially the crevice of his bicep, dipping down to the armpit. How I had loved to kiss him there, and he would smile and kiss my eye.

'You aren't worried now about doing something illegal, are you, Lil?'

'No, it's…'

How could I tell him my fears or of my guilt when I could hardly understand it myself? But it didn't matter. Maybe he did not care to know.

'I've, umm, I have to go, Lil. I'm holding up the line. But I'll meet you Friday, okay?'

'One o'clock?'

'Sure, that's fine. Bye, Lil.'

'Goodbye.'

I was lonely then, the sound of Teddy's voice recent and recalled.

But it was set. At least there was that.

I took up Mallory's bicycle. I decided I'd drop by her room when I returned to let her know. Perhaps a drink and a cigarette would taste all right. I just thought they might.

*

Teddy met us as he said he would. I'd waited until Thursday night to ring Lara. Otherwise she'd have backed out of it. I knew that much about her.

'It's hot,' is how she greeted me in the concourse. I arrived first having skipped my classes. Lara, rather bizarrely, attended her anthropology lecture before setting off.

'I needed something to do. I was going crazy,' she explained. 'I'd like a cup of tea before we get on the next train.' She sounded every bit the prim governess about to take her pupils away for the summer holidays.

'Lar,' I said. 'Now please remain calm, but Teddy is meeting us here.'

'What?' Dashed was the governess act. 'You didn't, Lil, please don't tell me you told him.'

'Lara, I had to. I didn't have enough money.'

'But why?' She hung her head in despair, involuntarily shaking it back and forth. 'Of all the people to ask for money. He'll tell Jack.'

I took her by the shoulders but stopped short of an embrace.

'He won't. Teddy is, for whatever else he is, loyal. I needed the money, and he said he'd drive us, all right? Won't you like that better?'

She would not cry. She must've resolved that today was not the day for tears, though the hint of them glimmered in her eyes.

'It sounds hellish to be alone with you and Teddy. Lil, how could you?'

'Fine,' I snapped. 'If you...' But I could not continue on in such a tone. It was cruel. She did not deserve that. 'It will be all right, okay? We'll get you there and we'll get you situated in the back of the car with blankets, and you can sleep the whole way back to New York. If you like, Mallory offered her apartment to stay in for when you know, it comes on.'

'No,' she said. 'I wouldn't like that. I'll go back to school, I think.'

'But, Lar, what if you have a fever, or, you know, it doesn't happen right away? You have to wait for the miscarriage.'

This was news to Lara. She lacked even my own shoddy knowledge of the affair to come.

'Whatever you do,' I warned, 'you mustn't go to the infirmary. You'll be expelled if you do. They'll know it right away. You're better off at the state hospital, or that's what Mallory said. You'll remember that, won't you? Unless you want for me to come…'

'No.'

She said no more.

We went in search of tea and coffee, passing our time until Teddy came.

*

Teddy brought two bottles. One of vodka and the other of whiskey. Lara chose the vodka.

'It's clear,' she mumbled.

She clamored into the back of the musty '32 Buick, sipping at it until Teddy told her she'd be better off taking big gulps. There mightn't be any anesthetic, he said. Between us in the front sat the whiskey, which I dared not to touch until the drive back. Neither did Teddy.

None of us spoke on that two-hour drive to Princeton. That was a relief, for what could have been said? Lara knew nothing of what was to happen to her, and my thoughts kept returning to my own fears. Perhaps Teddy knew about this sort of thing too well. Had he played a part in one before?

I did not ask.

We made good time, and when we arrived in the sleepy town of Princeton, it felt as if we might be coming for a weekend stay at the university. But of course we weren't.

I remember it being I who spoke to the receptionist, the

same tired one from the telephone. I think she had fading ginger hair, pinned neatly beneath a nurse's cap. But I doubt much of my memory from the day.

I must've given the name of Angela Allen and explained that it was not I but my short, fat friend with the auburn hair who was in need of help. I remember feeling particularly pretty, though I had hardly slept well. If anything, I believe I had the faint sick of hangover creeping over me, but it lent a shine to my eyes and a womanly swell to my breast.

We were told to take a seat and the doctor would call for Angela presently.

Never once did Lara moan that she could not go through with it. I'd expected a fuss, but none came. She was quiet throughout, until the name of Angela was summoned. I meant to squeeze her hand, but she was gone. I did not know if I would see her again, my best friend. We did not even know if it would work.

And then it was Teddy and I together. And I knew not what to say.

'Are you cold or something?'

I looked around the waiting room. There were a few other women, mostly alone, with unstyled hair and ratty coats of thick winter wool. It seemed funny with the weather so nice, but I don't know. Some people are fairly thin blooded. I wasn't cold, though and I told Teddy as much. He used to use that line when he wanted to kiss me.

I wondered what these women's stories could be, though I could barely stand to look at them. They were older than us, and they had the sad pallor of grief etched on their faces. Despite everything, my cheeks were rosy and my lips painted. Could Teddy smell the decayed alcohol oozing from my pores? I thought not. I couldn't smell it on him.

I bowed my head close to his. 'Do you think we're, well,

do you think this is wrong?' I asked. 'I mean do you think she'll go to hell for this and that I'll go too and…'

Teddy was amused.

'Always scared of hell, aren't you?'

'Well…'

'I wouldn't worry too much about that. What does it matter now? The right or the wrong of it. She's doing it. It's being done right now. You can't go changing it.'

'But…'

'Lil,' and I could feel his hand reaching for mine, but it never crossed the divide which I had so long ago driven between us, 'stop.'

'But…'

'If you believe in your God, then believe in your God. If you believe in punishment, then believe in your punishment. But don't go trying to make yourself believe that bullshit if you don't just to make yourself into a sinner and a martyr all in one.'

He was right. I had given up my God and could not call him back for the sake of inflicting my own punishment.

'Poor Lara.'

'We're all pretty poor these days. And that's a fact.'

'Teddy?'

'Yeah?'

But I said no more.

'Lil, I know.'

Our eyes met, and we were together again. But my guilt was too great. With or without God, I could and would feel guilt. For I had done this to Lara. And I couldn't go making love to Teddy while waiting for Lara to well … There isn't a commandment against it, but it would've been a sin. A sin against Lara. And that I could not allow myself to commit.

Lara came out without ceremony when it was done.

Her eyes were dead, her body limp. She looked a child again. Her voice was small and that of the defeated – a little girl exhausted from her day out and begging to go home.

'The doctor said the, the bleeding should ... It will be over by tomorrow morning, he thinks.'

That was all.

I return to this moment often enough. How she could bear it, I do not know. The discovery of a grey mass in my own panties several years later haunts me. It had been wanted, as much as it is possible to be wanted, but the child was gone. The blood began, black at first. It had been dead for quite some time. Life could not be lived in me. I, like Lara, did not speak of this to anyone, except to my husband. And in that way, I was not like Lara.

They married, of course, Jack and Lara, after the war, with Charlie Vaughn as best man and I as bridesmaid. Jack converted soon before, and Father Kavanaugh presided over the Mass with great joy. The reception was held at the Island's Knights of Columbus hall, the biggest party it had seen since the V-J celebrations two years prior. Mrs. Marcelli made pasta for a month in preparation and Mr. Marcelli cried like a baby throughout. It was a happy day.

But she did not tell Jack, and I do not think she will. What purpose would it serve now for him to know his wife? And so she keeps her secret hidden in a vain attempt to seal her heart from regret. I do not know how often she thinks of it.

We have never spoken of it since. She did not ask this of me, but I knew it from her dull eyes when she emerged from the surgery. We never speak of Teddy anymore either. Though on the night before her wedding Lara did condescend to say, 'I know it should be Teddy and not Charlie tomorrow. You won't get too sad and mope around, will you? Promise?'

'I won't.'

But it didn't matter me promising. I saw him there that day as he should have been in a blue suit, his hair freshly cut, his stubble emerging by the evening party, beer on his breath as he took me outside the hall to share a cigarette. Another secret to keep pressed to my heart.

You'd probably like to know that Lara and Jack are happy, or at least they put up the front of happiness. They live in Westchester, as you might expect, and have two children together, a boy and a girl. I suppose there needn't be room for regret. Their lives are filled with conventionality, the very things they both longed for in youth.

Lara acted as she needed to, or as I consulted her. Then why when we are together, which is rare in itself, is she reluctant to speak of the summer we shared? She, after all, had the happy ending. I did not.

Although it is against our doctrinal teaching, it is not the abortion itself for which I feel the weight of guilt. When their first child was born in the late autumn of 1948, I did wonder if what we had done was rendered more wrong or if it had been righted by the birth of Jane, my supposed namesake. But I came to no conclusions and, over time, my feelings of guilt for it have waned. At nineteen, I found myself haunted by the idea that my actions had indirectly led to murder. But this is no longer the case.

I corrupted Lara long before the abortion. Without me, she would have married a nice boy, perhaps not Jack but his generic equal, and led an untainted life. But I introduced her to sin and placed the apple within her reach. I took her innocence. Not Jack. A sin against God can be forgiven, but a sin against man sometimes cannot.

I try to live with my guilt, and as my penance for my own sins, I have adopted Lara's, Jack's, and Teddy's as well. I like the torture of this cumulative guilt; it is my hair vest, the last remnant of that summer.

There is a void inside of me and these few, damning fragments of a life once lived are what I have left. I hoped that by telling these stories of schoolgirl romance, I might release myself from the cycle of purgatory, but I see now I do not want the release. I crave the continual damnation too much.

I must now confess to you my last great sin. It may seem a trifling one at first. Perhaps it is a mere venial sin, but no amount of Hail Marys will purge me of my guilt. I'm certain of that.

*

We put Lara on the train at quarter to eight. She would be home by eleven, hopefully before the bleeding. She called Mallory, as I had told her to, just before midnight to let me know it had started. I spoke to her in the morning. There had been no fever. It was over. Our girlhoods were too.

It was Teddy who suggested he and I go for a coffee and a sandwich. He did not want to leave me, and despite the day and the sickening stench of whiskey on my hair and his lips, my heart swelled with love.

We went to a diner across the way, and once we ordered, he offered me a cigarette which I gladly accepted.

'Well,' he said, sizing me up, 'you're not as pretty as you used to be. You're too thin.'

'Yes,' I answered. I took a long pull on my cigarette. It tasted good.

I knew he preferred plump girls, girls with dark eyes and

full breasts, and the look of a nursing gypsy. He was not one for a skinny girl with wild hair and wild eyes, pale skin, and thin lips. And yet it stung.

'Come on, Lil,' he grinned, suddenly, 'don't go fishing. If you ate something, you'd be very sexy, you know that.'

But I could not eat. I'd lost my hunger with the summer.

Another summer was coming, and I wanted to play no part in it. I'd agreed to spend the months with Mallory in New York volunteering at USO centers, picking up strange men and stranger habits. It seemed worthwhile enough, something to relay to my inevitable daughter of what I did during the war.

I could not face the Island and the heat, the memories of the previous year radiating through the black asphalt at three in the afternoon, seeping into my skin, poisoning my mind.

'Listen, Lil,' said Teddy, lifting my mind from its reveries, 'I've got to tell you something.'

I took a sip of coffee and looked at the gross, sickly tomato creeping out from the white bread of my sandwich. I would not touch it.

'Sure.'

Teddy reached first for a cigarette, his brows knitting together when the match would not strike.

'Let me.'

He passed the cigarette and matches to me. I lit it and handed it back to him.

'It should be the other way around,' he offered with a gentle laugh.

We stared on, silent. He searched for words I did not want him to say but needed him to break the fairytale I almost thought possible.

'What is it, Teddy?'

'Lil, I've enlisted.'

'Oh.'

I said no more.

'I know I promised, but I did it … yesterday. I have to tell my parents still. They won't be happy, you know, but it's the Marines.'

'Right.'

How can the dying think to have last words? Are they ever poetic or are they damned to be prosaic, as so much of our speech is?

'Lil, I…'

He scratched at his neck, hidden beneath a light blue oxford collar. He must have picked at a pimple for when he brought his hand back to the table to lift his coffee cup, I saw the smallest trace of blood on his thumbnail.

'It's what you wanted, isn't it?'

To play soldier, to be the hero of the books he adored. Of the books he did not have the strength to write, though certainly the talent.

But I held my tongue.

'Thanks, I…'

I glanced across to his wristwatch. Half past ten. I told Mallory I'd be with her that night in New York. If I were to say I was catching the train back, though … I must go.

'Teddy, I have to … my train.'

'Right. I'll, let's get the bill.'

We each paid our own and left without a tip. I'd forgotten.

The night air was thick, oppressive. That of late August rather than mid-April. How long ago it seemed that March night at the Yale Club.

Teddy lit us each a cigarette, placing one between my lips.

'There, that's right. Let's walk slow.'

We only had a block to go, but it was the longest walk we were to take together.

'Lil,' he murmured at my neck.

I turned. And he kissed me. And I loved him. And he loved me too. Of that I am certain.

But I could not.

'Teddy.'

I met his green eyes with my own, and he smiled.

'I know.'

And that was our end.

I have often wondered whether or not I would have liked to have known it was our last kiss. Because I didn't.

Because I had hope.

And now I have memory.

Sometimes I think, was the summer that glorious? Or have I constructed its beauty out of the fragments which remain behind in my memory? I do think there are perfect moments, and I do believe many of such existed that summer. To say it was a perfect summer, although I am tempted to believe it was, would be a lie. I was sad and scared then too. Loneliness, even in our happiest of moments, cannot be held at bay. I know that now. I accept it.

Yet, I do believe that there were times – the day at the falls or the first time Teddy kissed me – where the beauty does not lie in the construction of my memory. We can feel such perfect moments as they are happening. We sense that death is creeping behind them, and so we cling to them. But we know these moments cannot and will not last. We hopelessly try to translate them into words in order that they might, but this too is a failure. And the tragedy arises from our own inabilities to capture the ethereal. The beauty is in the physicality, the acts, and once given words, there is a loss.

And so I lay across the glass, pressing it to me. Absorbed in the reflections, willing the past to come alive again. But to recollect is a solitary act, and the images of happiness are a mockery of the brilliance which once was.

I know now, though. I didn't know then, but I know now. That was the last time Teddy McCalman kissed me. It was the last time I saw Teddy McCalman alive.

Epilogue

Teddy died on November ninth, 1942, namelessly at Guadalcanal. There is no tombstone to mark his grave; no epitaph to sing his beauty and his youth. He died like so many others, having done nothing in his life to bear remembrance other than possessing a minor talent in a small New York town.

I learned of his death on the sixteenth. It was a Monday.

I went to Main to post some letters before classes. Lara and I kept up our habit of correspondence, though we revealed less than before. Our lives had separated. I grieved this as Lara must have, but we wrote nothing of it to the other.

There was a letter for me there too. It was from Mrs. McCalman. I opened it without expectation. Death has an air of emptiness which proceeds its announcement.

And there it was scrawled in black ink, a hand unsteady and rendered almost unreadable. But I did not need to read it. I knew.

I walked along, through the wide corridors built in the last century to accommodate the hoops of the students' skirts. I did not cry. I would not for some time.

I exited the building to a grey November day, but it was mild. I wore nothing for warmth but a mustard yellow cardigan, stolen from Mallory's closet. It was a rather unfitting outfit for news of death. I'd need to go back to my room to change.

I stared across the sunken lawn, yet untouched by snow. Five more months of this and then…

'Fuck it all.'

No one could hear me. No one cared, bustling off to breakfast and to classes and to a world filled with the reckless joy of youth I had not known since I was fifteen.

I took out a cigarette and lit it. It was going to be a long day, and I knew not when sleep would come.

Acknowledgements

Thank you to the lovely team at Valley Press for championing this manuscript from submission to publication. A special thank you to Jamie McGarry for his publishing vision in creating Valley Press, to Sam Keenaghan, who is a dream editor and found the perfect title, and to Peter Barnfather for his design.

To my father and to Mary for their constant love, support, and utter enthusiasm for this project. To my mother, my first editor from the time I could write, who never tired of listening to my stories. To Maria for reading a very early draft of the novel. To JJ, Kiera, and Emily for never doubting. And to Charlie: 'For love … makes one little room an everywhere.' Thank you for everything.